Amelia Ford gr
with a degree in l........ ....g .o. ....een years
decided to turn her hand to writing contemporary women's
fiction. She lives with her husband and three children in the
heart of Kent. Tagan's Chase is the third novel in the Tagan
series.

For more information about Amelia and her books visit
www.amelia-ford.com
www.facebook.com/AmeliaFordAuthor

ALSO BY AMELIA FORD

Tagan's Child, Book 1

Tagan's Change, Book 2

Tagan's Chance, Book 4

Coming Soon

Damned and Damaged

TAGAN'S CHASE

THE TAGAN SERIES - BOOK 3

AMELIA FORD

COPYRIGHT © 2018 BY AMELIA FORD

ISBN 978-0-9929882-9-6

Acknowledgements

Thank you to my fantastic editorial team, @sirjotajota and of course my lovely readers who have helped me achieve this third book. I am so grateful for the time, expertise and patience you have freely given to help me make this book and The Tagan Series the best it can be.

For Rachel. Thank you for your constant support and guidance.

"You can open your eyes now," Elaya said, with a hint of uncertainty.

"Ihrranna," her mother breathed, clearly overcome by emotion.

"You look so beautiful," I said, echoing Belayne Elessar's appraisal.

Elaya stood in front of us in her wedding dress. "I don't look too tall?" she asked as she turned around.

"Don't be ridiculous." I looked at the woman who over the last two years had become one of my closest friends. She was the epitome of refined elegance. In her heels, she was at least six foot two and she towered above me. Women her height were not unusual here in Ramia and I couldn't understand where her sudden lack of confidence had come from. After all, her height was of little consequence when the man she was marrying was a good six inches taller. There was no doubt that she looked absolutely stunning.

Her dress was the most delicate cream with a fitted

bodice made from the finest silk. It clung to her hips and then dropped to the floor in elegant folds, pooling at her feet. The neckline swept from one shoulder to the other emphasising her incredible bone structure and beautiful beading created a waistband accentuating her figure. A swathe of fabric formed a long train, which was attached at the shoulders and hid a plunging backline. Her hair was much longer than when I had first met her and it was styled in a chignon, adorned with a cluster of orchids, exactly matching the colour of her dress. I stepped towards her, and careful not to smudge her freshly applied make-up, kissed her cheek. The last two years had not been easy for either of us and I couldn't have been more happy to see Elaya stood here about to marry the man she had lost her heart to.

"You wait until Tigor sees you, he is going to think he's the luckiest man alive."

The girl who had done such a lovely job with Elaya's make-up stepped forward and swept a brush across Elaya's cheek.

"He *is* the luckiest man alive," she said, with a wink that was at odds with the elegant picture she presented, but so part of what I had come to love about her. Elaya was a loyal friend and one of mine and Ahran's most vociferous supporters, especially where their father was concerned. Over the last year, Driscan Elessar and I had come to a mutually awkward alliance, he was really no closer to accepting me as Ahran's girlfriend, but after not speaking to his son for over a year, he had come to a reluctant acquiescence after persistent coaching from his gentle, magnanimous wife. He and I exchanged pleasantries when necessary, but I was pretty sure he lived in hope that the portal, which I travelled through a little less frequently these days, would grant him his wish and swallow me up!

Belayne snapped out of her happy trance and kissed Elaya on the cheek. "No mother could be more proud of their daughter than I am of you," she said, softly.

I could feel tears welling up as I looked at them both. Elaya's mother was just as elegant in a beautifully cut pale grey suit, her own beauty still very much in evidence. The photographer had been snapping away happily and I had no doubt that the photographs would be gorgeous, he was a renowned photographer often used by the royal household, but Elaya and her mother were also making it very easy for him.

"I'm going to leave you two girls to finish getting ready and tell the High Priestess that you won't be long."

"I haven't had my make-up done yet," I said, feeling slightly panicked. It was the first time Ahran and I had seen each other for a couple of weeks and I was excited, but also rather nervous. I had allies in the royal household, yet there were still members of the royal court who were suspicious of anything Sapien. As far as they were concerned I was an outsider and, therefore, a potential threat to their world.

"Don't worry Sophe." Which sounded more like "Soff" in her accented English. I liked that she had shortened my name; it was what my best friend Bennie called me. "Let's have a glass of *hyorsa* whilst Teela does your make up. I need it to help calm my nerves."

Elaya was the most confident and sorted person I knew, but standing in front of an audience of Ramia's most noble and distinguished, with the man she had chosen over and above her father's wishes, scared the bejesus out of her. She had confided in me not so long ago that there was a part of her that wished they could have eloped and got married on the quiet, but she knew it would have broken her mother's heart and denied her Aunt Leylana the opportunity of throwing a royal wedding.

I sat at the dressing table with my face upturned towards the gifted Teela as she began to apply foundation across my cheeks.

"Here," Elaya said, handing me a champagne flute. I blindly reached out and took the glass she offered. "It will be your turn one day," she said with an air of promise.

I gave a wry smile at the thought of marrying Ahran, it filled me with pure joy, but still too many obstacles stood between us and our fairy-tale wedding.

"Hmm, over your father's dead body." I took a sip of what was the Ramian equivalent of champagne. "Besides I haven't been asked yet." I knew that the time wasn't right and yet I couldn't help but feel a pang of disappointment.

"I am sure that once you have made the permanent move to Ramia, my brother will waste no time in securing you as his wife."

I chuckled at her turn of phrase. I wanted nothing more than to move to Ramia and live with Ahran like a proper couple.

I sighed and changed the subject. "I hope Toby will be all right today." He had taken it upon himself to write a short speech that, in his role as Prince of Saleth and future King of Ramia, he wanted to read out during the wedding ceremony. Elaya and Tigor were more than happy for him to do this, and of course the King was overjoyed that he had settled into the role that was his birth right. I, however, still struggled with the legacy Tagan had left his son. I was unquestionably proud of my nephew, he spoke the language like a native, studied hard to learn about Ramian culture and had taken on the cloak of responsibility that came with being the heir to the throne with a maturity that belied his ten years. However, I couldn't help feeling that he had been robbed of his childhood and even though the King and Leylana had been very careful to ensure that he still did the sort of things that boys his age should do, or certainly boys his age in Ramia do, he had lost that carefree right that the average boy on Earth had. And that made me feel sad. Elaya touched my arm. "He will be fine. You worry too much."

"I know, but he's still a child." Before my sister Katie died, I promised I would take care of him and would do everything in my power to ensure that he had as happy a childhood as possible. I knew I could never replace Katie, but I felt like I had failed her and him, he had been forced to grow up far too quickly.

"He's happy Sophie, don't be so hard on yourself."

I felt a tear roll down my cheek; the thought of Toby losing his childhood, mixed together with what I'd had to do towards the sale of the house over the last couple of weeks, being apart from Ahran and the emotion of the day all caught up with me momentarily.

"Now stop that, you don't want to be responsible for smudging my mascara do you?"

"I'm so sorry Elaya," I said, reaching for a tissue and

wiping my eyes, realising I was being utterly selfish. "This is your day and here I am sabotaging it."

"Well, let's just say you've taken my mind off my nerves."

"See, that's exactly what I was trying to do," I said with a good-humoured sniff. I made a concerted effort to pull myself together and be a better bridesmaid, reassuring myself that it was now only a matter of minutes before I would see Ahran and be able to draw on his quiet strength. I was finding it harder and harder to spend time away from him these days.

Teela indicated for me to look up. "I'm not used to this kind of luxury. It usually takes me thirty seconds to do my make-up in the rear-view mirror of my car."

"Enjoy it," Elaya replied as one of the small army of people that were in the room adjusted the flowers in her hair.

Teela stood back seemingly satisfied and handed me a mirror. She had emphasised my eyes; the colours perfectly suited the slightly darker skin tone I had acquired since spending more time here and I was pleased with the overall look. "Thank you Teela." I gave the mirror back to her.

"You look lovely Sophie," Elaya said.

Suddenly, she looked a little wobbly. "Are you okay?" I asked.

"I can feel the adrenaline pumping."

"I can remember a time when we shimmied down a castle wall with the threat of being lasered to death at every turn and then rowing across a crocodile infested swamp.

You were as cool as a cucumber then," I said with a chuckle.

"Believe me Sophe, this is a hundred times more scary."

I laughed. "Just think about the wonderful man you are marrying and try to forget everyone else," I said, trying to reassure her.

She nodded. "I never thought this day would come."

I knew she was referring to Mr Elessar senior. "Your father has come a long way."

The photographer had been snapping away over the last hour and now that we were both ready he wanted a few more shots before we headed down to the groom and wedding party.

"Okay, all set?" I said, when he had finished.

She nodded. "I think so." Her hand was shaking as she took her bouquet from one of the attending team. It consisted of more cream orchids and a stunning flower that co-ordinated with the subtle coral of my dress.

"Wow! It's gorgeous Elaya."

"It is, isn't it? Tigor did well."

"What did Tigor do?" I asked, not quite sure what she meant.

"In Ramia, the bridegroom is responsible for providing the bouquets."

"Really?" So you haven't seen your bouquet until today?"

She shook her head. "No, but I knew he had used one of the best florists in Dinara, I wasn't worried about it," she said, turning the bouquet in her hands and inspecting the blooms more closely. "It's a tradition that goes back to a time when peasants had their own land and the groom would have grown the flowers himself. But of course, nowadays, things have changed."

"Golly! I'm not sure I would trust a man to provide my flowers."

She laughed. "It's tradition that the groom provides the bouquets as a promise of love and fertility, but I don't think there is a man in Ramia who would actually take on the responsibility of providing the flowers these days, they usually leave it up to the florists. Between you and me," she said behind her hand hinting at secrecy, "I know the florist and I had already spoken to her about what I wanted."

"I see," I said and took my bouquet, which was a more modest version of Elaya's, but beautiful in its own right. It was more than just chance that everything co-ordinated perfectly. I smoothed the lines of my skirt. It was a simple, floor-length affair with a sleeveless, wrap over bodice, and a satin ribbon at the waist. Elaya had matched the dress with a pair of strappy, high heels, which made me a good few inches taller. *I* was feeling nervous; I couldn't imagine how she was feeling.

"Ready?" I said to her.

She nodded. There was a slight flush to her cheeks and I took hold of her hand and squeezed it. "You're going to knock 'em dead!"

She frowned a little. "I'm not sure that's what I want to achieve."

I chuckled. "It's a figure of speech. You look absolutely stunning!"

"Thank you Sophie." She gave me a brief hug.

I grabbed a handful of tissues and hid them under my bouquet. We made our way along the corridors of the palace and to the vestibule which led out into the garden where the ceremony was to take place. Elaya's father was waiting for us. He approached his daughter and spoke to her in Ramian before giving her a kiss. For a brief moment, I saw a rare flicker of emotion across his face, if I was not mistaken he was actually quite choked. He cleared his throat and acknowledged me with a perfunctory nod before holding his arm out to Elaya. The lyrical sound of a small orchestra, which had been drifting through the open doors, seamlessly switched to the beautiful arrangement Elaya had chosen to walk down the aisle to. I took my position behind father and daughter and we stepped out of the cool of the palace into the warm Ramian sunshine. I concentrated on leaving the building without falling flat on my face and it was a moment or two before I looked up and ahead.

The waiting guests bowed their heads as was custom and I sighed at the stunning job Leylana had done of making the already beautiful palace garden into a breath-taking location for a wedding. There were trees where there had not been trees before and they were beautifully woven together to create a canopy of shade over the whole congregation, protecting them from the hot sun as it shone in the cloudless sky. There were white and coral flowers everywhere interspersed against a backdrop of cool greenery that reminded me of an enchanted glade in some magical fairy-tale forest. And as if the music and scenery were not enough for my poor earthly ears and eyes, every now and then I caught the most delicate floral scent as it wafted across my path. I took a deep breath and sighed again as I discreetly sought out the man I hoped would one day be standing at the altar, waiting for me.

He was stood at the front with the King and Queen, and unlike the rest of the congregation who, according to wedding ceremony etiquette, were not to look up and cast their eye on the bride until she was stood side by side with her groom, he was turned towards us and doing a terribly job of hiding the fact that he was looking in our direction. It was typical Ahran who felt less bound by convention than a person in his position had any right to. Our eyes met. And there it was, that little frisson of excitement I always felt when I saw him accompanied by a jumble of other emotions; all-consuming love, security and a sense of well-being the likes of which I had not felt before I met him. A smile stretched across his face and he gave me a heart-fluttering wink. I returned his gesture with my own little disapproving smile and looked away; if I didn't concentrate on walking in these heels I was sure to fall and I certainly didn't want to add 'Incapable of Conducting Herself in Public' to Ahran's father's list of reasons why I was an unsuitable daughter-in-law and future Princess of Carenna. We made it to the front with all falls avoided and Mr Elessar handed his daughter to her husband-to-be, who was waiting with a huge grin on his face. He was indeed one of the luckiest men alive.

The strings played their last few notes and everyone sat down ready for the ceremony to begin. I stepped forward and took Elaya's bouquet and sat down next to Toby who was seated in the front row alongside the King and Queen.

"Wow Auntie Sophie! You look lovely!" Toby said, a little too loudly as he misjudged the length of time it would take everyone to settle. It earned him a few chuckles from those around us. Leylana smiled at him and squeezed his arm. She was completely besotted with her grandson; there was no crime she would not forgive him for and nothing she wouldn't do for him. She had even managed to persuade Halsan to allow Toby to bring his dog, Mungo to Ramia, even though the King had an aversion to dogs. Needless to say, the mutt had made himself at home; slept on Toby's bed and begged for food at any given opportunity.

"Thanks, Tobes," I whispered.

Leylana reached across and dropped a smooth soapstone pebble into my hand and I remembered what she had told me. It was believed that it absorbed the love and good wishes of its bearer whilst the ceremony took place, and then as the congregation followed the newlyweds out they would put it into a basket. The couple would later receive this basket and take it into their new life along with all their guests good wishes. I turned my pebble over and it felt cool in my hot hand.

The ceremony proved to be not too dissimilar to wedding ceremonies on Earth, except of course it was in Ramian. Ahran was trying to teach me the language, but languages had never been my forté and so it was a long and painful process. Fortunately, he was a very patient teacher.

At one point the High Priestess paused to allow Elaya, who was overcome by emotion, to gather herself. I assisted in my bridesmaid duties and stood up to hand her a tissue. Elaya wasn't prone to outward displays of emotion, but she knew, as did anybody who was close to her, that she and Tigor were soulmates. The significance of the ceremony was not lost on her. Indeed, it was obvious to those sat in the front row that Tigor himself was struggling to hold it together. I had been sobbing like a baby from the moment they had turned to face one another and I knew I was not alone as I caught Leylana dabbing a tissue to her eyes.

Toby had embraced his life here in Ramia. He had found a loving family he never knew he had, and as I sat there watching the ceremonial union of these two people, I realised I too was part of that family. I had lost my precious sister three years ago, and although she could never be replaced, I had gained a sister in the form of Elaya as well as a family who had accepted me as their own.

Tigor dipped his head and gave Elaya a lingering kiss which elicited applause and whoops from the congregation. There may have been several hundred dignitaries in the audience, but there were also lots of their friends; Tigor was not of noble birth and it was clear that many of them did not feel constrained by any strict royal protocol. It brought a smile to my face. This family was pushing the boundaries of Ramian tradition, whether some of its elders liked it or not.

Elaya and Tigor turned to face us, their happiness plain to see and as they walked down the aisle as man and wife, people threw petals in their path. Everyone began to file out and I caught the eye of Ahran's Uncle Herck. He gave me a swarthy grin and I smiled back. It was a while since we had seen him, he was always jet setting off, chasing the latest diamond discovery or doing deals with precious stone dealers who I understood were notoriously cut throat. Somehow, Herck always came out on top, preferring to spend his time engaging with these ruthless merchants and the more desirable side line of high class women who were easily seduced by a shiny rock, rather than doing his duty as brother to the King. Relations between Herck and Halsan were strained at the best of times, but according to Leylana his visits were a little more frequent than they used to be which she attributed to the arrival of his great-nephew Toby onto the scene. I always enjoyed his company and so did Toby's grandmother, but then I think Herck was much more comfortable among women than men. In his company, he had the ability to make you feel like nothing else mattered to him other than hearing about what had been going on in your life even though, compared to his, one felt it was considerably more mundane. Halsan was a king and statesman, but Herck was a well-respected businessman and a devout ambassador of women. I looked forward to catching up with him later.

I caught my toe on a ruck in the carpet that had been laid in honour of the bride and groom and I would have fallen had it not have been for the arm that slid round my waist and caught me.

"Steady Mootya."

My eyes closed briefly as I felt the heat from his arm spread across my back and with it that wonderful sense of belonging I had grown accustomed to.

"Do I get the first dance?" he said.

I turned and looked up into his blue eyes, which were no less mesmerising to me now than when I had first met him.

"I'm afraid there's a queue, you'll have to get in line," I said which earned me a squeezed bottom cheek.

"Ahran, behave yourself!" I hissed under my breath. I took a quick look over my shoulder to see if anyone had noticed his little indiscretion.

"And as you well know, I find that very difficult around you."

I reached behind me and took hold of his hand just to be on the safe side.

"You look absolutely ravishing, that colour suits you," he said.

Ahran and I dropped our pebbles in the basket along with the other guests and took a moment to bask in his compliments. He flattered me often and I never tired of it, but as happy and secure as I felt I still hadn't managed to silence the voice of insecurity that reminded me, I was still not one of them. In a moment of self-doubt, I had recently shared with Elaya, she told me an old Ramian saying which roughly translated meant, *The more exotic the flower, the greater it will be cherished.* It was a lovely sentiment, but as a Sapien, I'm not sure it really applied to me.

"Thanks. You scrub up pretty well yourself." This of course was a monumental understatement. His dark blue morning suit emphasised his height. It was matched with a cream waist jacket, a cravat and grey fitted trousers that defined his long muscular legs. He made my mouth go dry and my mind flitted forward to tonight when the festivities were all over and I would have him to myself. I really had to pinch myself sometimes.

2

R apturous applause broke out after Toby's speech. He had been very secretive about it and the only person who had heard it, before today, was Sulaan; he and Toby had developed a close bond over the last couple of years. Sulaan had devoted his life to serving the King and Queen and had no family of his own. Even though he never talked about her, Leylana suspected he had been having a relationship with one of the royal clerks for years. However, it was clear that the King's right-hand man thought a great deal of Toby. I had been told that together they had been working on this speech all week and Sulaan looked just as proud of Toby as Toby's grandparents did. I even caught him giving my nephew a little secret thumbs-up as he made his way back to his seat.

"Are you okay?" Ahran said, stroking my back with the hand that was casually draped on the back of my chair.

I blew out my cheeks. "If I eat any more, this dress might just give way under the strain!"

His eyes dropped to my cleavage. "Not necessarily a bad thing."

I gave him a little jab in the ribs and rolled my eyes. I took in another breath to see if I could find any more give in the fabric. We had just worked through an eight-course meal. Mealtimes, particularly during special occasions here, felt like an endurance test; it was survival of the fittest or *the most evolved* and I failed every time. I had however, learned to adapt in my own way, and accepted the smallest of portions every time I was offered food. There was no guessing how many courses one had to consume. Fortunately, Toby, who had always eaten well, had embraced this aspect of Ramian culture with gusto and instead of putting on weight was getting taller almost by the week. He had grown a foot since he first came here and was now nearly as tall as me.

I made the most of the breather the customary singing between each course gave me and although I didn't understand the words, I enjoyed the harmonies around me as the guests sang words of support and encouragement to the happy couple.

When the last notes of what I thought was a rather melancholic song for a wedding died down, Tigor's best friend stood up.

"Do you want me to translate?" Ahran whispered. Leylana had offered me a translator, but I had declined. It was nice to remove myself from the proceedings once in a while and be alone with my thoughts. "No, it's fine, you can give me an abridged version later."

"I can think of better ways of spending our night together," Ahran said with a glint in his eye.

"And what might they be Mr Elessar?" I said, turning to face him with a look of innocence.

I knew that expression and it sent delicious shivers down my spine.

"A dip in the pool, followed by a warm bath together, a glass or two of something bubbly and then who knows what next?" His voice had dropped an octave and his hand was gradually working its way up my thigh under the table. I could feel myself being drawn in, like the defenceless victim of a hypnotic cartoon snake, as his words and the warmth of his hand weaved their magic spell. I knew I was powerless against Ahran's seduction, not that there was one part of me that tried to resist. I had been on Earth for nearly two weeks prior to the wedding busy with the sale of the house and coffee shop and Ahran had been tied up on the farm, it had been the longest we had ever been apart and I craved his touch. I hated being away from him, it made me feel uneasy and out of sorts.

"Well, your luck might just be in," I said smiling and turned my attention back to the proceedings to find that we had moved on to Tigor's speech which was obviously humorous, judging by the frequent outbursts of laughter around the room, although some of the older, stuffier members of the court didn't appear to be overly amused. Once the speeches and more singing were over, people began to mingle and I took the opportunity to go outside and get some air whilst Ahran spoke to a friend and neighbour of his. In the dark, a million little lights twinkled in the interwoven trees where the ceremony had taken place, the whole area beneath had been turned into a huge dancefloor with a stage and a live band at one end.

It was a warm, balmy evening and the band were a couple of songs into their set. I sat down and slipped my shoes off and watched some couples dance to a lively track. They reminded me of the dancing I had seen al fresco on the banks of the river Seine when I had been travelling. At the time, I had thought Paris a pretty spectacular backdrop, but the sight of the brooding twin mountains residing over the palace, a golden moon suspended like a large antique pocket watch between them and its reflection glistening in the river below, was altogether rather special. Leylana had really surpassed herself in the staging of this wedding; she had capitalised on the drama Mother Nature had provided, but at the same time had managed to make it feel charming and intimate. Ordinarily, Ramians would get married at their parent's home, but because Leylana no longer had any children of her own, she had asked Elaya if she would be happy to have the wedding at the palace. Elaya was, of course, more than happy to grant her aunt this wish even though it wasn't a particularly popular decision with her parents.

"Are you okay Sophie?" Leylana asked as if my thoughts had conjured her up. She took a seat next to me.

"Yes, just giving my feet a break from these shoes," I said, stretching out my legs and wiggling my toes. "I was admiring what you've done here Leylana, it's breath-taking."

"Thank you. It has come together very nicely I think."

"I see Talina is here," I said, nodding towards Ahran's

ex-fiancée who was dancing with a man I didn't recognise. "Did Elaya invite her?"

"No, but her parents are part of the royal court."

"Yes, of course." It wasn't the first time Talina had been at a royal gathering. Leylana knew I wasn't comfortable with Talina's presence, but a while ago explained that they were bound by protocol and that I shouldn't take it personally. Even though the King and Queen were the heads of state, there were still powerful families who could not be ignored, I understood that. It reminded me of the Elizabethan court I had studied at A-level, but with less bed-hopping and treachery, at least as far as I was aware. No, Talina barely represented any kind of threat to me these days. She'd married a rich and powerful Dinaran businessman and it seemed the trappings of their extravagant lifestyle suited her well. She had moved on. However, she still had an irritating habit of kissing Ahran whenever they met. I tried not to rise to the bait.

"What with the wedding preparations I haven't had a chance to ask you how everything is going back on Earth," Leylana asked.

"Nearly there, Mr Collier is a friend, he dealt with my mother's probate and he's coming tomorrow to bring the paperwork to sign and then contracts can be exchanged."

"This is excellent news, I know how much Ahran and Toby are looking forward to you moving here permanently."

"I'm looking forward to it myself. The last two years haven't been easy, what with the police investigation into Toby's *disappearance*," I said, air-quoting speech marks with my fingers. "They have questioned me more times than

I can count. As far as I know the case is still open, but they're not actively looking for him."

"Well, that's a relief," Leylana said.

This topic of conversation brought back some difficult memories. It had been tough at the beginning of mine and Ahran's relationship. I had to return home often and pretend that I had no idea where Toby was. I was convinced that the lead investigator thought I had something to do with it, but he had no evidence to pin anything on me. The relentless round of interviews, press coverage and the constant fear that I was being followed really took their toll. But now that the case had gone cold, I was able to travel back and forwards to Ramia a little easier and without feeling like I had to constantly look over my shoulder.

Leylana covered my hand with hers. "Well my dear, duty calls. I hope it is all settled quickly and that you'll be here for my party."

"Yes, so do I," I replied. It was Leylana's 125th birthday in a couple of weeks, it would no doubt be an extravagant affair and I was looking forward to it.

"Good. I'll see you then if I don't see you before," she said, standing up.

I stood up and kissed her on both cheeks before she left me to fulfil her role as host. I sat back down to enjoy a few more moments on my own.

"You look a little lost. Would you care for a dance?"

I looked up at the man who had just spoken to me and recognised him from other royal functions. He was tall, dark and very good-looking.

"Yes, why not?' I said, slipping my feet back into my

shoes. I took his hand and we made our way to the dance floor.

He moved beautifully. "You've danced before?"

"Guilty as charged," he replied. "I live in Paris and dancing is big there."

"It's funny you should say that," I said, as he swept me around the dance floor. "I was only just thinking of the couples I had seen dancing by the river when I was on my gap year."

"Ah, yes, the beautiful Seine. A very special place to dance."

"I'm sorry, I didn't catch your name."

"It's Evo. And you are Ahran's girlfriend Sophie, if I am not mistaken. He is a lucky man."

I blushed. I was being flirted with and felt terribly flattered.

"So, will you be joining the party tomorrow out by the lake?" he asked.

"No, I can't, I've got business to attend to on Earth in the morning. I've got my solicitor coming with some documents for me to sign, he's going on holiday and…oh, it's all very dull," I said with a wave of my hand. I cursed myself for sounding so boring.

He nodded. "Well, that is a shame," he replied.

At that moment, I noticed Ahran appear at the edge of the dance floor. He didn't look particularly happy and returned my smile with a brooding look. I felt guilty as Evo continued to sweep me around the dance floor.

"I hear Ahran's business is doing well."

"Yes, he works very hard." I had been taking care of the

farm accounts and the farm was going from strength to strength. Ahran had a knack for rearing strong livestock that always fetched a premium at market, the arable side of the business was doing just as well. I often teased him that he was so charismatic that even a field of wheat wanted to grow for him. Here in Ramia, farming was a highly-respected profession and many young children aspired to be farmers much like they aspired to be doctors or astronauts back home. It was hard work, but the yields were high, which was a good thing considering how much Ramians loved their food. There was no killing of the golden goose here.

"I think I had better hand you back to your boyfriend," Evo said, looking like he was enjoying Ahran's discomfort. The last few notes of the song played out.

"Thank you, Sophie. I enjoyed that very much." He kissed my hand.

Ahran walked towards me with that long, sexy gait of his.

"Evo," he said with a curt nod.

"Ahran, good to see you."

Ahran turned back to me. "I haven't had a dance yet," he said, looking a little hurt.

"I can probably squeeze you in now," I said, looking up into his fathomless eyes. Evo may be attractive, but he was no match for Ahran.

"Thank you, Evo," I said, as Ahran took my hand. Evo gave me a little bow before Ahran led me back onto the dance floor.

"Did you enjoy that?" Ahran said flatly.

"Evo dances well."

Ahran looked unimpressed. "There is an expression in Ramia." He thought about this for the moment. "The dancing can come when the work is done."

"I'm not sure what you mean," I said.

"The trouble with Evo, is that he cares too much about the dancing."

I chuckled at Ahran's disapproval. He was jealous.

We danced to the next song with an upbeat tempo and then the band took it down a few notches to something much slower. Ahran held me close and we swayed to the music. The electricity between us had not lost any of its intensity over the last two years. It thrummed between us with each step we took and I closed my eyes as we slowly circled the dance floor. I was at my happiest when we were together, it was as if there was a force field around us that no one or no thing could penetrate. I knew that if this song went on forever I would never tire of the absolute complete- ness I felt in Ahran's arms. The last few bars of the song played out and we stood still, not wanting to pull apart and accept that we couldn't actually stand there forever. Ahran kissed my forehead and the band launched into a faster number and the moment was gone.

Tigor, Elaya and a number of their friends had joined us on the dance floor and we danced for the next hour until my legs ached.

A little while later, I grabbed Ahran's hand and reached up on tiptoe. "I need a glass of water," I said, trying to make myself heard over the music.

"Do you want me to get one?" he said.

"No, you stay here, you're enjoying yourself. Want one?"

He nodded just before Elaya grabbed his hand and spun him off across the dance floor.

I smiled and left them to it knowing I would have to have a break if I was to keep up with them.

Ahran's Uncle Herck was standing at the bar, talking to a gentleman who I knew to be a close advisor to the King, but as soon as Herck saw me he brought his conversation to an end and turned towards me.

"Sophie, you look stunning!" he said, kissing me on both cheeks.

"Thank you Herck. It's good to see you."

"How are you? We haven't seen you for a while."

"I've been particularly busy of late, but I've managed to take a few days this time."

"Oh good! Have you brought anyone with you?" I said, looking over his shoulder, in the hope that there might be a lady in tow. I couldn't understand why he always came alone, he was one of Dinara's most eligible bachelors.

"Why would I bring a woman, when I have you, Leylana and Elaya to keep me company?" He gave me a wink.

"Luckily for me, I am the only single one left," I said, raising an eyebrow and engaging in his banter.

"My nephew is a fool. If I was a few decades younger, I'd whisk you away so fast your feet wouldn't touch the ground."

I laughed, flattered by his compliment.

I glanced across at Ahran who was doing some kind of

up tempo waltz with one of Elaya's girlfriends. "If he carries on like that," I said. "I may be tempted to come with you regardless of the age difference."

Herck threw his head back and laughed, clearly enjoying my flirtation. "I may have to hold you to your word. Now, what will you have to drink?"

"Oh, just water please."

He asked for a glass of water and ordered himself another drink. "Shall we sit down and you can tell me all about how the farm is doing and what Toby has been up to?

"Yes, let's."

We found a table a little way away from the dancefloor and sat down. My eyes did a sweep of the emptier tables surrounding the dancefloor. "It's just the hardcore party-goers left I see."

"Yes, the sour faces have left thank goodness."

"Do you mean the court elders?" I knew that Elaya's marriage to Tigor was not a popular one.

"Yes, the elders and even some of the younger courtiers need to keep up with the times," he said.

"I know Elaya has broken with tradition by choosing Tigor, but surely love counts for something? I think Tigor is a perfect match for Elaya. Anyone can see that they are completely in love with one another."

"It's not about tradition or love, it's about blood."

"Blood?" I asked.

Herck nodded. "By marrying Tigor, Elaya is diluting the royal blood line."

"Surely that's a good thing?" I said, thinking about some

of the royal misfits in history who had come about from parents who were too closely related.

"No, it isn't. It is better to maintain the purity of the royal bloodlines than to mix with that of the less pure. Any undesirable consequences can be screened and dealt with through genetic purification."

"Oh," I said, not sure I wanted to know any more, it sounded a little too much like playing God. "I guess it's important to protect the royal family," I said distractedly, reminding myself that Toby was now part of it.

"Yes, absolutely. It goes back to our founding forefathers. Soon after they arrived there were many who mixed with the native tribes and went on to become the wider population, but there were some who were very careful to maintain their heritage and it is believed that we are their direct descendants."

I let this information sink in. "And Tigor and Elaya's marriage is not popular because his blood is not as pure as Elaya's?"

"Exactly. It's why arranged marriage is seen to be the best route so the royal bloodline can be maintained." Herck paused for a moment. "It's also why Toby is such an acceptable heir. He is both royal and Sapien."

"But I thought Sapiens were considered inferior?"

"They are, but the purists among us believe that the royal family are superior because we are the closest genetically to our original ancestors. It is an uncomfortable irony for Ramians that their royal families are considered the most superior when in fact they are the genetically closest to those who are believed to be ruining our homeland."

"I see, well at least I think I do." I thought about this for the moment. "If their homeland is so important, why are so many against an Earth/Ramia alliance then?"

"It's because they don't want an alliance, they want to reclaim Earth for themselves."

"*Jesus!* Really? You mean war?!" I asked feeling totally horrified at what he was suggesting.

Herck nodded. "It would be war if Sapiens didn't give them what they wanted."

I stared at him wide-eyed.

"I'm sure it won't come to that," Herck said, realising he had maybe gone too far and began to back track. "The factions here who want that are small and lack any kind of real powerbase. It's one of those scenarios that could happen, but the chances of it ever happening are very small."

I thought about everyone I knew and loved back home. "But it *could* happen," I said, not feeling reassured in any way.

"As I said, it probably never would, there are too many people here who want to work with Sapiens not destroy them."

I struggled not to feel too panicked by what he had just said, Earth wouldn't stand a chance if Ramia decided to attack, and hoped that maybe he had got it all wrong. "You seem to know a lot about all this. I didn't think it was some-thing that interested you?" I said, recalling Halsan's anger at Herck's apparent lack of interest in Ramian politics.

"Hey, Herck, are you moving in on my girlfriend?"

I looked up to find Ahran with beads of sweat on his

brow from his dancefloor exertions. He was smiling down at us. "I thought you were just getting some water?" he said.

"I…yes. Here have this," I said passing him my glass and feeing scandalised by the prospect of the War of the Worlds.

"I was just giving Sophie a history lesson," Herck said, not answering my question and chuckling a little nervously. "But I think I've said more than I should have."

"Oh really? Like what?"

"Inter-galactic war and the total destruction of the human race," I replied.

Ahran laughed. "You mustn't take him too seriously. My uncle loves a conspiracy theory. Isn't that right Herck?"

There was something about Ahran's tone that made me doubt his light-hearted delivery.

"Absolutely right nephew, absolutely right." Herck replied, trying to brush it off as nothing but tittle tattle.

I narrowed my eyes at both of them. "Why do I get the feeling that you are hiding something?"

"You're reading too much into it," Ahran said, grabbing my hand. "Come on, it's time you got back on that dancefloor."

Before I had a chance to protest I was dragged out of my seat and there was just enough time to throw an apologetic glance over my shoulder at Herck.

We danced alongside Elaya, Tigor, and their friends for the remainder of the evening and I tried to put the potential downfall of my entire race to the back of my mind.

3

I leaned against one of the palace walls with my shoes in my hand. "I can't walk another step."

"Then I shall carry you," Ahran said, scooping me up in his arms. It was the early hours of the morning, most of the guests had left and the palace was beginning to settle down for the night. Toby had lasted until just after midnight, I found him curled up on a sofa in one of the drawing rooms on my way back from the loo. Yula, one of Leylana's personal bodyguards, had carried Toby to his room and I'd helped her put him to bed before re-joining the party.

I stifled a yawn and rested my head on Ahran's chest as I allowed him to carry me to our room.

"I'm guessing that swim is out of the question?" he said, laying me down on the bed.

"You forget that I'm a mere earthly Sapien, I don't have your stamina," I said with another yawn. "Can you undo my dress?" I said, sitting up and started the not inconsiderable task of take the four thousand pins that were in my hair, out.

"Sophie, you do ask the most ridiculous questions," he teased. I loved his accent, particularly when he said *ridiculous*. It was such an English word that he had clearly picked up from me, but it sounded so charming when it rolled off his tongue.

"What is ridiculous, is the amount of pins the hairdresser used," I said, struggling with a particularly stubborn one.

And then I felt his warm lips on the back of my neck as he worked the zip down at the back of my dress. My eyes closed and I stopped what I was doing. Two weeks were far too long not to feel those lips on my skin. He pushed the straps of my dress off my shoulders and brushed his fingertips down my back making me shiver with anticipation. I had never been with a man longer than six months before I'd met Ahran and I had often questioned how couples maintained the passion in a long-term relationship. Surely sex would become routine and predictable? How wrong I was. Of course, I couldn't speak for anyone else, but between Ahran and me, our lovemaking only became more intense, more satisfying, more potent. It was like our attraction for one another had been distilled into one, life-affirming force that we had no control over; all we could do was let it take us wherever it chose. Sometimes it was hungry, passionate and demanding, at other times it was slow, patient and wonderfully torturous. It was anything but predictable. It was intoxicating and addictive.

I slipped out of my dress and knelt on the bed facing him. It was hard to describe how I felt about him. Of course, I loved him, but it was more than that. It was like he had somehow become part of me. I felt him with every beat of my heart, with every breath I took and it made me feel more complete. I never tired of his company, it was like we were two pieces of the same whole, weaker apart, yet stronger together. On the farm, we were a great team and as a couple, despite our differences in our origins, it was like we were made for each other.

My mouth hungrily sought his.

"Oh God, I've missed this, I've missed you," Ahran breathed, kissing along my jawline heading for that spot just beneath my ear. I hurriedly undid his cravat and began to unbutton his shirt. He deftly undid his belt. He had this remarkable ability to strip off without his lips actually leaving my skin. I laid my palms on his chest and the strong beat of his heart reverberated along my arms until it mingled with my own heartbeat. I could no longer tell whether the feverish rhythm was his or mine.

"Do you have to go back tomorrow?" he asked, relieving me of my underwear, his lips against mine.

"Once I've signed those papers, other than to see my friends, there is no need for me to go back," I said, breathlessly.

"And then you can come *home*," he said meaningfully.

"I can't wait." There was no better word to describe being with Ahran. He was my safe haven, my present and my future. I was just as anxious as he was for me to move in and take our lives forward.

I put my arms around his neck and pressed myself into him hoping to convey just a fraction of how much I wanted him, wanted to be *here* with him. His mouth seized mine and he kissed me passionately. I had a feeling there was going to be nothing slow and patient about our lovemaking tonight. He ran his hands up and down my back and intermittently kneaded my bottom. I gently pushed him back until he was leaning on his elbows and I was straddling him. I began to circle my hips seductively. His eyes were closed and he lay still for a few moments as he allowed me to pleasure us both. I leaned forward and touched my lips to his and found his hot, demanding tongue. His hands gripped my hips, encouraging each movement I made. His mouth broke away from mine and found my breasts, paying equal attention to each. This caused my arousal to escalate and my breath to come hard and fast.

He spoke in Ramian, which he often did when we made love. I only caught the odd word, but they were gentle words of love and encouragement.

"Mootya, I need you now," he said finally, urgently.

THE NEXT MORNING, we breakfasted with Elaya and Tigor's more immediate wedding party and when it was an appropriate time for me to leave I said my goodbyes and Ahran walked me the portal.

"It's very poor timing," Ahran said, stopping and encircling me in his arms.

"I had no choice in the matter," I said, looking up into his eyes. "It's Mr Collier's twenty-fifth wedding anniversary and he is taking his wife to the Canaries, if I don't do it now it will be another two weeks and I don't want the sale to fall through."

He sighed. "I suppose you are right. Hurry back though, we've got some catching up to do."

I recognised that look in his eyes. "Can't wait." I gave him a lingering kiss and walked into the portal, I wanted to draw a line under my life on Earth and get on with my life in Ramia as much as he wanted me to. It was eleven in the morning on Earth, which would give me an hour and a half to make a quick trip to the coffee shop and then phone Bennie before the solicitor arrived.

I'd sold the business to a gay couple who had recently moved to the village. They had some really good ideas about what they wanted to do with it and I hoped that some of the older, more parochial members of the community would accept them. I stepped out of the portal into the wood to find that it was cold and drizzly in Hatherley. One could be forgiven for thinking that winter had already set in and it only made me more keen to get on with what I had come to do and get back to Ramia. I let myself into the house and put my bag on the kitchen table to search through my bag for my car keys, but after I had emptied the contents out onto the table, I realised they weren't there. I pulled my Ramian phone out of my back pocket to phone Ahran to see if I'd left them behind, but just as I was about to hit dial, I spotted them on the windowsill. I grabbed them and put the phone down on the kitchen side, before walking through to the hallway to grab a coat. Ahran had insisted on buying me a car after my old Land Rover had given up the ghost and so

I left the house and started the engine of my top of the range Audi sport to make the short drive to the coffee shop.

The couple who were buying the business had been managing it for the last six months so they could learn the ropes, which meant I had been a little detached from it of late, but as I opened the front door I felt a pang for what, in a few hours, would no longer be my little coffee shop. I felt a tinge of sadness and a smidgen of guilt that I had sold what had been a family business for nearly fifteen years. Mine and Toby's lives had changed so much in the last couple of years; we had both suffered tremendous loss, but at the same time, had gained a life beyond our wildest dreams. I went into the kitchen and picked up the cardboard box I had left on the counter when I had come in here the previous week to do a final clear up. I took one last look around and locked the front door for the final time. I shouldn't be sad, owning my own business had taught me so much and I could now use what I had learned in the next phase of my life to help Ahran run what was now *our* business. Not so long ago he had asked me if I wanted to be a partner in the farm. I did of course. It was an exciting prospect and testament to how much Ahran wanted to involve me. I had grown to love the place and I couldn't wait to help run it as an equal.

I drove back to the house and let myself in, noticing how different the house felt now I had all but moved out. Houses felt odd when there was no longer anyone living in them. It was like there was an energy shift or a vacuum ready to be filled by the energy of new people.

I glanced at the clock; there was still time to call Bennie.

As I waited for her to answer I tried to work out how long ago it was since I'd seen her.

She picked up.

"Hi Ben, it's me."

"Sophie, you must be psychic I was just thinking about you."

"Can you talk?"

"I'm in London today, but I was about to have some lunch, is everything okay?"

"Yes, all fine." I still hadn't told her where I was spending most of my time. I had come up with the story that Toby was living with his grandparents in the south of France, and that I would be staying there once I had sold the house and the shop until I decided what I was going to do and where I was going to live. I didn't like deceiving my best friend, we had always told each other everything.

"I'm just waiting for the solicitor and thought I'd give you a call for a catch up, it must be over a month since we last spoke." Now that I thought about it, it was probably longer than that and I felt a sudden pang of sadness. Were we growing apart? I hadn't called her, but she hadn't called me either, it seemed like she was always too busy these days. "How are you?"

"Oh, not so bad."

"You sound tired."

"I er...just had a late night last night."

"Are you still seeing that graphic designer?"

"Who was that?" she asked.

"Clint. No, Clive," I said, struggling to remember what she'd said his name was.

"Oh, you mean Clark. No, there have been one or two since him," she said with a laugh.

I frowned. "I've always known you had an appetite Ben, but that must be at least six men in as many months!"

"I know, you can't blame a girl," she said, brushing it off.

"I just hope you're being careful." I didn't want to sound all big-sisterly and judgemental, but she was getting through men like there was no tomorrow. The biggest surprise had been when she had ditched Matt Waterhouse, the guy she'd had an on-off relationship with, but had been in love with for years.

"You know me Sophe, careful is my middle name," she said, flippantly.

There was something about her devil-may-care attitude that wasn't quite ringing true. "Are you alright Ben?"

"Never better. Did I tell you about this new guy? He's a big cheese in the city. Completely smitten, keeps sending me flowers, took me out to dinner last night and gave me a pair of diamond earrings. You ought to see them Sophe they must have cost a bloody fortune. He's taking me away this weekend to his pile in the country. He's public school. Must be old money, he's even got a housekeeper!"

She said all this as one complete sentence without drawing a breath.

I frowned. Coming from a well-to-do family herself, she had never been that bothered about money. She sounded weird, like she was high on something. "Please be careful Ben."

I didn't like the idea of her hanging around with Champagne Charlies, they were too used to the high-life, often with a cocaine habit to boot.

At that moment, the doorbell rang.

"Look Ben, the solicitor's at the door, I've got to go. Can I call you later?" I wasn't ready to finish this conversation, but for the time being it would have to wait.

"Sure."

"Speak to you later okay?"

"Yeah, bye hun."

She ended the call before I'd had a chance to return her goodbye. I put the phone down and stared at it for a moment or two. Is this what our relationship had become? I blamed myself. Maybe if I had contacted her sooner, given her more time and not been so wrapped up in what was going on in my life, I wouldn't be feeling like I was losing her.

The doorbell rang again. "I'm coming," I said and opened the door.

I did a double take. I was expecting Mr Collier, but instead there were two men I didn't recognise stood on my doorstep.

4

—————

"Miss McAllister?" one of them asked.

"Yes," I replied. They were plain clothed, but had an air of authority about them.

"My name is Detective Superintendent Harris," one of the men said, showing me his badge, "And this is Mr Craven, an MI5 intelligence officer."

Mr Craven nodded.

My heart sank. *It had to be about Toby.* I couldn't help wondering why an MI5 officer would be interested in Toby.

"We would like you to come with us Miss McAllister to discuss something which is an important matter of national and international security."

I looked from one to the other. *Shit! It was worse than I'd feared.* I could feel the blood draining from my face. They had obviously found out about Ramia.

"Are you arresting me?" I asked, feeling like the wind had been completely knocked out of my sails.

"Do we need to?"

"Why…I…no," I stammered.

I looked over their shoulders to the nondescript, black car parked outside my house.

"What do you mean a matter of national and international security?"

"I'm afraid I cannot discuss that standing here on your doorstep."

"My solicitor is due any minute," I said, feeling the panic beginning to rise.

"You can make a request for legal representation once we get back to the office."

"But I haven't done anything wrong," I said in a rather pathetic attempt to defend myself.

"Can we go?" Harris asked with forced patience.

I looked at the MI5 agent, who hadn't said anything yet. Maybe he was watching my body language for something that might give me away. Oh my God, had I just touched my hair? Wasn't touching your hair a sign that someone was… I reined myself back in.

"Can you please tell me what this is about?"

"We believe you may have some information that might be useful for us. All you have to do is answer a few questions and then you can go. It shouldn't take too long."

"Can't we do that here? I have an important meeting."

"I'm afraid not, your meeting will have to wait. Shall we go?"

I felt like I had been given little choice. "Er…Yes, I suppose so."

Whilst I struggled to comprehend what was going on, I grabbed my bag and went with the two men to the awaiting car. Harris opened the car door and I quickly glanced around to see if anyone was witnessing this. It just so happened that, Mr Reynolds, my new and slightly odd neighbour opposite, chose this moment to walk his dog and watched me get into the car. I had only spoken to him once, but I can remember thinking at the time he asked a lot of questions and was always out in his front garden poking his nose over the fence. Had he been watching my comings and goings? I scowled at him and he looked away as if he hadn't seen me and continued with his walk.

I sat in the back seat. Harris sat in the front and the silent one, a Mr Ormerod, as it turned out, sat in the back with me. I smiled awkwardly at him. "Shame about the weather," I said with forced cheerfulness, saying the first thing that came into my head and immediately regretting it. This was not the time to be making small talk. *Just keep your mouth shut Sophie!* Paranoia began to set in as I worried I might say something that could be taken the wrong way.

"Yes," he replied, but made no attempt to further the conversation.

The car pulled smoothly away from the curb. We headed towards the town, but instead of going straight ahead at the roundabout towards the police station, the car turned left and onto the motorway.

"Where are we going?" I asked, puzzled.

"MI5," Harris replied.

"In London?!" I asked, unable to hide my surprise.

He nodded. "Yes."

Jesus! This was more serious than I had first thought.

"Look, are you sure you've got the right person? Is this about my nephew?"

"Save your questions for the interview room Miss McAllister," Harris said.

I sat back in my seat and looked out of the window and started to feel the ripples of panic. I took a few deep breaths and consoled myself with the thought that I would call Ahran when we got there and he would come and help me to explain that there must be some kind of gross misunderstanding.

I watched the scenery go by, and as we hit the heavier traffic of inner London, I felt less jittery. Common sense would prevail.

Vauxhall Bridge came into view ahead. If this trip wasn't quite so serious it would have been rather exciting. I'd seen the Secret Service's iconic building in films many times and it was rare that anyone got to go inside, but instead of turning right towards it, we continued over the bridge.

"Aren't we going to MI5 headquarters?" I said, turning around to look at the building.

"We are. The building you're thinking of is MI6, it's a common mistake."

We turned right along Millbank and down into a well-lit, underground car park beneath an imposing, neoclassical building. Electric gates allowed us access and we parked.

Mr Harris opened the door for me and we made our way to a featureless door where the silent Mr Ormerod tapped in a key code and pressed his fingertip to a pad next to it. The door clicked open.

We proceeded to walk along a stark white corridor that

felt clinical, like a hospital or a research lab. We made a number of turns before passing two people with identity lanyards around their necks who nodded to the MI5 officer next to me. We went through another security door before heading down some steps into the bowels of the building. Each corridor looked the same and the doors were identical except for the numbering system on them. I felt like I'd stepped onto the set of Alice in Wonderland, although it was less whimsical fairy-tale, more avant-garde, psychological thriller.

Finally, we entered a room that was bare except for a table and three chairs.

"Please put your bag on the table and empty your pockets."

I hesitated for a moment. "You don't seriously think…"

"Miss McAllister, please just do as I have asked," Mr Ormerod said.

I sighed and pulled out some spare change and a receipt from my pocket and handed him my bag.

"Thank you," he said, picking up my belongings. "You may sit down. Someone will be with you shortly." And then he left.

Harris stood by the door.

"I haven't done anything wrong," I said to him in the hope that if I said it enough times someone might believe me. Of course, I had lied to the police about Toby's where-abouts and kept an unknown parallel world secret, but I knew my reasons were justified.

He raised his eyebrows and nodded as if to say, *That's what they all say.*

I was overcome by a sudden pang for Ramia. Not only were the people I loved there, but I had grown to love the place. I missed the sunshine, the mountains and the farm. I sighed and looked around the room. Apart from the plain white walls and the bright lighting the only thing that prevented the room from looking like a cell was a panel of mirrored glass. I caught my reflection in it. The stark over-head light shadowed my features making me look like I hadn't slept for a week. I sat up straighter and re-did my ponytail. The door clicked and two suits came in. The older man of the two was thinning on top, had beady eyes and wore a pin striped three-piece suit. The younger man was taller and slimmer with a mop of dark hair and geeky black rimmed glasses.

"Oh good," I said, standing up. "I believe I'm entitled to a phone call." I'd seen cop films, I knew my rights.

"Sit down Miss McAllister. I'm afraid that's not quite how things work here," he said with a cultured English accent.

"Let me introduce myself. My name is Compton and this is Meakins."

Compton had an air of confidence about him; a man who clearly had been in the job for a long time. Meakins had an aura of intelligence, but was less confident, his body language was awkward, apologetic even.

"Can someone please tell me what's going on?"

"Take a seat," Compton said and gestured towards the single chair on one side of the table. If it meant I was going to get answers I would have done back flips around the room, I thought to myself as I sat down. Meakins also sat down and crossed one lanky leg over the other. Compton remained standing.

He took a deep breath as if what he was about to say pained him.

"Do you know what we do here Miss McAllister?"

I thought about this for a moment. "You protect the country from different kinds of threat?"

He nodded. "You're right. Do you think it's important for the citizens of this country to feel safe and protected?" He rested his chin on his thumb and placed his forefinger over his lips in contemplation whilst he waited for my answer.

"Um, yes of course," I replied.

He sucked in a breath. "Good, good, I'm glad we both agree on that."

I felt like I was in front of a Victorian headmaster about to be given the telling off of a lifetime. The impression he gave that he was conducting this interview regretfully was just a smoke screen, I was pretty sure he was getting some sadistic enjoyment out of making me squirm. My heart thumped in my chest. His tactic to make me feel intimidated was working.

"Do you pose a threat to this country Miss McAllister?"

"I...no," I stammered.

"Do you know anyone who could possibly pose a threat to this country?"

I looked to him and then Meakins. "No," I said more resolutely. I couldn't work out where he was going with this. Was he talking about Ramians?

He looked at me with narrowed eyes and pursed his lips

as if he was about to blow me a kiss. I recoiled at the thought.

He took another sharp intake of breath, after what seemed like forever. "Your nephew was kidnapped two years ago, wasn't he?"

"Yes." I replied, looking him in the eye. I could feel myself colouring as I began to feel the increasing pressure of his interrogation.

"And he has never been found?" Was there a hint of challenge in his question?

"I don't understand how my personal tragedy has anything to do with national security?"

He smiled and did that funny pursing of the lips in quick succession thing. It was obviously something he did when he was thinking; a habitual tic and it was most unattractive.

"I think it could have everything to do with national security."

I swallowed. *Oh God, here it comes*.

"What do you know about Tagan Halsan?"

His question caught me off guard.

"He is the father of my nephew," I replied. 'Why?'

"How would you describe him?" Compton said without answering my question.

"I never actually met him."

"But your sister had a relationship with him."

"It was a brief fling."

"Did your sister have any contact with him after that?"

"No, he wasn't interested in Toby." I sent up a silent apology. After learning more about Tagan over the last couple of years, I now knew that he would have been over the moon if he had known he was a father. However, I was prepared to say anything to protect Ramia and the people I loved.

"Do you know where he is now?"

"No."

"He carried a British passport, but wasn't British was he?"

"I…I don't know."

"So you don't know where he was from?"

"I'm not sure my sister ever told me."

"Think harder Miss McAllister."

I could feel tears of frustration beginning to well. "Can I have my bag? I'm sure I'm entitled to a phone call," I said rather pathetically.

"You will be allowed to make a call if and when I get some satisfactory answers," he said, sharply.

"I don't know what you want me to tell you," I said, my voice rising in exasperation. I took a deep breath. "Look, I never met Tagan Halsan and I'm not sure I can give you the answers you're looking for. Can I go home now?"

Compton seemed unmoved by my plea for freedom. "Meakins, what can we tell Miss McAllister that might help jog her memory?"

Meakins launched into a ten-minute address about Tagan's movements in the year prior to him meeting my sister. He didn't once consult any notes and was able to remember dates, places and names with impressive accuracy. He obviously had some kind of photographic memory and it suddenly made sense why MI5 would be interested in having this lanky, slightly awkward, barely out of adolescence, brain box working for them.

Other than travelling all over the world, it seemed Tagan had been rather handy with a computer, not that I was given any details. I wondered if he had somehow breached the government's central computer system, and maybe that was the reason why Compton was so miffed. What was also interesting, was that Leylana had given me the impression Tagan had spent a year out travelling around the world and I had pictured him partaking in the obligatory bungee jumps, elephant rides and beach bummery that was on your average gap year student's itinerary. It came as some surprise to learn that he seemed to have had a rather different agenda.

Ahran had once explained how Ramia hoped to make contact with the world that held the answers to the origins of their race, maybe Tagan had been gathering information to pave the way for some kind of Earth/Ramian alliance? I'm pretty sure that Tagan's motives would have been innocent, but I could see how this might easily be mistaken for espionage from MI5's perspective. So Tagan was, or had been, on MI5's radar, but he had died eleven years ago, so why me and why now? Were they interested in Toby? And what, if anything, did they know about Ramia?

My head began to ache and I started to wonder how long they would keep me here. "Please can I have a glass of water?"

"I'm sorry, you cannot."

"But surely I'm within my rights to have a glass of water?" I asked, trying to keep the edginess out of my voice.

"I'm afraid, Miss McAllister, from the moment you walked through that door you lost all your rights."

THE QUESTIONING WENT on for hours. I'd heard how the first rule of interrogation was to wear your subject down. Compton had obviously graduated from the School of Inquisition with Honours. He asked me more about Tagan, about Katie, about the coffee shop, about my friends. He hadn't, as yet, let on that he knew anything about Ramia. My head was pounding, I was hungry and thirsty and all I wanted, was to see Ahran.

"I've answered all your questions. Please can I go now?"

"I'm sorry Miss McAllister, you won't be going anywhere tonight. We have only just begun, but for now, I'm done."

I breathed a sigh of relief. "Where will I be staying?"

"Here, courtesy of Her Majesty the Queen."

"I didn't think I had been arrested."

"It's up to you what you want to call it. I'd prefer to think of it as helping with our enquiries."

I had begun to loathe this man. He had shown little humanity and his questioning had been relentless.

"Goodnight Miss McAllister."

He gave me a curt nod and left the room. Meakins followed on behind.

I looked to Harris who had been standing at the door and noticed he had been replaced by another man. I had been too involved in my interrogation to notice. "Follow me please," he said.

He took me along several corridors and we entered a room that was similar to the one I had spent most of the day in, except in this one, in addition to the table and chairs, there was a bed. On the table was a plate of food, which looked like it had been stood there for a while and I poked my head into a basic en-suite that consisted of a toilet and a sink.

"How long will I have to stay here?" I asked my escort.

He shrugged. "I'm sorry, I don't know anything about your case." He looked genuinely apologetic and turned to leave.

I grabbed his arm. "Please, can I at least make a phone call?" I knew I couldn't phone Ahran, if I remembered correctly I had left my Ramian phone on the kitchen side and so I had decided to call Bennie. I wonder if she would run a mercy mission to Hatherley and call him.

"I can ask, but I think it's unlikely." Although the guard seemed doubtful, he'd given me a glimmer of hope. Of course, there was every chance that Ahran was on Earth looking for me by now, in which case I could have phoned him directly, if I could remember his number.

"Oh, please do, I would be so grateful." He'd been the first person today who seemed to possess any kind of compassion.

"I'll see what I can do," he said with a smile.

My flagging spirits were momentarily buoyed. I went into the facilities, and splashed water on my face unaware of what the time was. I was scared and wanted to speak to Ahran more than I had ever wanted anything in this world.

I walked over to the tray on the table and drained the glass of water before picking over the cold food with the fork.

Surely they would let me go home tomorrow. I tried to take a few calming breaths. Compton had spent a long time questioning me about Tagan and Katie and I had begun to think that maybe they did know something about Ramia after all. Perhaps tomorrow would bring more answers, although the thought of spending another day here filled me with dread. I sat down on the bed and took off my shoes, suddenly feeling exhausted. I leaned against the wall and closed my eyes.

I must have fallen asleep because I woke up in the dark, cold and with a crick in my neck. It took me a moment to realise where I was and for the events of the day to come flooding back. A heavy sinking feeling hit the pit of my stomach. My mind flitted back to yesterday and last night. Ahran and I had been at Elaya and Tigor's wedding enjoying the festivities along with everyone else and then we had spent the night together. How was it that now I was in a dark windowless cell having spent the day being interrogated by a man who clearly modelled himself on Hermann Goering?

I felt chilled and without taking off my clothes, slipped under the blanket. I lay there in the dark, feeling completely impotent. There was no way of contacting anyone and my mind went around in circles trying to make sense of what was happening and how I was going to get out of it. Had my luck finally run out? Once Toby's kidnap case had died down I had travelled freely between Ramia and Earth enjoying the best of both worlds, *literally.* I had kept my head down, busied myself with the coffee shop when on Earth, and when in Ramia, helped Ahran to build his business and the foundations of our future.

We had a wonderful relationship, he was everything I wanted in a man; loving, caring, compassionate, and he had awakened something within me that I had never known existed. When we were in each other's arms I felt alive, carnal almost. I had no inhibitions, no insecurities, I just felt the purest form of me. It was in those moments that I was stripped back and became the person I was supposed to be without that constant feeling of trying to keep my head above water whilst my fears and the general baggage that my life experiences had left me with tugged at my ankles threatening to pull me under. It was during those times that I felt truly present. I didn't need mind altering drugs to give me a heightened sense of life, nor did I need any form of meditation to find my true self. All I needed was Ahran.

And now I was without him and fairly confident that he would be going spare. Letting out a sob, I gave into my emotion for a few moments and then took a deep breath as I tried to draw on all my resources. Toby's kidnap came to mind, I had been in worse situations than this, and I knew I felt stronger for the experience. I had to stay calm, trust my instincts and exploit any opportunity that would get me out of here. I'd already decided that I wouldn't contact Ahran directly; it would put him in too much danger. If they were after Tagan, I was pretty sure they would be interested in

Ahran. No, for this one, I was on my own. In the past, this would have frightened me, but now it only made my resolve strengthen. I had been far too cooperative so far. I was here courtesy of the British government, they weren't some terrorist cell for God's sake. What was the worst they could possibly do to me?

5

"You can play the silent game Miss McAllister for as long as you like, you will find I am a very patient man," Compton threatened. It was the next day and we had been sitting in stalemate for the last few hours.

"And as I said to you, Mr Compton, if you allowed me to make a phone call I think you might find me a little more co-operative," I said, for the umpteenth time.

If I thought Compton was bluffing, I was disappointed because I spent the entire day in the interrogation room and then the next day in my cell on my own. I was still wearing the clothes I'd arrived in and my determination was wavering. Bloody hell! If I ever got out of here the papers were going to hear about this!

On the morning of the fourth day I was escorted back to the interrogation room.

"Ah, good morning Miss McAllister. I trust you slept well," Compton said.

I gritted my teeth. "Thank you, I did." I wasn't going to give him the satisfaction.

"Has having some time to yourself made you any more obliging?"

"I will answer your questions Mr Compton as soon as you allow me a phone call," I replied as calmly as I could when all I wanted to do was scream at him.

He did his lip pursing thing for a few moments.

"Very well. I can see that you are a determined woman. I will allow you to make one call."

I nearly burst into tears with relief.

Compton nodded to the man stood by the door who left and returned with a phone in his hand.

"I will leave you to make your call in private," Compton said, standing up before leaving the room.

I didn't think for one minute it would be private, but I wasn't about to argue after three days of living in hell, which in retrospect, was pretty much how I imagined being held captive by the KGB would have been like. Compton was every bit as ruthless even if he was a tweed wearing, Etonian toff.

I decided calling Bennie was my safest bet and my hands shook as I dialled her number. She picked up on the third ring.

"Cordelia Blythe-Smith."

"Bennie, it's me, Sophie."

"Hi Sophe, I'm really sorry it's not a good time. Can I call you later?"

"Ben. I need your help, it's urgent."

"What is it?" she said, sounding a little less flippant and more concerned.

How could I ask her to contact Ahran without giving anything away?

"I'm being questioned at MI5 headquarters in London."

"What?! Really? What on earth for?!"

"It's something to do with Tagan Halsan, Toby's father."

"Shit, Sophe. Why are MI5 interested?"

I glanced at the mirrored panel. "I think they suspect he's some kind of spy? Look, can you help me Ben?" I asked.

"What do you want me to do?"

"Where are you?"

"Er, I'm at home."

"In Clapham?"

"No, in Hatherley."

"Perfect! can you get hold of my solicitor?" I knew MI5 would expect me to say this. "And can you tell my boyfriend where I am," I said, feeling a strong urge to protect him. I knew the only way Bennie would be able to get in touch with Ahran was to go to my house and use my Ramian phone. "I've left my mobile at home."

And then the line went dead.

"Ben?"

Nothing.

Compton came back into the room followed by Meakins.

"You said I could have a phone call," I said, rounding on him.

"And didn't you just have one?" he replied.

"Yes, but I hadn't finished."

"Perhaps when you tell us more I will allow you to have a longer call."

I threw my hands in the air in frustration. "I've told you a thousand times, I don't know anything!" I could feel tears brimming.

"Let's talk about Toby," he said.

I closed my eyes and took a deep breath. "What do you want to know?" I said with an exasperated sigh.

"You became his guardian when your sister died."

"Yes," I replied wearily.

"Did Toby ever meet his father?"

"No."

"And you never tried to find him for the boy's sake?"

"No."

"And yet, you have had contact with an associate of Tagan's." Compton looked at Meakins questioningly.

"Mr Ahran Elessar," Meakins said, dutifully obliging.

My heart sank.

I cleared my throat. "He came to my house once or twice."

"And when was that?"

I paused pretending to think about it, but used the time to temper my nerves. "Oh, it must have been about two years ago," I said shakily, I was beginning to feel like I was sinking. Compton gave nothing away and I still had no idea what he knew.

"Did Toby meet Mr Elessar?"

I hesitated. "Um, yes he did."

"And did Mr Elessar discuss Tagan Halsan with him?"

"Not that I recall," I said, making out that I was giving this some thought.

"So what was the reason for his visit?"

I hesitated. "He was trying to find Tagan and wanted to know if I knew of his whereabouts. I told him I hadn't a clue where he was." This of course was complete fabrication.

"Did Mr Elessar leave any forwarding contact details?"

"No."

Compton took in a sharp intake of breath. "You see, the problem we face Miss McAllister is that we can find no trace of Tagan Halsan or Ahran Elessar. It would seem they have disappeared off the face of the Earth. No birth records, no national insurance number, nothing. It's like they never even existed."

"What exactly is it that you think they've done?" I asked.

"It is our job to investigate anyone who poses a threat to national security. A man who travels widely, with fake passports, is able to bypass governmental security systems, and who no one seems to know is indeed someone we are interested in." He perched on the edge of the desk in front of me. "And unfortunately, Miss McAllister, currently you are our only lead."

It didn't sound like they had any inkling of Ramia and I breathed a small sigh of relief. "You can't keep me here like this. I haven't been offered legal representation, you've barely let me make a phone call and I haven't changed my clothes in four days!"

"I'm sorry if you have been inconvenienced," he said,

not sounding in the least apologetic. "But you must under-stand our concern."

"You wait until the papers hear about this."

"Are you threatening me Miss McAllister?"

"I. DON'T. KNOW. ANYTHING!" I cried, glaring at him.

Compton paced the floor and then planted himself in front of me his face only inches from mine.

"But I think you do," he said menacingly, his halitosis hitting me like a brick. I stood my ground and eyeballed him back.

"I think you know where Tagan Halsan and Ahran Elessar are. I would hazard a guess that you even know where your nephew is," he challenged.

I felt a ludicrous urge to laugh. It was panic of course. It had gotten me into trouble many times at school and would in no way help me here. I managed to remain silent.

"You know more than you are letting on and I *will* get to the bottom of it!" he said, angrily. My lack of co-operation was clearly starting to piss him off.

"I have a search warrant for your house." He looked at his watch. "And they will be going in about now. Perhaps you'd like to give up the wide-eyed innocence act and tell me the truth before I have you arrested for being an accom-plice to terrorism."

I went cold. I frantically did a mental check to try and remember if there was anything incriminating at home. All there was, was my Ramian phone. Would Bennie have had time to go into the house, retrieve my phone and call Ahran before the search team arrived? And would they go after her next? I regretted getting Bennie involved and was beginning to doubt whether there was any way out of this one. I felt completely trapped.

"But I haven't done anything!" I squeaked.

"Take her back to her room," he said in disgust.

"This is ridiculous!" I said in frustration as I was frog-marched out of the room by the guard who had been standing at the door.

Back in my cell, I sat on the bed at a loss as to what to do next.

What had Tagan been up to? Whatever it was, it had seriously got under Compton's skin and like a rabid terrier he was not letting go. Was Tagan simply gathering information about Earth to pave the way for an Earth/Ramian alliance or were his intentions more sinister as Compton seemed to be suggesting?

I hit the bed with my fists because quite frankly, I didn't know what else to do. Would Bennie have been able to get hold of Ahran before MI5 searched my house? Or had I just helped to deliver him to them on a plate.

Sometime later the door opened and I sat up. It was the guard who had brought me here earlier.

"Your solicitor is here."

"Thank God for that!" I said, standing up. I sent Bennie a silent thank you, she had obviously managed to get hold of Mr Collier.

I was taken to another room, the guard opened the door and the man who was waiting for me turned around.

To my surprise, it was the King Halsan's attaché, Sulaan. I didn't know whether to feel happy or upset.

He offered me his outstretched hand. "Miss McAllister."

I shook it. "Er..hello, it's good to see you." My mind raced, dare I feel hope that he was here to secure my release?

"Take a seat," he said, gesturing to the chair on the other side of the table. On the table was a pen and an A4 notebook.

"Obviously, I'm here to offer you advice and legal representation," he said, pointedly. "If you don't mind I would like to ask you a few questions first and then we can take it from there."

All I wanted him to do was tell me that he had a plan and it was going to be alright, but he was playing the role of the detached professional rather too well and I felt like screaming at him *Just get me out of here!*

"I understand you were detained four days ago. Can you tell me what you have been questioned about so far?"

He looked up from his notebook with his pen poised.

Suddenly the penny dropped as to why Sulaan was here. Maybe Bennie had managed to get hold of Ahran after all, but worried about Ramian security, the King had sent Sulaan to find out what the British government knew, rather than secure my release as I had thought. It made me angry, but what made me even more upset was that I had no idea where Ahran was and I couldn't ask.

"Please do what you can to get me out of here," I asked, through my teeth.

"We'll come to that in a moment. If you could just answer my questions first."

He was being infuriating. Where had the kindly uncle

figure gone that I had so often witnessed when he had been in Toby's company. It made me begin to doubt whether the kindness and hospitality of Toby's grandparents had all been a pretence too. Did I really not mean anything to them? Had my capture presented Ahran's father with an extremely convenient way of finally getting rid of me? Perhaps I had been a fool to think that I could ever really be a part of their lives in Ramia. Did Leylana know where I was? Surely, she wouldn't allow me to stay here any longer than I had to. And where the hell was Ahran?!

The nasty little voice in my head suggested that perhaps Ahran's father had finally been able to persuade Ahran that I was no good for him. I felt sick.

"Why have they called you in for questioning?" he asked.

I shrugged. "They seem to think that I know where my nephew's father is?"

"And do you?"

"No! I don't know anything," I said, eyeing him suspiciously.

"Why are they interested in him?"

"They haven't actually said, but I think they think he's a spy or something."

"And why would they think that?"

I sighed deeply and sat back into my chair. He obviously wasn't going to help me until I had answered all his questions. "They seem to think that he spent time travelling from country to country."

"Why do they consider that unusual?" he asked.

I threw my hands up in the air. "Because they seemed to think he was doing more than just sight-seeing."

"So, you haven't been able to give them any information about your nephew's father?"

"No, I don't know anything about him. The whole last few days have been a complete waste of time," I said in exasperation.

Sulaan closed his notebook.

"Can I suggest you don't say anymore unless I am present? In the meantime, I will make a case for you to be released, it is clear that you are unable to help them with their enquiries."

"At last. *Thank you*," I said with a frustrated edge.

Sulaan stood up. "I'll be in touch."

"Please do whatever you can to get me out of here," I said, grabbing his arm and giving him a meaningful look.

He looked at my hand on his arm and then back at me.

"As I said Miss McAllister, I'll be in touch."

I stared in disbelief at his back as he left. It would seem he had every intention of leaving me here. I was taken back to my cell where I cried myself to sleep.

6

I woke up, what must have been several hours later as the door opened and the stark light overhead, lit up the room. I sat up blinking.

"Get up," commanded a male voice.

"Now what?!" I said, getting to my feet

"Shut up!" he barked.

It was then that I realised it wasn't one of the uniformed MI5 security guards, but a man wearing a black boiler suit and a balaclava.

"What's going on?" I asked.

"It would be better for you if you don't say anything," he said, as he strode towards me. I glanced at the black rucksack he was carrying and couldn't help thinking his cultured accent jarred with his overall appearance.

"You need to come with me."

"Am I being released?" I asked, doubtfully.

"You're being moved," he said, walking towards me.

"Moved?! Where to? Who's ordered that I be moved?"

"Enough of your questions," he said.

My mind fogged as I struggled to understand what was happening. I watched his gloved hands unzip the rucksack he was holding and he pulled out a roll of duct tape. He dropped the bag on the floor. "Turn around. Put your hands behind your back," he demanded.

Stunned into silence, I did as he said, too frightened to do anything else. He roughly taped my hands together.

"Look, I think you've made a mistake," I said, finding my voice. "My solicitor was here today securing my release. I'm due to leave very soon."

"You leave me no choice," he said, tersely and turned me around to face him.

He pulled off a strip of tape and stuck it over my mouth. Any hope that I was being released began to fade. He grabbed my arm and pulled me roughly towards him. There was something vaguely familiar about him, but I couldn't put my finger on it.

It was clearly the middle of the night because the corridor lights outside my cell were dimmed. We walked quickly and he used a security pass to gain access through a number of doors. My mind raced. Why hide his identity? Was it another of Compton's tactics to intimidate me? Where was he taking me? Eventually, we came out into the underground car park. There were a number of cars parked and my captor pressed the remote-control button on his keypad. The indicators of one of the nearest cars flashed.

"Get in," he said, opening a rear door and looking over his shoulder to check that we hadn't been followed.

I soundlessly did as I was told and sat in the back seat,

my knees knocking together with fear whilst I waited for the man to get into the driver's seat. There was something about him that was at odds with his attire. I couldn't help thinking this wasn't normal behaviour for him because he seemed anxious and a little scared. It was a dangerous mix and it worried me. I didn't want to antagonise him because in his state of heightened anxiety, I really wasn't sure what he was capable of.

I tried to talk myself out of being so melodramatic. Maybe I *was* being rescued. Perhaps Sulaan had been unsuccessful in securing my release, but had arranged for someone to help me escape? It would explain the clandestine behaviour of this man and his dress. I felt a glimmer of hope and then it faded. If that were the case, why would he need to tape my hands and mouth? No, I had a bad feeling about this. Maybe Compton was even more ruthless than I thought and after realising that I was of no use to him had decided to do away with me. But this was the British government they wouldn't be allowed to do something like that. Would they? My thoughts began to ricochet off in all sorts of directions. Didn't thousands of people go missing every year never to be found again? I had threatened to go to the press and perhaps I was being taken off somewhere to be silenced for good. All sorts of grizzly scenarios began to play out in my mind.

Arghhh! I was sending myself silly. I had clearly watched far too many films. That sort of thing doesn't really happen and then I reflected on the last couple of years and reluctantly realised, anything was possible.

I sat back in my seat as we travelled quickly through the

streets of London. Not too fast as to attract attention to ourselves, but fast enough to get where we were going as quickly as possible. I looked into the rear-view mirror and made eye contact with the dark gaze of my captor. I looked away. What could I do? Thanks to the tape I couldn't try and talk myself out of this one, and tied up, there was absolutely nothing I could physically do, so I sat there watching the townscape go by, quietly shaking, and fearing the worst.

It was late and there were few people about, just the odd person standing at a bus stop minding their own business or the shapeless mound of a homeless person shrouded in a sleeping bag in a shop doorway uncared for, unnoticed even, by those who walked past them. But for a moment I envied them, they were at least free and no matter how much they had been let down by the state, they weren't about to be ruthlessly dispatched by it. I tried to put these thoughts out of my mind and silently watched the scenery go by. London was indeed a soulless, lonely place at night.

We had been travelling for about thirty minutes when we pulled into a shadowy back street behind a warehouse. There was no street lighting and the place was deserted. My captor turned off the car engine and waited. Inside the car was warm, but I struggled to stop myself from shivering. I had no idea where we were or what we were waiting for. The driver tapped an impatient rhythm out on the steering wheel with his thumb, when suddenly a set of headlights appeared, lighting up the street. The car stopped behind us. My captor got out and I could hear raised voices. I jumped when the door next to me opened.

"Get out," he said.

I climbed out of the car and stumbled. With my hands tied I underestimated how much one used arms for balance. He marched me over to the waiting car. In the driver's seat was a balding and slightly overweight middle-aged man, who unlike the guy in the balaclava made no obvious attempt to hide his identity.

"Can you do what I've asked without fucking it up?" said the man who had kidnapped me.

"Yes, yes," the driver in the car replied.

This put the fear of God in me. What had he been asked to do? I had visions of being taken somewhere remote, being brutally murdered and my body dumped in a ditch only to be discovered by some poor, unwitting dog walker a few days later.

The next thing I knew I was bundled into the back of the car, my worst fears seemingly being realised. Suddenly it occurred to me who the man in the balaclava was. It was Mr Ormerod the MI5 officer who had accompanied me to MI5 HQ. Why was he hiding behind a balaclava and a boiler suit? The minutes passed and I tried to make sense of what was going on. There was only one thing I could do and so I began to thrash about.

"Hey, that's enough lady," the driver said in a cockney accent. He was obviously some kind of East End hit man. I ignored him and thrashed about some more, swinging my legs up to kick the door.

"Oi! What d'you fink you're doin'."

And then I had an idea. I slipped off one of my shoes and managed to hook my toe under the door handle. With one pull the door flew open and I could hear the rush of tyres on tarmac.

I wasn't quite sure what my plan was, but jumping out seemed as good a plan as any, the only downside was that this time I didn't have Ahran to protect me. However, whatever was about to happen, I wasn't about to make it easy for this *bozo*. I inched myself towards the door.

The driver shot a glance over his shoulder. "*Jesus Christ!*"

He pulled the car over and we came to an abrupt halt. I rolled off the seat and got wedged in the foot well behind the front seats. With my hands bound, I was well and truly stuck.

The driver got out of the car and leaned in through the open door.

"Wha' are you playing at?" he said.

I tried to scream and thrash about some more, but only managed to wedge myself in even tighter.

He went back into the front of the car and racked the seat forward before pulling me out.

"You could've got yourself killed," he said angrily. "Not to mention ruin me business."

I caught sight of his hackney carriage driver identity badge clipped to his belt. He was a cabby. This surprised me. Why would MI5 hire a cabby to dispose of me? Was he moonlighting to supplement his income by doing MI5's dirty work at night? Or was it just a disguise?

I tried to scream.

"Alright love, just calm down, 'ere let me take this off." He leaned towards me and I shrank away from him.

"Sorry, this might 'urt a bit," he said as he slowly peeled off the tape covering my mouth. I winced at the sharp burn of it.

"Now are you gonna behave yourself?"

I nodded. "Yes, and thank you, but please don't kill me," I said, my voice hoarse from all the screaming.

"I ain't gonna kill ya," he said, sounding bemused.

"Then where are you taking me?"

"I've been paid to take you to an address."

"What address?"

He shook his head. "Nah, nah, you ain't going to trick me love. I ain't supposed to tell you anyfink."

"I just want to know where you are taking me."

"Look lady, don't you give me no trouble. As far as I'm concerned, this is just a job. I've been paid to take you somewhere and that's what I'm gonna do."

I could hear him muttering to himself as he flicked the child lock switches on the doors. "I ain't got time to mess about."

He got back into the driver's seat and started the engine. We began to pick up speed as we re-joined the dual carriageway.

I struggled to figure out what was going on. It was all very odd. "Look Ron, I don't want to cause you any trouble."

"'Ow do you know me name?"

"It's on your identity badge."

"Shit!" he said, sounding cross with himself.

It appeared he wasn't used to ferrying passengers bound with duct tape around.

"Whatever that guy has paid you, I will pay you double," I said.

He shook his head and gave a humourless chuckle. "I'm sorry love, I value me balls. I ain't getting involved in this any more than I have to. I've gotta wife with MS and three kids to feed, I can't afford to be knee-capped." We pulled up at some traffic lights. "That bloke back there may have sounded like Prince Charles, but I wouldn't trust him as far as I could throw 'im."

"Please can you just stop at a phone box? I promise I won't cause you any more trouble."

"I'm sorry love. I'd love to 'elp ya, I really would, but it ain't worf the risk."

"Pleeease, you don't know what I've been through over the last few days."

He shrugged apologetically. "Look all I can do is take ya to where I've been told to take ya. It ain't much furver now."

He clearly wasn't going to budge. I sighed and looked out of the window. We were leaving the lights of the suburbs behind us and were travelling along quieter, darker, country roads. I hadn't been paying much attention to the road signs so I made more of a concerted effort to try and work out where we were or where we could possibly be heading. There weren't many landmarks, just hedges and field gateways. We took a left turn and the car began to slow.

"I fink it's 'ere somewhere," Ron said, peering at some woodland as we drove past it.

We came to a halt at the end of a track.

"This is it?" I asked, looking out into the gloomy darkness.

"Yup. Out ya get."

"But there's nothing here," I said, feeling panicked.

"That ain't my problem. Now get out of the car."

"You can't leave me here, it's in the middle of nowhere."

"Look love, this ain't my business. Are you gonna get out of the car or do I have to drag you out?"

"Come on Ron, you're not a bad person. You wouldn't leave a defenceless woman here on her own. Just take me to a police station, I'll testify that you were blackmailed."

"Just get out of the fucking car," he shouted. I was obviously testing his patience.

"I can't, in case you hadn't noticed my hands are tied and you put the child locks on earlier," I spat.

He huffed and got out of the car to open the door. I climbed out and glared at him. "Can you at least cut the tape off my hands?"

He didn't say anything and quickly got back into the driver's seat.

"Please Ron, please don't leave me here," I begged, when I realised he was actually going to leave me here on my own.

The engine roared to life and the wheels spun before he shot off down the road, leaving me standing there all alone. Some woodland creature gave out a blood curdling screech. If I hadn't been so scared, I would have laughed at the cliché.

Unfortunately, it was a cloudy, moonless night and I strained my eyes in the dark. Now what? I had thought at first that I was being transferred, but the guy in the bala-clava was far too edgy for it to have been an official trans-fer. And then there had been Ron who couldn't get rid of me quick enough and now I was standing here in the middle of nowhere. A horrible thought stuck me, maybe I was about to be disposed of after all. As if to confirm my suspicions, I heard footsteps coming from the track. My heart began to pound as I realised with dismay that this dark lane in the middle of nowhere was about to be the location of my execution.

I started to back away frantically looking for a place to hide. The most obvious place was in the hedge, but the tangled mess of brambles standing in my way made that option impossible, so I ran. I ran as fast as my tied wrists would allow.

The next thing I knew a pair of arms wrapped around me.

"Get off me, let me go," I screamed as I struggled to break free.

"Sophie, it's me Ahran."

Suddenly I lost all my fight. "Ahran! Oh God, Ahran," I said, my legs buckling beneath me. I nearly died with relief and burst into tears.

He scooped me up into his arms and laid his cheek on my forehead.

"Shhh," he said as if soothing a child.

"You bastard! Why didn't you come and rescue me?" I sobbed. "I've been in that hell-hole for four days and, and, you... you just left me there!" I knew I was being completely unreasonable. There was no way I would have wanted him to have even tried to rescue me at the risk of him being caught.

"You don't know how much I wanted to, but that place is impenetrable."

I lay heavily in his arms. The fear and panic of the last couple of hours began to dissipate and it left me feeling weak.

"Come on, let me take you inside."

He carried me back down the track. I wanted to ask so many questions, but didn't have the strength to voice any of them for now. What mattered was that Ahran was here. He carried me in silence until we eventually reached a small thatched cottage. The sweet smell of wood smoke was in the air and the light glowed invitingly at the window. For now, I was safe.

7

Once we were inside the cottage, Ahran put me down and lowered his lips to mine.

I pulled away. "Don't kiss me, I need a shower. I haven't had a proper wash in days."

"I couldn't care less," he said, kissing me again. "I've been so worried."

"Are you going to untie me?"

"I wasn't going to immediately, I thought it could be interesting," he said with an arch of an eyebrow.

I stamped my foot. "Ahran, you are not funny!" Although, not quite able to keep the smile from my face. I felt so relieved. Not only was I safe, but he still wanted me.

"Let me get something to cut that tape," he said, as he went into the kitchen.

He came back out brandishing a pair of scissors and cut the tape from my wrists.

"Ah, my shoulders," I said, circling them a few times

and rubbing where the tape had been. "Why on earth did I have to be tied up?"

"I had no idea you would be," Ahran said apologetically and began to massage my stiff muscles.

"What did Sulaan say to them?"

"It wasn't Sulaan who got you out."

"Who was it then?"

"Bennie. Sulaan tried his hardest, but they weren't having any of it. They think Tagan is a dangerous terrorist and you and Toby are the only ones with any connection to him, they weren't going to let you go without some answers."

"Terrorist? Bennie?" I said, repeating the two words that had taken me by surprise. "Since when did Bennie hold any sway with MI5?" I said, picking the detail that was more of an immediate concern. I'd often thought she looked like a Bond girl, but a double agent? I couldn't quite see it.

"She doesn't, but her boyfriend does. Apparently, he mixes in those kind of circles and was able to pull a few strings."

I still couldn't understand why I had been bound and gagged, although I felt a certain sense of satisfaction that we had outwitted Compton. He would do his nut when he found out.

"So, they think Tagan was a terrorist?"

Ahran nodded. "He'd hacked into government computers; they believe he was planning some kind of attack. The British government have a price on his head and you were their only lead."

"I don't get it. Why now? It's nearly twelve years since

Tagan disappeared, surely they realise he's no longer a threat."

"That's what I've been asking myself. It seems such a coincidence that you should be arrested the morning you arrive back."

He turned me around and gave me a brief kiss on the lips. "Let's talk about this later, we need to get back to Ramia."

"Can I at least have a bath? I said, looking around at the cosy interior. Faded chintzy curtains matched the sofa and armchair and a fire roared in the hearth. "Where are we anyway?"

"We're about half an hour from Hatherley. I wasn't sure when you were being delivered and I wanted somewhere remote and away from CCTV cameras." He paused. "I suppose you can have a bath; they won't know you are missing until the morning."

He led me up to the bedroom and went into the bath-room to turn on the taps. I began to undress. When Ron the taxi driver had brought me to a remote wood, I really thought my number was up. And now I was here with Ahran, anticipating a lovely warm bath. It seemed life had a habit of taking the most unlikely of turns. I padded naked into the bathroom and was met by the warm smell of roses. I cleaned my teeth and then slipped into the suds with a deep sigh. Ahran had gone downstairs and judging by the noises coming from the kitchen, was up to something.

I closed my eyes. Like a cat with nine lives, it seemed I had survived yet another close shave and I wondered when my luck would finally run out. I quickly suppressed the thought. I had come so far on my journey of self-improvement, but from time to time the old negativity found its way through, usually when I was tired and my resources were low. These days I was better equipped to deal with it, more able to block such thoughts before they started to spiral out of control. Just being here with Ahran gave me strength. He was like my own personal energiser and just being in his company made me feel stronger and more resilient.

He came into the bathroom holding a mug of tea and a bacon sandwich.

"You know your way to a girl's heart," I said, pulling myself up out of the water.

"I know my way to *this* girl's heart," he said with a heart-thumping smile.

He sat next to the bath and I sank my teeth into the bread before taking a swig of tea. "Oh my God, that's good."

"I can't quite believe you're here. That's the last time you travel back to Earth on your own. We have become too complacent," he said.

"To be fair, we had no idea that they were after Tagan. Did you know what he was doing here?"

"I did. But I'm not sure how much the King and Queen knew. Tagan had this romantic notion that one day Earth and Ramia could become allies. He also hoped to find answers to the questions about our origins so that we could fully understand who we are and where we come from."

I digested this information, I had obviously been right about Tagan's reasons for being here.

"Tagan loved Earth," he continued. "He said it felt like

home to him and he hated that we had to hide our identity here."

"I thought MI5 had found out about Ramia, about Toby." I paused for a moment or two. "Does it really matter that much to Ramians, you know, finding out about where you come from? It seems to me that you would stand to lose more than you'd gain if Earth ever find out about your world."

Ahran nodded. "It matters a great deal."

If I didn't know the origins of man, I'm not sure it would bother me that much, but I had to respect that it was important to them. I finished the last of my sandwich and drained my mug.

"Now I'm feeling more human."

"Let me wash you." He squeezed some shampoo into his hands and began to massage it into my hair. I closed my eyes and leaned back. He was always so in tune with me, always knowing the right thing to do or say and I bathed in the love I felt for him. He worked in silence, giving me the time I needed to recover from my ordeal.

"You were wasted in the army, you would have made a wonderful hairdresser," I said, enjoying the feel of his fingertips massaging my scalp.

He chuckled, but didn't reply and after rinsing the suds from my hair, began to soap my neck, shoulders and back with gentle strokes.

"Lean back," he instructed.

He turned his attention to my chest and soaped my breasts and tummy, then quickly rinsed me off and sat back on his heels.

I turned to look at him. "Why have you stopped?"

"Because if I don't stop I know how this is going to end and I don't want to stay here any longer than we have to."

I knew what he was saying made sense, but another hour wasn't going to make any difference.

"We're safe for now. You said yourself that they won't know I'm gone until the morning." I reached out and took hold of his hand and kissed his knuckles.

"No seduction, Sophie," he warned and pulled his hand away to grab a big fluffy towel from the radiator. He held it out for me and I sighed and pulled the plug out. I stepped out of the bath and found myself wrapped tightly in a towel and his arms.

"I cannot risk losing you again," he said solemnly.

"Believe me, I have no intention of coming back here on my own."

"Ah, what is it you say? That is a song to my ears."

"You mean, *that is music to my ears*," I chuckled.

"Are you laughing at me?" he said with a glint in his eye,

"Yes! What are you going to do about it?" I said, dropping my towel before turning and shrieking as I ran into the bedroom with him hot on my heels. It felt so good to be here with the man I loved more than life itself. Less than an hour ago I'd had no idea when or if I was ever going to see him again and all I wanted now was to feel his arms around me. He took me down on the bed.

I squealed as he pinned my arms above my head.

"You need to learn to respect your elders," he said as he began to nuzzle my neck.

His lips were beginning to work their magic and I struggled to concentrate on what he was saying. I pushed his sweater up and ran my hands over his beautiful torso. He broke away from my kiss and whipped his sweater over his head and wriggled out of his jeans.

I felt the sudden desire to possess him and be possessed by him as my lips sought his. The love I felt for him poured out of me and with every lap of my tongue and stroke of my hand I branded myself into him. When we were making love, it was like we operated on a different level. Our hands and our mouths fed an altogether different existential plane, we were not only together physically, but we were unified spiritually. Our delicate souls sang together, danced together, embraced each other until nothing beyond the field of *us* mattered. From the outside we were like any other couple enjoying physical lovemaking, on the inside it was an all-consuming inner revelry of what we meant to each other.

I kissed the spot over his heart and felt the quickened thud of it beneath my lips. I closed my eyes and inhaled the smell of him. He smelled of soap, faintly of wool and that slight hint of the sun. I loved his scent more than any other smell in the world. I took the hard bead of his nipple between my lips and tugged gently. This elicited a groan from him that hit me in the pit of my stomach like a thunderbolt of arousal. I brushed my lips across his chest and down his stomach until he grabbed hold of my shoulders and pulled me up his body. His heavenly mouth worked against my lips and his tongue began to tease. His kisses were always the deliciously hot precursor to what his body was about to do to mine and I could feel myself drifting into that special place with him. No move I made was a conscious one, every touch of my fingers and kiss of my mouth was driven by instinct. Tonight love was not being made, it was already there in abundance, each caress of our hands and whisper of encouragement only served to reinforce and affirm the feelings we had for one another. I yielded to the gentle pressure Ahran was applying and we began an exquisite duet where every stroke bonded me to him and him to me.

As we lay in each other's arms a little while later, I began to realise that after what had happened over the last few days, I no longer had a life here on Earth, my life was in Ramia now with Toby, with Ahran, and with my family.

"SOPHIE. Mootya. It's time to wake up," Ahran whispered gently in my ear.

It felt like I hadn't slept for a week and the last thing I wanted was to be dragged into consciousness.

"Just a while longer," I mumbled, turning over.

"Come on sleepy head, we need to leave."

Other than a weak wave of my hand, I didn't move.

Ahran chuckled. "So, you want to go back to MI5 and get to know those bastards better?"

That did it. I sat up with a groan, "What time is it?"

"Four thirty. We can't stay here any longer."

There was an urgency to his voice that seemed to do the trick.

"Okay, I'm up," I said, getting out of bed, squinting as I searched for my clothes.

"Here." Ahran said, handing me a pile of new clothes. "I got these for you, I figured you might need them." He was already fully dressed and his hair was slicked back from where he'd washed his face and combed it through with his fingers.

"Thanks." I said, taking them from him. "You don't know how much I could do with some clean clothes." I started to dress. "Can I just grab a cup of tea?"

He handed me a travel mug and smiled.

"Oh, you're goood," I said with a satisfied nod. "Have I ever told you, you will make a wonderful husband?"

"Often," he said with a cheeky grin. "Now get your butt into those clothes."

"Okay, okay, I'm on it," I said, thrusting a foot into the jeans he had given me.

Ahran and I had enjoyed a wonderful courtship even after a shaky start. We had overcome so many obstacles, more than the average couple, and we had discussed marriage a number of times although it was rarely me who raised the topic. I knew that one day he would ask me, when the time was right, but it was never a subject I pushed. I was just thankful that, against all the odds, we had found one another. Although, I couldn't deny there was a part of me that wanted him to be absolutely sure that he was making the right choice by settling for me, not only was I a mere Sapien, but the chances of us ever being able to have kids were virtually non-existent.

A few minutes later, I stood on the doorstep in Ahran's

jacket with my hands around my mug whilst he locked the cottage. It wouldn't be long before it started to get light. It was a pretty little house and under different circumstances I would have loved to have spent a few days holed up here with him, but it would be foolish to stay here any longer.

"Whose place is this?" I asked.

"It belongs to a friend of a friend."

"Maybe when we get back home we can go away for a few days," I suggested as we got into a silver hire car. "We could go to that place you used to go to with Tagan when you were kids. What was it called? Marka something."

"Markoosh," he replied.

"Yes, let's go there."

Ahran smiled and started the engine and we drove down the track. "It sounds far more exotic than the static caravan in Wales I used to go to with Bennie," I mused.

And then a thought occurred to me. "Why did you go to Bennie for help?"

"Do you mean with your rescue?"

I nodded.

"I didn't, she offered. She said that her boyfriend had connections in high places and persuaded me to let her at least try," he shook his head as if he couldn't quite believe it, "And she delivered."

I thought about my best friend. We were inseparable as kids, in fact we were pretty inseparable as adults for a while, but life took over, we got jobs, she moved to London and then landed a job with the BBC which took her all over the world. We still managed to stay close, and then I moved to Ramia and we contacted less often and met up even less. I felt a pang of guilt. And now I was going back to Ramia and I had no idea when I would see her again. There was every reason to believe that I might not come back to Earth, ever. This brought a lump to my throat. I couldn't quite get my head around never seeing her again.

We were about ten minutes away from Hatherley. "I need to see Bennie," I said quietly.

"I'm sorry Sophie, that's not possible," Ahran said, dismissing the idea.

I swivelled in my seat to face him. "I need to see her Ahran. Not only has she virtually saved my life, she is my closest and oldest friend. I may never see her again." The prospect of this hit me right in the chest and I let out a sob.

Ahran looked at me with sympathy, but I could see determination in his eyes. "We cannot stay here any longer Sophie. It's not safe."

I thought back over our recent conversations. "I can't leave without seeing her. Something's going on in her life and I can't leave without knowing that everything is alright."

"You can call her from Ramia," he said more insistently.

"I've tried to talk to her over the phone and she always comes up with some excuse to end our conversation."

"No, Sophie, we don't have time."

I placed my hand on his arm. "Please Ahran, if Tagan was alive and you thought he was in trouble, you would want to see him, talk to him."

"This is different. It's not safe."

"You're with me, it's not as if I will be alone and unprotected like before," I petitioned.

84

He took a deep breath and sighed, knowing he was fighting a losing battle.

"Okay, but only if she is still in Hatherley. If she has gone back to London, it is out of the question."

I wiped my eyes, pleased I had won him over. "Can I have your phone?"

"It's in my jacket pocket," he said, resignedly. He was clearly not happy about this at all.

"Do you have her number?"

He nodded.

"Bennie," I said into the phone. It dialled automatically and began to ring.

She answered. "Ahran? Is everything okay?" she said, sounding a little groggy. It was still very early and I had obviously woken her up.

"Bennie, it's me."

"Ah Sophie! You don't know how good it is to hear your voice. Ahran sent me a text to say that you had arrived safely."

"Safe and sound," I said. "Although, don't quite understand why the mystery man and the duct tape."

Bennie chuckled. "Oh God! He tied you up?! I'm so sorry, Giles Ormerod is a mate of Tristan's. I think he liked the idea of the money, but was scared shitless."

"Tristan's your boyfriend?"

"Yeah."

"He must think a lot of you Ben."

"Got him eating out the palm of my hand," she said with an air of smugness.

She may have been a self-confessed man-eater, but I

knew she was a hundred times more loyal to her friends than the man in her life. I was relieved to hear that she sounded a lot more like the old Bennie I knew and loved.

"Don't you think it's about time you kept your nose out of trouble Sophe?"

"Oh God, tell me about it! Drama is overrated as far as I'm concerned. Look hun, I know it's bloody early, but I don't suppose you could meet us?" I said, getting to the point of my call.

"What time is it?" She paused. "It's 5 o' clock!"

"I know, it's just that we are due to catch a flight," I said, cringing at the lie, as far as she was concerned, Ahran and his family lived in southern France. She knew nothing about Ramia. "And I don't know when I'm going to see you again." Perhaps it was time I told her the truth. "I don't suppose you are still at your mum and dad's?" I asked, subconsciously crossing my fingers. I knew I wouldn't be able to persuade Ahran to make a detour back to London.

She hesitated. "I...yes."

"Fantastic!" I said, feeling relieved. "Can you meet us at...?" I looked at Ahran knowing he could hear our conversation.

"At the truck stop just off the A21," he said.

"At that greasy spoon by the garden centre."

She didn't reply.

"Ben?"

"Yes, okay then," she said eventually. I detected her lack of enthusiasm and it hurt. Maybe this really was goodbye.

"See you in a bit."

"Okay, see you in a bit."

"Bye." I ended the call.

"Something is definitely up. I think she's cross with me about always being away, maybe it's time I told her about Ramia."

"Sophie, we haven't got long," Ahran warned.

"I know, I know."

FIFTEEN MINUTES later we pulled into the car park of *Pete's Place* and I spotted Bennie's black Golf.

To my surprise, I had butterflies in my stomach. I wasn't quite sure what I was going to say, but I was looking forward to giving her a hug and hoping to get some reassurance that everything was alright between us.

I unclicked my seat belt and got out of the car. The car park was quiet, but there was a light on inside the café indicating that the cafe was already open.

I walked towards Bennie's car with a smile on my face which quickly began to fade when I saw her get out.

She was wearing sweatpants, a heavy woollen jumper and Ugg boots. Her hair was scraped back in a messy ponytail and she looked tired and washed out.

"Hi Sophe," she said, slightly awkwardly and sounding more than a little guarded.

I gave her a hug and noticed how much slimmer she felt.

"Is everything okay?" I said, holding her at arm's length.

"You can't expect a girl to look like a movie star when you drag her out of bed at the crack of dawn," she said jokily, even though her eyes were wary.

"Hi Ahran, it's good to see you." She gave him an awkward peck on each cheek.

"Come on, let's go inside," I said, taking her arm and glancing back at Ahran.

His face was expressionless.

We ordered some tea and coffee and sat down at a table in the corner. I noticed Bennie glance at Ahran, as if she was waiting for him to say something, but he had started to take a great interest in the laminated breakfast menu on the table. The atmosphere between us felt odd.

"What's going on?" I said, looking from Bennie to Ahran. I had the distinct feeling that there was something they weren't telling me. Neither of them spoke immediately. Bennie and I weren't in the habit of pussy footing around one another so I just came out with it. "You look worn out, are you okay?"

She added two sugars to her coffee and started stirring slowly. "Don't start getting all over-protective. I've been burning the candle at both ends and just need to take some time out," she said, not looking me in the eyes.

"Is it drugs?" I said in a hushed voice. It would at least explain her poor complexion and why she looked so washed out.

She let out a little snort as if what I had said amused her. "Nothing I can't handle."

I leaned towards her, "Is it that bloody toff you're seeing?" I said, thinking back to my earlier suspicions that he had somehow drawn her into a world of champagne and drugs.

She shook her head and gave a half smile. "It's that *bloody toff* that saved your arse."

I felt a pang of guilt. "I know. I'm sorry. I should thank him."

She nodded in agreement.

I placed my hand on her arm. "I'm worried about you."

"You don't need to worry about me," she said, her gaze meeting mine. "You just concentrate on looking after Toby."

"But I do worry about you. You're my best friend and I feel like we're…we're drifting apart."

She glanced at Ahran again. "Things are just a bit complicated at the moment." And then she looked at her watch. "Hadn't you better get going? It won't be long before MI5 realise you've gone and you need to be on that plane."

I got the distinct impression she didn't really want to be here and the furtive looks between her and Ahran puzzled me.

"Bennie's right, we need to go," Ahran concurred. He seemed just as uncomfortable being here as Bennie did. At first I thought his reluctance to meet Bennie was because he wanted to get back to Ramia as quickly as possible, but now I wasn't so sure.

I looked at them both and started to feel irritated. They were keeping something from me, and yet neither of them seemed prepared to offer any explanation.

"Why do I get the feeling I'm missing something?"

"You are, the last four days!" Bennie said flippantly. "We've been so worried about you, haven't we Ahran?"

There was something about the way she said *we* that made me start to draw conclusions that just seemed too weird to even contemplate. Was there something going on between Ahran and *Bennie*?

Suddenly, I felt peculiar and more than a little sick. I tried to tell myself I was being ridiculous.

"It's time we left," Ahran said and stood up.

"Phone me when you get there," Bennie said, following suit. This meeting was clearly over. Bennie hugged me and I returned her hug a little stiffly. It was unlike Bennie to initiate a hug. "We'll have a proper catch up when everything has settled down."

I nodded, feeling like I had been winded. I had come here worried that something was going on in her life and I was leaving fearing that the something I was worried about was *my* boyfriend.

I hesitated, looking from Bennie to Ahran, not sure what to do or say next.

"Go!" she said forcefully.

I watched her kiss Ahran and him give her a hug in return. "Bye Ben," I said numbly, wondering when they had become such good friends.

"Call me," she called after us as Ahran steered me out of the café.

We had just got to the car when Bennie came running out. "Sophe, wait!"

Had her conscience got the better of her and she'd decided that she couldn't let me leave without telling me?

She held out her phone. "It's Audrey, she's been looking for you," she said out of breath.

"Audrey?" I said, looking at the phone and wondering what could possibly be the matter for Audrey, one of my oldest friends, to call me on Bennie's phone at this time of the morning.

I had visions of my oldest friend having fallen down the stairs or maybe there was something wrong with her partner, Paul. "Audrey? Are you okay?" I said, holding the phone to my ear, my own drama momentarily forgotten.

"Sophie, thank God I've got hold of you. You weren't answering your phone.

I glanced at Bennie who looked troubled.

"What is it Audes?"

"It's Toby."

I felt a shot of adrenaline. These were two words I wasn't expecting to hear.

"What do you mean?"

"Toby is *here*."

I looked at Ahran in horror and he shook his head in fearful disbelief.

"I can't get any sense out of him," Audrey said. "He doesn't seem right. He says that you have been captured and that he's here to offer himself in return for your release. I asked him how he got here, but he wouldn't tell me. What on Earth is going on?"

"Have you told anyone else he's there?" I asked.

"No, not yet, but I wondered if I should call the police. Are you in some kind of trouble?"

I froze to the spot. "No, no, no, whatever you do, don't call the police!"

"Can you please tell me what is going on?" Audrey said with an edge of frustration.

"There's nothing to worry about I promise, he is

completely mistaken. Just keep him there and we will come and get him straightaway."

We got into the car and Ahran started the engine. I handed Bennie her phone back. "I'll call you," I said, getting into the passenger seat. In the next moment we wheel spun out of the car park and left Bennie standing in the car park.

"If MI5 find out that Toby is here…"

"I know, I know," Ahran said, putting his foot to the floor.

"Why did the King and Queen tell Toby I had been arrested?"

"I'm not sure they did."

"So how the hell did he know?" I said angrily.

"I have no idea."

Ahran's phone rang. "It's Halsan," I said, reading the display.

I was half tempted not to answer it, I knew he would be doing his nut and it would only be five minutes before we had Toby and were on our way back to Ramia.

"Answer it," Ahran said, noticing my hesitation. "If you don't, things could get out of hand."

I answered the call. Halsan didn't even give me a chance to speak before he launched into a flurry of angry and panicked Ramian.

"Halsan, it's Sophie," I said, when he paused for breath.

"Put me onto Ahran," he said in English.

I was a little hurt that he hadn't asked how I was, but understood his fear and worry. Hell, I wouldn't be able to breathe easily until we were at Audrey's.

"Ahran is driving. But don't worry we know where Toby is and we'll be there in five minutes."

"You know where he is?" he asked. "I have agents searching for him as we speak."

"He's with a friend of mine. He's safe."

"He's on Earth?! No one can find out he's there," Halsan warned.

"I know and they won't," I promised. "Left here Ahran," I said, directing him towards Audrey's. "We'll be back in Ramia in fifteen minutes."

There was a perceptible sigh of relief down the line. "Be careful. Oh, and it's good to hear your voice Sophie."

"Er…thanks," I said, pleased that he had actually acknowledged me. "See you shortly."

I hung up feeling jittery, I was just as worried as Halsan and wouldn't be happy until we were safely through the portal. "Her house is just at the end, Hunter's Cottage."

Ahran came to a halt outside Audrey's house. I couldn't help looking back down the street to see if anyone had noticed our arrival, but apart from the milkman who was going about his morning deliveries, Audrey's road was quiet. I glanced at the clock on the dashboard it was six twenty. Thank goodness it was still early. I put my concerns about Bennie and Ahran to the back of my mind as I galvanised into action and ran up Audrey's front path with Ahran close behind. I knocked on the front door and Audrey opened it in her dressing gown.

"Sophie love, come in."

"You've met Ahran haven't you," I said as we walked into her hallway.

"Yes, nice to see you again Ahran."

"Good to see you too Audrey," he said, bending to give her a kiss on each cheek.

"I haven't had a chance to get dressed," she said, clearly feeling embarrassed that she was still in her nightclothes. She seemed a little flustered. Even women in their sixties weren't immune to the *Ahran Effect*.

"Where's Toby?" I said, looking over her shoulder.

"He's in there having some breakfast."

"Is Paul here?" I asked.

"He's upstairs having a shower," she said as we made our way down the corridor towards the kitchen. "He'll be down in a minute."

"Would you like a cup of tea?" Audrey asked

We entered the kitchen. "I'm afraid we can't stop Audes. I know you must be wondering what on Earth is going on, but it's…" I stopped in my tracks as I noticed Toby's half eaten piece of toast on the table, his vacant chair and the back door wide open.

"Oh my God!" I could feel the blood draining from my face.

Ahran shot out of the back door.

"Toby?!" I screamed as I ran out after him.

8

To my complete relief, Toby and Ahran were walking back across the lawn, Ahran's arm around Toby's shoulders. Toby had one of Audrey's cats in his arms.

"Auntie Sophie!" he said when he saw me.

"Ah Toby, please don't ever do that again!" I put my arm around him and kissed his hair. "You really frightened us."

"Do what? I only went outside to get Audrey's cat."

"Where do I start?" Going into Audrey's back garden to chase the cat was only half of it, there was the small matter of him coming back to Earth, on his own!

"Marmalade was meowing to come in, but when I opened the door she ran away, so I went into the garden to find her," he explained.

"Why have you even come here? You know it's not safe," I said, pulling him from me and holding him at arm's length.

"Magdala told me she had overheard a conversation that you had come back and been arrested and I guessed it might be because of my kidnap, so I thought if I went to the police they would see that I was alright and let you go."

"Magdala told you?" I said. Magdala was Toby's tutor, she was a sweet, intelligent young woman and I was surprised she had given this away. She knew better than to tell him anything that might compromise his security. "Where was your bodyguard?"

"Magdala said she would help me get back to Earth and told Enriq that we were going on an early morning nature trail around the palace gardens and that there was no need for him to come."

"She took you to the portal?" I asked.

"Yes," replied Toby.

I looked up at Ahran, and gave him a look as if to say *Why would she do such a thing?*

"She was only trying to help," Toby said in his tutor's defence. "Please don't tell Paps, I don't want her to get into trouble."

"Don't worry you're not going to get her into trouble," I said, knowing full well that she had done a pretty good job of that herself.

Audrey had joined us. "Can someone please tell me what is going on? What's a portal?" She asked looking totally confused.

Dammit! I'd made a careless slip. Like Bennie, she knew that Toby hadn't really been kidnapped, but she had no idea about Ramia. I took hold of Audrey's hands. "We need to talk Audrey, but we can't do it now." I said pleadingly. "We've got to get Toby back to safety. I know it is all terribly confusing, but there are people out there who still want to get hold of Toby and we cannot afford to stay here any longer. There's no time to explain. Please don't tell anyone you've seen us and make no mention of a portal." I gently squeezed her hands, willing her to understand and feeling guilty that this wasn't the first time I had done this to her.

"I don't like the sound of it Sophie."

In the distance, I could hear a police siren and it panicked me. "I know, it's all very confusing, but the sooner we get going the better. I promise that one day I will explain everything to you." I couldn't bring myself to tell her that this day could be a very long time from now.

Audrey's face was a picture of concern and worry. She looked like she was about to argue, but obviously thought better of it. "Alright dear, but look after yourself and Toby." She looked at Ahran. "I feel happier that they have you. You're a well-built young man."

"Don't worry I will protect them," Ahran replied. "We need to go Sophie."

"I know." I looked at Audrey apologetically. "I'll be in touch."

She nodded.

We made our way to the front door. Both Toby and I said our goodbyes whilst Ahran checked that the coast was clear.

"Please don't worry, we'll be fine," I said, giving her a hug.

"We miss you Sophie, it's not the same around here without you." She looked like she was on the verge of tears.

I felt terrible. We'd turned up out of the blue and were leaving as quickly as we had come with no word of explanation. I knew it wasn't fair on her. "I'm so sorry Audes, I hate leaving like this, but the sooner we go the better. I'll be in touch."

I hoped she wouldn't make me feel any worse than I already did.

"Don't leave it too long," she said, waving a stern finger at me.

"I won't, I promise."

She waved us off from the lounge window.

"Did you hear that siren?" I said to Ahran once we were back in the car, before I'd realised it was a stupid question. Of course he'd heard it.

"Yes, it was heading in the opposite direction."

"Thank goodness!" I felt decidedly jumpy.

"Are you alright Auntie Sophie?" Toby asked.

I turned around to look at him in the back seat.

"I'm fine," I said, trying to put on a brave face. "But please don't go pulling anymore stunts like that again."

"I won't," he promised.

We pulled out of Audrey's road and through the village towards my house and the portal. We drove past the coffee shop and I felt a little pang for my old life which had been so much simpler and much less fraught with fear and worry even though it hadn't felt like it at the time. But I didn't have Ahran then and I knew I would accept whatever life had to throw at me if it meant we could be together. Once back in

Ramia, we would all be able to get on with our lives. Although, my heart felt heavy at the thought of not seeing my friends, I also had no idea how I was going to complete on the sale of the coffee shop from Ramia.

Ahran glanced in the rear-view mirror as if something had just caught his attention.

"What is it?"

I turned around to see two unmarked police cars shoot past us. They turned left ahead of us, down my road. I looked across at him. "That's not good."

"No, it's not, get down both of you."

We drove past the road leading to my house and saw the police cars parked outside, along with the two unmarked cars that had just passed us.

Ahran swore and drove on by.

"What about the portal?"

"We can't take the chance."

It wasn't until we were on the dual carriageway, heading away from Hatherley, that Ahran picked up speed.

"Okay, you can sit up now."

"What are we going to do?" I felt hot and cold with panic.

"Go to the nearest portal."

"Where's that?"

"Paris."

"Paris?!" I exclaimed. "Surely there is another one in the UK."

Ahran shook his head. "After you were arrested all the other UK portals were closed down except the one in your wood. The plan was that as soon as we were safely through, that would be closed too. There is an emergency protocol that if there is any hint of a threat to Ramia all portal access is closed in that region."

"But France?! How are we going to get there without being found out? Can't a portal be opened up for us somewhere on this side of the channel?"

Ahran shook his head. "It can take up to a week for a portal to be fully operational. Our best bet is to get to Paris."

My poor brain struggled to process this latest piece of information.

"We don't have any passports," Toby said from the back.

Toby had a point. "How are we going to get on a plane without a passport?" I asked.

"We have a better chance going through the Channel Tunnel," Ahran replied.

I had visions of clinging to the underside of some articulated lorry. "Are you sure?"

He nodded. "We need to get some fake passports. It's much easier to get through security on the tunnel than it would be at an airport," he said distractedly.

"Where do we get fake passports from?" I asked.

He thought about this for a moment, "How about Bennie? If her boyfriend was able to get you out of MI5 HQ, maybe he can get us some passports. Call her," he said, passing me his phone.

After this morning's meeting, I felt apprehensive about asking for her help again and as I waited for her to pick up I tried not to think about why Ahran had thought of her before anyone else.

"Hi Ben, its Sophie."

"Hi Sophe, did you get to the airport okay?"

I tried to put my worries about the nature of her relationship with Ahran out of my mind and focussed on the task in hand. "There's been a slight change of plan, we are now officially on the run and heading to Paris. Do you think your boyfriend can sort us out with some fake passports?"

I chewed my lip waiting for her response.

She hesitated. "I don't know. You've got yourself into some deep shit this time Sophe, and you think I live a faster pace of life!"

"Can you help or not?" I didn't mean to sound quite so abrupt, but I couldn't help it.

"I'm not sure I can ask Tristan again. Leave it with me."

"Thanks Ben."

"Just as long as the next time I'm caught by MI5 and need to escape and flee the country with fake ID you're there to help me out."

"Totally," I said with a chuckle, unable to help myself. It was as crazy as it sounded, but Bennie didn't seem to be too fazed by it.

"I'll call you in a bit," she said and hung up.

"What do we do whilst we're waiting?" I said to Ahran after ending the call.

"We eat."

In spite of the gravity of the situation I rolled my eyes and laughed; as far as Ramians were concerned food was the answer to everything.

We drove to the nearest McDonald's drive through and sat and ate it in the car whilst we waited for Bennie's call.

"This tastes sooo good," Toby said, tucking into a bacon and egg McMuffin.

I had completely forgotten that it was two years since Toby had been on Earth and sampling the delights of the world's most successful fast food chain was clearly something he had missed.

"Why is there no McDonalds in Ramia?" he asked, sounding slightly disgruntled.

"There's Oerlanda's," I said mentioning the closest thing to McDonalds in Ramia.

"Oerlanda's burgers don't taste anything like this," Toby replied.

"That's because the Big O's food is actually good for you."

"There's no way anyone would get away with serving food like this in Ramia," Ahran added.

I sipped my tea and scalded my tongue. "I'm sure they do something to the tea, it's always so hot," I complained.

Ahran's phone rang and he put it on loud speaker.

"Hi Ben, any luck?"

"Yeah actually. I've found someone who can sort you out with fake passports, but they come at a price."

I looked at Ahran and he nodded in encouragement. "I don't think we have much choice. Are they any good?"

"At £10,000 each I would bloody hope so," she replied. "I've been assured by Dodgy Dave that this guy is the best around."

"Coming from someone called *Dodgy Dave* I'm not sure that's much of an endorsement. Was your boyfriend able to pull a few more strings?"

"I didn't ask him. Apparently, this guy used to sort out passports for my colleagues in the industry. Brits aren't always welcome in some of the countries we film in."

"So they get fake passports?"

"You've got it."

"I had no idea filming wildlife was so riddled with corruption."

"You'd be surprised. Look, I need you to send me photos of you all."

"Ok, sure."

"Oh yes, and you're going to need to stump up thirty grand *cash*."

I looked across at Ahran. He gave me a nod.

"Tell him to go ahead."

"Right then, send me the photos as soon as you can."

"How long will they take Bennie?" Ahran asked.

"I'm not sure. As soon as I know, I'll call you."

"Thanks Ben," I said.

"Bye Sophe." She hung up.

"We need to change our appearances," Ahran said.

"How?"

"Cut and dye our hair, change clothes that sort of thing."

"Ok," I said somewhat reluctantly, although I couldn't let vanity stand in our way of getting back to Ramia as soon as possible.

Ahran stuffed our food wrappings into a bag. "Let's head back to the supermarket, we passed on the ring road and get what we need." He started the car engine. "And then we'll head to a motel, lie low and wait until the passports are ready."

We drove to the supermarket and parked near the entrance. "I'll go in and get what we need, you two stay here and keep your heads down."

"I need to go to the toilet Auntie Sophie."

"Just pee over there," Ahran said, pointing to some newly planted shrubbery nearby.

Toby looked at me pleadingly. "No, I need to *go*." He said, beginning to look panicked. I knew that look.

"Can't he come in with you Ahran? MI5 don't know he's here and he needs to use the facilities."

"Okay, but you are going to have to be quick."

"I will," Toby replied, the relief evident in his voice.

I slid down in my seat and watched the two most important people in my life walk into the supermarket. Knowing that we couldn't go back to Ramia immediately was horrible, but the thought that we were going to have to try and get through British border control without being recognised was even worse. Maybe we could lie low for a couple of days and then slip through the portal near the house. The trouble was, if they thought that Tagan was a dangerous terrorist and their only lead had just escaped from MI5 HQ, my house and maybe the surrounding area would be under surveillance. I was sure that as far as they were concerned, I had just confirmed their suspicions that I did know something after all.

In a matter of minutes, Ahran was striding back across the car park with Toby trotting by his side, looking decidedly sheepish.

"What's the matter?" I asked as they got into the car.

Ahran slung the bags in the back, climbed into the

driver's seat and pulled out of the car park with a stony expression on his face.

"Ahran, what is it?"

"Somebody recognised Toby."

My heart sunk. "Who was it?"

"Mrs Taylor from school," Toby replied.

"Great! Could this get any worse?" I said, recognising the name of Toby's teaching assistant from his old primary school.

The muscle in Ahran's jaw flexed. "I told her that she was mistaken, that Toby was my son. I think she believed me, but we can't take any more chances."

I nodded. "You're right."

"I'm sorry Auntie Sophie. I really needed to go to the toilet." His bottom lip quivered as if he was about to cry. He wasn't prone to tears, but I think he was beginning to realise how much trouble we were in.

I turned around to give him a reassuring smile. "It's not your fault."

"Is there a motel nearby?" Ahran asked.

"There's a couple just off the motorway heading towards the Channel Tunnel if I remember correctly."

"We'll head to one of those."

We drove in silence as we made our way out of East Sussex and onto the motorway leading to the coast. When we were about half an hour away from the Channel Tunnel terminal we followed the signs to the services and pulled into the car park of a motel.

"We can't risk either of you being spotted again," Ahran warned. "At the moment, I'm guessing they don't have a visual of me so I'll check in, head to the room and set the fire alarm off. Once everyone is outside, I'll signal to you the number of the room and once the Fire Brigade has checked the building you and Toby join the crowd as they return to the building, that way no one will notice you.

"Okay, got it," I said.

He gave me a quick kiss and left us in the car. After what seemed like an age, the fire alarm went off. Everyone who was inside the building started to gather in the car park near to where we were parked and it was only then that I noticed the green assembly point sign that we were parked next to. I spotted Ahran in the crowd of people and he signalled a 'one' and a 'five'. It was twenty minutes before the Fire Brigade arrived and another fifteen before the all clear had been given for everyone to re-enter.

"Ready Tobes," I said.

"Yep," he replied.

We got out of the car and joined the throng of people heading back into the building. I couldn't help but smile at how clever Ahran was, it was genius. He had gone on ahead and the door of room number fifteen opened as we approached.

I looked nervously up and down the corridor and spotted the CCTV camera at one end.

"There's a camera at the other end of the corridor," I said once we were safely in our room and the door was closed.

"Apparently, that CCTV isn't working." His face was a picture of innocence until he winked.

"You're such a vandal," I said, letting out a sigh of relief and gave him a hug. After the morning's events, I needed to feel his warmth for a moment, recharge myself with him. He squeezed me back and kissed my head. "It's going to be alright."

I nodded against his chest. I trusted him.

We broke apart and Ahran walked over to the bed where the supermarket bags were sitting. "Right, we better get started."

Toby was already on the bed flicking through the channels on the television. "Its ages since I've seen any proper T.V.," he said with glee.

The recognisable voices of the presenters of BBC Breakfast suddenly filled the room.

"Hey look Auntie Sophie, you're on T.V."

My head snapped round to see an unflattering still of myself that must have been taken whilst I was being interrogated.

"Sophie McAllister a suspected terrorist, escaped custody late last night. She is also wanted for questioning in relation to the disappearance of her ten-year-old nephew two years ago. The police have reason to believe she could be armed and dangerous, and advise you not to approach her, but to contact the police immediately."

I stared into the solemn face of the familiar presenter who had been a part of my morning routine for many years, "A terrorist? Dangerous?! How ridiculous!" I said, feeling bitterly let down by her.

"It was only a matter of time," Ahran said with a knowing expression.

"But they're lying."

"Don't be naïve Sophie, they'll say whatever they have to if it makes people turn you in quicker."

I felt a stupid sense of betrayal by my fellow countrymen and angrily marched into the bathroom. "Come on, let's do this," I said.

9

I stared at myself in the dressing table mirror. My long, blonde, wavy hair had been replaced by a dark, slightly uneven pixie cut, thanks to Ahran's untrained hands. The style accentuated my cheek bones and my eyes looked even bigger than usual. I changed the angle of my head to try and see the back.

"I suppose it will have to do," I said, trying not to sound too upset.

"With some heavier make up, I think even Bennie would struggle to recognise you." I tried not to dwell on why Ahran chose her as he tipped out the remainder of the supermarket bag. "I'm no expert, but I picked out some stuff that might do," he said, handing me some dark eyeshadow, some gaudy looking lipstick and a mascara.

I laughed through the tears that I was struggling to hold back.

"I'm going to look like a drag queen! I'm sure passport

control will be only too relieved to see me leave the country with this lot on."

"You'll look just as beautiful as ever," Ahran said, giving me a quick kiss. This only served to release the flood gates holding back my tears.

"Hey," he said, pulling me into his arms.

"I'm being ridiculous," I said, wiping my nose on my sleeve. "Just ignore me."

"It's understandable," he said and held me at arm's length. "I know you're scared, but we'll be back in Ramia in no time, I promise."

I nodded, not quite believing it was as straightforward as he was suggesting. He was doing his best to reassure me and my heart swelled. If ever I was sad, he was there for me, if ever I was scared he was there for me, if ever I was uncertain, lonely, or upset he was always there for me and in that moment, I loved him more than ever. Of course, I couldn't tell him that the reason for my tears on this occasion wasn't because I was worried about our safety, but because I was mourning the loss of my hair!

"It's gone ginger!" Toby said, coming out of the bathroom, sounding most displeased.

Sure enough, my nephew was sporting a mop of red hair.

"It said *blonde* on the packet."

"Welcome to the game of chance that is do-it-yourself hair dye," I said, disentangling myself from Ahran's arms.

"I rather like it, you look like Prince Harry."

"More like Ron Weasley," he said, grumpily.

I pulled the chair back in front of the dressing table and

brandished the scissors. "I'd like to welcome you to *Hair Today, Gone Tomorrow*. Please take a seat," I said in my best hairdresser's voice.

Toby walked towards the chair and rolled his eyes at Ahran who was struggling to hide his smile. There obviously comes a point in a child's life when their favourite Auntie's jokes are no longer funny.

I set to work and tried not to think about how distraught Katie and Leylana would be if they could see Toby's curls falling to the floor. I gave a big sigh at the thought of my beautiful sister and Toby's equally beautiful grandmother. There wasn't a day that went by when I didn't miss Katie, she would be mortified if she knew that her son was once again in grave danger. Fortunately, although I no longer had my sister, I did have Leylana who had become a close friend and confidante and she would be going just as spare at the thought of Toby being at risk once more. Both Halsan and Leylana had gone to great lengths to protect him and keep him safe. Who'd have thought that it would have been Magdala, the daughter of a well-respected and trusted friend, who should encourage Toby to do what he had done? I couldn't understand it.

"There. What do you think?" I said, as I put the finishing touches to Toby's short back and sides.

Ahran came over to inspect my work. "You've missed a bit here," he said, tugging at a wayward tuft.

"Goodness me, one haircut and already you're a critic," I said as I gave the bit of hair in question what for.

Ahran laughed his deep rumble of a laugh. *God, I loved that sound.*

I knew that I had to try and keep things as light-hearted as possible for Toby's sake. I didn't want him to feel any worse than he already felt or any more frightened than he already was.

"Change into the clothes I bought you and then I'll take a photo of each of you against that wall," Ahran said, pointing to the pictureless expanse of whitewashed wall next to the T.V.

I was pleased to see that Ahran had done a slightly better job of choosing some clothes for me than he had done with the make-up. I slipped into the charcoal pair of skinny jeans, a white vest top and a light knit sweater that went with the jeans rather well. Together with my tan, the make-up and the flat pumps he had selected I looked decidedly Mediterranean, possibly not Parisian, but as stylishly European as a British supermarket could stretch to.

Using his phone, Ahran took photos of me and Toby and once I had taken one of him, he emailed them all to Bennie.

It was now just a waiting game.

SEVERAL HOURS LATER, Toby and I were sat on the bed, he was engrossed in some car programme, but my mind was elsewhere. I looked across at Ahran who was sat in the chair doing something on his phone that, unlike mine, was still going strong. In the time I had known Ahran technology had moved on and it was no longer necessary to charge a Ramian phone, they recharged themselves somehow harnessing the movement of the user.

I felt guilty. Harvest time on the farm was over and now it was time to plough and sow winter crops. Ahran had a competent team working for him, but I knew he would be finding it difficult being away from the place. *I* was finding it difficult being away from the place. My misgivings in the early days about whether I would ever feel at home there had been completely unfounded. I loved it and wished more than anything we were back there now.

"I'm sorry," I said to him.

Ahran looked up from his phone. "What for?"

"For putting you through all this again."

"It's not your fault *Mootya*. You weren't to know." He came and sat on the edge of the bed.

"Consider this a minor hiccup." He ran the back of his hand down my cheek. At times like these he would often kiss me on the nose or tuck a loose strand of hair behind my ear, one of those insanely intimate gestures I had grown to love and take comfort from, but it suddenly occurred to me that he could no longer tuck my hair behind my ear. I felt angry again. "It's so bloody unfair. I just want us all to get on with living our lives, without all the fear and drama."

"And we will. Tomorrow we'll all be safely back in Ramia," he said.

I took a deep breath and sighed. "These passports had better be good."

"I'll go out and get us something to eat," he said, standing up. "You hungry?"

"Starving," Toby piped up.

"Nothing new there then," Ahran said with a chuckle and picked up his jacket.

"Don't be long, will you," I said as he bent down and gave me a kiss.

"I'll be as quick as I can. Don't open the door to anyone," he warned.

"I won't." I didn't like that he had to leave us, but I guess we had to eat, or at least they did. The door clicked behind him.

I settled back on the bed. "Come here," I said and put my arm around Toby and watched some inane daytime quiz show. A little while later there was a knock on the door. Dammit, I was pretty sure we had put out the 'Do Not Disturb' sign. I jumped off the bed and went to look through the spy-hole, which much to my dismay had misted up and all I could see was a shadowy figure of medium height standing on the other side. I heard a key-card slide into the reader. I grabbed the door handle, fearing MI5 had caught up with me.

"Can I help you?" I said through the door.

"It's the maid," said a female voice. "I've come to service the room."

"Oh, thanks, but there's no need."

"Okay, have a good day."

"You too," I replied. I leaned my head against the door feeling dizzy with relief and then put the chain across as a precaution before padding back to Toby on the bed.

"Are you okay?" I said, only to find him looking like he was about to burst into tears.

He nodded. "Coming back to Earth has made me realise how much I miss mum."

"Oh sweetheart," I said, putting my arm around him.

"It's only natural that you feel like that."

"When I'm in Ramia, it's not so bad," he said, his voice breaking. "But coming back here makes me feel sad." He began to sob into my chest.

I stroked his hair. "You have a good cry," I said through the lump in my throat. "It won't be long now." If I had any doubts about Toby living in Ramia, hearing this made me realise that the legacy Tagan had left him was the best thing that could have ever happened to him. I never wanted him to forget his mum, but the life he had with his new royal family had not only taken his mind of his loss, but had given him the most wonderful future. I had no doubts he would become a well-respected, capable and compassionate leader. I also no longer felt guilty about him not coming back to Earth. He would always be at risk here.

"Why don't you try and have a little snooze? It's been a long morning."

His tears began to subside and I could feel myself starting to drift.

I was in a long floaty nightdress, my wrists bound by heavy metal cuffs and I was walking barefooted, feeling like I had been drugged. Every now and then I would nod off and the long chain that was attached to the cuff tightened, jolting me awake. I opened my eyes to see Compton standing there pulling on the chain. Meakins was on a leash and on all fours like a dog. "Stay awake Sophie," Compton said, with a lecherous grin plastered across his face and he rattled the chain between us.

"Sophie, open the door," Ahran's voice demanded bringing me back to consciousness.

I leapt off the bed realising I had been dreaming and he couldn't get in. I unhooked the door-chain and felt more than a little relieved at the sight of Ahran entering the room with a takeaway. I shook my head as if to shake off the disturbing dream and went to redo my ponytail only to be reminded that I no longer had long hair. *Ugh!*

"Smells good," I said as my stomach rumbled at the aroma coming from the bag in Ahran's hand.

"Just fish and chips I'm afraid."

"I shall have to go on a serious diet when we get back to Ramia."

"Don't you dare," Ahran said as he took the warm paper parcels out of the bag.

Toby woke up, obviously lured by the smell of the food. "Oh yum, fish and chips."

The boys tucked into their lunch with gusto, I picked at mine, rattled by the dream I'd just had.

"PERHAPS WE OUGHT TO CALL BENNIE," I said as it approached nine o'clock that evening. It had been a long boring wait and we still hadn't heard anything. "Maybe she didn't get the photos."

"She sent a text confirming she'd got them," Ahran replied.

"You didn't tell me that," I said, feeling a little hurt. So now they were texting each other without my knowledge.

Ahran shrugged.

This only seemed to fuel my earlier suspicions. "Ah!

The waiting is making me crazy. There are only so many quiz shows you can watch!" I paced up and down, channelling the feelings of hurt and frustration.

"I know. The best thing we can do is settle down for the night and then call in the morning."

"Let me call her." I held out my hand for his phone.

"It's getting late," he said, reluctant to do as I was suggesting.

"It's only nine."

He hesitated.

"Ahran, just hand me the bloody phone," I said testily.

His expression darkened slightly, but I ignored it. He handed me his phone and I dialled Bennie's number.

"Hi Ahran," she answered breezily.

"Ben, it's me."

"Sophe, is everything okay?" Her tone changed when she realised it wasn't Ahran. This bothered me.

"Have you heard anything yet?"

"I've just had a message as it happens, the passports will be ready tomorrow and will be couriered first thing in the morning, so I should be able to meet you about ten."

"Good!" I said, feeling pleased that we had some news, but frustrated that we would have to wait until the morning.

"Shall I come to the hotel you're staying in?"

"I guess that's as good a place as any, it's the motel on the A20 near Stonely."

"Okay, cool. Can I speak to Ahran?" she asked,

"Er, yeah, sure." She clearly didn't want to speak to me anymore.

I handed Ahran the phone. "She wants to talk to you."

He put the phone to his ear.

"Do you think that's a good idea?" he replied, turning away from me.

I frowned at his back. What was going on between them?!

If only I had superhuman hearing.

"I know Ben," he said in a quiet voice.

And I couldn't help but be struck by how tender his voice had become, he was talking in hushed reassuring tones. I felt insanely jealous and was fast reaching the point where I would have to confront Ahran with it.

"What's the problem?" I said when he hung up.

"Oh, nothing," he replied.

I felt the urge to cry and brooded whilst Toby watched a documentary about the blue whale. When he had fallen asleep I brushed my teeth and stripped down to my vest top and knickers before climbing into bed myself. Ahran was still sat in the chair, where he had been for most of the afternoon and evening, on his phone co-ordinating his team back at the farm and arranging payment for the passports to be delivered to a safe deposit box at Waterloo station.

"Are you coming to bed?" I asked, still bothered by the conversation he'd had with Bennie.

"Yeah, in a minute," he said, without looking up.

I pulled the covers up under my chin. It had been a very, very long day and I was not only physically exhausted, but I felt emotionally drained. I looked over at Ahran. I know he had been busy with work for most of the day, but since the phone call to Bennie he had also been distant. I didn't like it. I didn't like it one bit.

10

I woke up early. Toby was still fast asleep and Ahran was on the other side of the bed gently snoring. I hadn't been aware of him coming to bed last night even though I had lain awake for what seemed like hours not only worrying about getting across the borders to France, but wondering whether I was about to lose my boyfriend to my best friend. Surely, she wasn't seeing two men at the same time?! I shook my head. In the cold light of the morning, it seemed like such a stupid assumption and as I looked across at Ahran's resting features I gave myself a mental dressing down for being such an idiot.

I scrambled out of bed, cross with myself, there was no reason to doubt Ahran's feelings for me. I switched the kettle on and went into the bathroom to wash my face. I caught my reflection in the mirror; it was still a shock to see my dark brown crop. I scrutinised my appearance for a moment or two. It seemed like my tan had faded overnight and my eyes looked tired and hollow. I'd had enough trauma in my life to last several lifetimes, the last thing I wanted to do was add to the ordeal by suspecting my boyfriend was having an affair. In an attempt to wash away my painful thoughts, I splashed some cold water on my face. We would be seeing Bennie this morning, maybe she would finally shed some light on what was going on.

I poured hot water over the teabags and emptied the sachet of hot chocolate into a glass. Just as I was stirring the abomination that was UHT milk into our teas, Toby came to and stumbled out of bed.

"Morning Auntie Sophie. For a minute, I thought we were back home," he said groggily as he made his way to the bathroom.

"In Hatherley?" I asked.

"No, in Dinara."

I nodded, digesting the fact that he now considered the palace his home.

"Wakey, wakey," I said, placing a cup of tea by Ahran's bedside.

"I am awake," he mumbled.

"You were still snoring."

"I don't snore," he argued.

I raised my eyebrow at him, feeling buoyed by the fact that things seemed to have returned to normal between us. Maybe the strain of the recent events had taken their toll on me and I had just imagined everything between him and Bennie.

He sat up and was about to get out of bed when I noticed he didn't have a stitch on and he was resplendent in all his morning glory.

"Ahran!" I said between my teeth, my eyes darting to the bathroom where Toby was.

"It's nothing he hasn't got," Ahran replied, never more at ease than when he was naked.

"Ahran, please, he's only ten." I threw him the towel that had been left on the chair and turned away. My pulse had increased in tempo and I wondered whether it was normal to still be so attracted to him. Weren't the fireworks supposed to fizzle out after a while?

He came and planted a kiss on the back of my neck. "I can't wait until we are back home, *alone*," he said pointedly.

"Nor can I." I turned around and put my arms around his neck. "I love you, I don't know what I'd do if anything happened between us."

"Nothing is likely to," he said and kissed me on the lips.

I frowned. I'd wanted him to be more certain than that.

Toby came out of the bathroom and we stepped away from one another.

"I've made you a hot chocolate," I said, pointing to the glass on the dressing table.

"Okay, thanks," he said, picking it up and taking a sip.

"What time are we meeting Auntie Bennie?"

"Ten o'clock,' Ahran said.

I sat on the bed and drank my tea. "What did you do with the controller?" I said to Toby, scanning the room for the T.V. remote.

"It's here," he said, picking it up off the floor.

I had avoided the news yesterday, but there was a part of me that was morbidly curious to see if I had made the news today.

I switched on breakfast T.V. and watched an interview with the new shadow health secretary in which she tore the current health secretary to shreds over his handling of a recent crisis in a Midlands hospital. My attention began to wander as I contemplated seeing Bennie again. It wasn't until I saw an old photo of Toby pop up on the screen that my attention snapped back to the T.V.

"Following the disappearance of suspected terrorist Sophie McAllister, a new development has come to light. Police have reason to believe that Miss McAllister's ten-year-old nephew, who disappeared two years ago, was sighted in an East Sussex supermarket yesterday. He was in the company of a man who claimed to be his father. Police suspect that this man may know the whereabouts of Miss McAllister or may be part of the terrorist cell she is thought to be involved in."

Ahran stood in the doorway of the bathroom listening to this worrying development. A pencil drawing of a face that was vaguely familiar flashed onto the screen. Then I realised it was supposed to look like Ahran, although there was something not quite right about it.

"This is an artist's impression of the man. He is said to be tall, of athletic build with blonde hair and wearing jeans and a dark coloured jacket. He is wanted for questioning in connection with the disappearance of both the boy and his aunt."

"Are they going to capture us?" Toby asked, sounding terrified.

"No, of course they aren't," I said, looking to Ahran for reassurance.

"The sooner we leave the country, the better," he said tight-lipped.

"You're going to need to do something about your appearance." Up until now, we had assumed that no-one knew what Ahran looked like but now we risked, him being recognised too. "You could shave off your hair," I suggested. The first time I met Ahran he had just left the army and his hair had been very short. I looked at his thick blonde hair now which was damp and swept back from where he had washed his face and run his wet hands through it like he always did. "It would be something."

"You're right."

"Let's do it now," I said, feeling the need to be proactive.

Ahran went to his bag and brought out his electric shaver. He snapped on one of the attachments which transformed it into clippers.

"Do you want me to do it?" I asked.

"Don't worry, I can probably do it quicker than you, I've had years of practice."

He went into the bathroom and after a few minutes emerged looking like the hot soldier I had found on my doorstep two years ago. He didn't look any less attractive, just more militarian, just as mouth-watering, but a little more lethal.

"Can I shave my hair off?" Toby asked, also a little in awe of Ahran, but for completely different reasons. He idolised his uncle and aspired to be like him in any way possible.

"No, you cannot," I said, quashing any ideas of Toby's

to turn himself into a ten-year-old Action Man. "Grams would never forgive me!" I picked up the room service menu. "Let's order some breakfast."

Ahran placed our order over the phone whilst I had a shower. It didn't do to dwell too much on how much trouble we were in. Once we'd eaten I put on some make-up, trying to match it to how I'd applied it in preparation for our passport photos yesterday.

By the time we had all showered and had our breakfast, it was nearly time to meet Bennie.

"How are we going to leave the hotel without anyone recognising us?"

"As long as we aren't seen together, I think we should be safe. I'll check out. You wait here for a few minutes and then make your way to the services on the other side of the car park. I'll wait for you there." He zipped up his bag. "Okay?"

I nodded.

"Good." He gave me a quick kiss on the lips and ruffled Toby's hair before he left. He seemed remarkably cheerful considering we were all now officially wanted.

I sat down on the bed next to Toby.

"It will be alright Auntie Sophie," he said. He must have noticed the worried expression on my face.

I smiled. He was growing up so fast. "Course it will." I put my arm around him and gave him a squeeze.

I let a good fifteen minutes pass before Toby and I left our room and slipped passed the girl on the front desk who was busy checking out a young couple. We followed Ahran's instructions and crossed the car park to where there was an unofficial gap in the bushes and a well-trodden bare earth path which had been created as a short cut to the main services. I scanned the large car park for Ahran and the silver hire car. Considering there must have been a hundred silver cars parked there it was not easy to spot until my eyes settled on a couple standing about fifty feet away in the far corner. The guy was tall and he had his hand on the woman's shoulder, her face was upturned towards his and it looked like they were having an intimate conversation.

And then I realised it was Ahran and Bennie!

All my doubts and fears that I'd had last night hit me in the chest like a large blunt arrow. I pulled Toby closer to me for support.

Neither of them noticed us until we were only a few feet away. Ahran dropped his hand from Bennie's shoulder.

I plastered a fake smile on my face. "Hi."

She looked much better than the last time I'd seen her. Her hair was down, it was longer than I remembered and her make-up was as immaculate as it always was.

"Hi Sophe," she said. "Loving the rock chick look!"

I could barely summons a smile I felt so angry. Betrayed.

"Have you got the passports?" I said with a coldness I couldn't hide.

"Er, yes," she said, slightly thrown off balance by my abruptness. She opened her bag and pulled out a brown envelope.

I took it and examined the contents. "They look good enough to me," I said in a clipped tone.

I had yet to look at Ahran.

"I can't see how anyone would notice the difference," Bennie said noticeably underwhelmed by my response.

"Sandra Turbot?" I remarked, looking at my passport, feeling completely dispassionate about my new name.

Bennie shrugged apologetically.

"We should go," I said, turning to Ahran. His expression was unreadable.

I struggled to turn back and look at Bennie. In my mind's eye, all I could see were grotesque images of her and Ahran's bodies in the throes of passion. I began to feel claustrophobic and short of breath.

"Good luck," Bennie said.

"Um, yeah, thanks," I replied.

She gave me a quick hug, and then embraced Ahran for a little longer than I deemed necessary.

How long had I been held at MI5? Four days? It was such a brief period for Bennie and Ahran to become so close. Oh God! Maybe it had been going on for a while. There was no debating that Bennie was absolutely gorgeous, and much more like the Ramian women Ahran was used to. All those times when he had been off to farm sales and veterinary courses, had he really been coming here to see Bennie? Maybe it explained why I hadn't heard much from her lately.

Oh Jeez! I felt like I was going to be sick.

"Are you okay Auntie Sophie?" Toby said, touching my arm.

"I'm fine. Let's go." I opened the car door.

Bennie gave Toby a squeeze. "Be brave sunshine, maybe I can come and visit before Christmas?"

What if I was about to lose Ahran? Was there any point in me going back? Perhaps I should just hand myself in now? And then I thought of Toby, he needed to be in Ramia, I would never forgive myself if he was captured by the British government to become some freaky scientific side show. No, I would ensure his safe return, I wouldn't confront Ahran now and rock the boat, at the very least I owed it to Toby to get him back safely without burdening him with my own drama. Had I been a fool to think that Ahran would settle for me?

11

We headed for the Channel Tunnel terminal.

"What has got into you?" Ahran said, breaking the stony silence that had settled between us.

"Nothing."

"You were actually quite rude to Bennie," he said, taking his eyes off the road for a second. "She has done a lot for us."

Now he was defending her. *The bastard!*

"I just didn't want to hang about, we needed to move on." I turned and looked out the window, this wasn't a conversation I was prepared to have in front of Toby. Neither of us said any more and I continued to sit there and stew. Not long now and we would be on our way to France and the portal.

On our approach to the terminal, there was a car that had broken-down on the slip road. An elderly woman stood on the other side of the safety barrier and her husband had his head under the bonnet.

Ahran slowed down and pulled up behind them.

"What are you doing? We haven't got time. What if they recognise us?!" I said uncharitably.

Ahran frowned and shook his head before getting out of the car.

"*For fuck sake*!" I muttered under my breath. Ordinarily, I would have been more than happy to stop and help an elderly couple in need, but on this occasion, it just so happened that we were wanted by the British government and there was no telling whether our plan to flee the country to get to a portal to another world would actually work. No, this was not the time to play Good Samaritan.

"What's he doing?" Toby said, peering out of the window, equally concerned by Ahran's untimely diversion.

I shook my head, feeling hot tears prickling my eyes. "God knows!"

The next thing I knew, Ahran was putting their bags in the boot and the couple were getting into the car.

"Hello," said the lady, looking slightly embarrassed.

"Er, hello," I replied and raised my eyebrows at Ahran as if to say, *What the hell are you playing at?!*

"This is Derek and Dorothy Cartwright, I'm giving them a lift to France," he said.

"It is so kind of you," Mr Cartwright said. "We just couldn't believe it, our son is getting married in Lille in a couple of days and we are having a big family gathering this evening. It's been two hours and the AA still haven't arrived."

"What will you do when you get to the other side?" I asked, wondering whether Ahran had decided that we were now a taxi service and had completely lost his mind. I had visions of him agreeing to join in with their festivities, that's if we actually got across the border.

"Our nephew is going to pick us up."

"What are you doing?" I mouthed to Ahran as he started the engine and headed back up the slip road.

A slow grin worked its way across his face, but he didn't answer. I rolled my eyes. He could be so infuriating sometimes.

I sat there with my arms tightly crossed, trying to be polite to the couple who were doing their best to make small talk, but clearly feeling uncomfortable by the atmosphere I was doing a pretty good job of creating.

There were two cars ahead of us at passport control and we were only a few minutes away from finding out whether Dodgy Dave's passport forging mate was really worth thirty grand. I pulled down the sun visor and looked at myself in the small mirror. My heart was beating like I had just run a marathon and there was a nervous red rash spreading across my neck. I rooted around in the bag at my feet for the lipstick Ahran had bought. I wasn't really sure why I thought a layer of lipstick would protect me from capture and a life sentence in prison, but I felt a little war paint was at least worth a try.

The barrier lifted up and let the first of the two cars ahead of us through.

"Oh God," I muttered.

Ahran took my hand and gave it a squeeze. For a

moment, I forgot I was angry with him and tried to take comfort from his touch.

"At least we've got Mr and Mrs Cartwright for company. Five is much better than three when you're travelling, don't you think," he said, pointedly.

I turned to smile at our new passengers who were sitting either side of Toby. And then it dawned on me what Ahran had done; to the chap in the passport control booth, we looked like nothing more than a family on a day trip to France. He hadn't picked up Mr and Mrs Cartwright because he had felt sorry for them, he had picked them up because the police were potentially looking for a man, a woman and a boy travelling on their own. Adding an innocent elderly couple to the mix was the perfect decoy. I felt guilty that we were using these kindly people, but I had to marvel at Ahran's quick thinking.

The car in front of us went through the barrier and we pulled up to the booth. After the UK border control guy had given our passports a cursory glance and bothered himself enough to poke his head through the booth window for a somewhat disinterested perusal of the car's occupants, the barrier lifted and he waved us through.

We drove towards the awaiting train. I couldn't believe it, we had done it, we had actually done it!

I glanced across at Ahran who winked in return.

With all concerns about getting through border control having been laid to rest, my thoughts returned to my current relationship crisis.

If he had been unfaithful, could I walk away from him? It had taken me so long to trust him, to accept that he had chosen *me* despite the trouble it had caused between him and his father. Could I live a lie that went against all my hard won inner battles? I laughed at myself. What was the point of trusting someone? What I should have learned was that no one can be trusted, not even the love of my life and my best friend.

ONCE WE WERE on the train, I had to get out of the car to stretch my legs and put some distance between Ahran and myself, even if I risked being spotted. Toby was happily playing hangman with Mr Cartwright and Mrs Cartwright was reading her book. I walked along the carriage momentarily observing other families and their excitable children as they sat through this leg of their journey.

I stopped to read a poster on the wall of the train and stared at it unseeingly. To my horror, I realised I was now in the same position Talina had been in two years ago. Talina had lost Ahran to another woman and that woman had been me. It was no doubt the work of karma that I now found myself in that exact same position. Huh! Once a cheater, always a cheater. Ahran had told me that he hadn't been faithful to Talina when he was in the army, even though he said that if they'd have got married that would have all stopped. I should have run for the hills as soon as I had learned that he had cheated on her even before he had cheated on her with me. God! I was such an idiot!

I eventually got back into the car. I couldn't look at him.

We barely said a word until we left the train and drove to the final barrier on our journey to the French portal.

"Have you got the passports?" Ahran said, holding out his hand.

I reached into the glove box and handed them to him.

"Our nephew should be waiting for us on the other side," Mr Cartwright said as we pulled up to French border control.

This time I didn't give much thought to being spotted on account of the ease with which we had passed through British border control and our added insurance policy in the shape of our unwitting travel companions. That was until the French official gestured for us to get out of the car.

Ahran replied in fluent French.

"What do they want?"

"They want to check the car and for us to go through security."

I processed what he'd just said. "This is it! We're going to be captured, aren't we?" I said, voicing my fears.

"Captured?" Mr Cartwright said from the back.

Dammit!

I turned around and laughed. "Oh, we just have this running joke…," I said, trying to laugh it off. "My husband isn't a European citizen, and I always tease him that if he doesn't behave himself I'll have him deported."

Mr Cartwright gave me a half smile, not quite seeing the funny side of it.

Ahran pulled over, "Come on, let's get this over with."

We left French customs searching the car and all walked into the main building. My knees began to shake.

Ahran put his arm around me and kissed my hair. "Don't worry, try to act normal."

He pulled me to his side. "That's easier said than done," I whispered.

I glanced at Toby who looked scared stiff and reached for his hand. "It'll be fine," I said, trying to ignore my own fear.

They checked our passports again, this time taking more time to study them. Mr and Mrs Cartwright's first and then mine, Ahran's and Toby's.

"It's a terrible picture," I said nervously, feeling the need to fill what seemed like an interminable silence as my passport was scrutinised. The humourless customs officer looked up with an apathetic expression.

Just shut up Sophie!

"'Ow long weel you be staying en France?"

"Pour un jour," Ahran replied.

The official nodded his expression unchanging. *Boy!* If he was trying to make us feel uncomfortable, he was succeeding.

After what seemed like a lifetime, he nodded, handed me back the passports and finally allowed us through.

I felt slightly dizzy as we walked towards the security scanner where we took off our belts and shoes and emptied our pockets. Thankfully, we all passed through it without any alarms sounding and I breathed a sigh of relief. I smiled up at Ahran as we waited for our things. No matter how angry or hurt I felt, it was good to know we were now free to go. In a few minutes, we would be on our way.

The tray with Ahran's belongings rolled towards us and his phone bleeped with a message.

I picked it up to hand it to him and glanced at the screen. If it had been from anyone but Bennie, I wouldn't have read it.

Have you told her yet? x

My heart lurched and my world began to crumble around me.

I blindly handed Ahran the phone, but didn't let on that I'd seen the message. "Everything okay?" I asked as all the feelings of hurt, betrayal, sadness and despair threatened to engulf me.

He looked at the screen. "Yes, fine," he said and slipped his phone into his pocket, whilst making no attempt to elaborate.

Her message and his answer seemed to confirm all my suspicions.

I blindly walked out of the building, unaware of anything that was going on around me.

"Meez Turbot?"

I put one foot in front of the other.

"Meez Turbot?!"

We had almost reached the sliding glass doors which would lead us outside and to our car, when someone grabbed my arm. I turned to see that it was one of the custom officials. "Are you Meez Turbot?"

I turned and looked at him blankly. "No, I…."

"Yes, she is," Ahran interrupted as he shot me a warning look.

"Oh yes. Sorry, I was miles away," I said, shaking my head to try and focus on the man standing in front of me.

I flinched as he raised his hand.

A voice in my head sighed wearily. *He's got a gun, you're being arrested.*

"Your passport, meez."

I stared at the burgundy booklet he was holding and took a moment to realise that he wasn't actually holding a gun. "You dropped it over zer," he said, pointing to where we had stood waiting for the trays containing our belongings.

"Oh," I said, feeling like my knees were about to buckle.

"You must be carefool, if you lose zis, you weel not be able to retoorn to En-gland."

After Bennie's message, I'm not sure I cared where I was going. "No, quite. Thanks," I said, taking the passport from him.

Ahran took my elbow and steered me out of the building.

"Ah, there's Graham," Mr Cartwright said, pointing to a man who was frantically waving at us with a big smile on his face.

"I'll just get your bags," Ahran said.

We all walked to the car and Mr Cartwright stopped and turned towards us. "We can't thank you enough," he said with his hand outstretched.

"No, thank you," Ahran replied, shaking his hand. "You kept our son occupied on the train. You know how restless children can get on long journeys," he said, rolling his eyes like a seasoned father.

"I remember it well," Mrs Cartwright replied.

Ahran lifted their bags out of the boot, but I was still reeling from Bennie's message and stood and stared at them all feeling like I was in a tunnel, their voices echoing around me.

"We'll say goodbye then," Mr Cartwright said, holding his hand out for me to shake.

My brain failed to fire the necessary signal to my hand to actually do what he was suggesting, instead I just stared at it.

"Sandra," Ahran encouraged.

"Oh yes." I shook Mr and then Mrs Cartwright's hand and they left to join up with their nephew.

"What's the matter?" Ahran said.

"Nothing," I snapped.

"There is clearly something."

"I don't want to talk about it."

Ahran's eyes searched my face, but neither of us moved.

"Can I get the magazine we bought yesterday Uncle Ahran?" Toby asked.

"Yes, sure," Ahran replied, pressing the boot release again.

I climbed into the passenger seat.

"Please talk to me," Ahran said once he was in the car.

"It's not there," Toby complained, getting into the back seat.

"Not now," I whispered dismissively.

For about forty-five minutes we sat in silence driving along the E15 to Paris.

"Will you please tell me why you aren't talking to me?" Ahran said, quietly.

I glanced around at Toby to find that he had fallen asleep and then turned back towards Ahran. "Have you got something to tell me?" I said in a quiet, barely controlled voice. I raised my eyebrows waiting for the answer and braced myself for the worst possible news ever.

"About what?" he replied in a measured voice.

"About Bennie."

12

Ahran closed his eyes briefly.

I knew it. "You're having an affair with her, aren't you?"

He gave a humourless snort. "Is that what you think?"

"Well, it would explain the secret messages, the furtive looks and the way you touch her when you think I'm not looking."

Ahran looked back at the road, and shook his head slowly as if in disbelief.

"So you're not denying it?"

"Of course I'm bloody denying it!" he said angrily. "I cannot believe you think I would have an affair with your best friend. I love you Sophie. You seem to have such a hard time accepting that!"

"You cheated on Talina," I said, dragging exhibit A into the argument.

Ahran ran his hand over his hair. "That was different, I didn't love her, but you are my whole world."

"And you haven't been having a relationship with Bennie behind my back?" I wouldn't allow myself to feel the joyous feelings of relief until I heard him actually say it.

"I am not having an affair with Bennie," he repeated and picked up my hand to kiss my knuckles. "I love you Sophie, you and I are meant to be together, why would I jeopardise what we have?"

"I don't know," I said, shrugging. "When I saw her message asking you whether you had told me yet, I was convinced she wanted you to tell me about you and her." And then my initial conclusion after seeing her at the greasy spoon yesterday morning sprung to my mind. "Is it drugs?"

Ahran shook his head, he had gone very still.

"Oh God, I was so sure something was up, it's been eating away at me," I said, laughing at my own stupidity. "I'm such an idiot!"

Ahran wove his fingers with mine, took a deep breath and then paused.

"What?" I said, sensing something was up.

He hesitated some more as if he was struggling to find the right words.

"What is it? You're scaring me."

He took his eyes off the road for a moment. "Bennie has cancer."

"What?"

"Bennie was diagnosed with cervical cancer, six months ago."

I stared at him unable to voice any of the questions that were suddenly bombarding my brain.

"Unfortunately, the disease has not responded to chemo and they have downgraded her treatment to palliative care. She has been too frightened to tell you. She loves you Sophie."

"I don't understand," I said, feeling like I'd been hit by a bus, broadside.

"She only has months to live."

"You mean she's going to die?" I said, not quite able to believe what he was saying.

He nodded.

Suddenly, I wondered whether I would have preferred him to tell me that he and Bennie had been having an affair after all.

"Oh My God! I can't believe it." I groaned. "The last thing she needed was to sort out all my problems," I said, feeling dreadful about dragging her into all of this on top of what she was already going through.

"She wanted to do it for you, she said she had nothing to lose."

A tear rolled down my cheek, maybe it explained her erratic behaviour with men recently, she was living the high life before it was too late. Another thought occurred to me. "We can take her to Ramia, she can be treated there," I said, not quite understanding why Ahran hadn't thought of this already.

"It's a lovely idea Sophie, but we can't."

"What do you mean we can't, of course we bloody can," I said, feeling anger swelling inside me. "Give me your phone. I'll get her to meet us in Paris and she can come back with us." I couldn't understand why Ahran was being so obstructive, this was nothing that a phone call and a visit to a Ramian doctor wouldn't solve.

"It is forbidden," he replied.

"What do you mean it's forbidden?" I said, baulking at how ridiculous that sounded. This was Bennie, my best friend, we had known each other since we were five years old. If there was any possible way I could help her, I would.

"There are strict laws about who can come to Ramia, not to mention who can receive treatment there. Can you imagine what would happen if every Ramian on Earth took every sick person they felt sorry for back to Ramia to get better? Our world would be inundated, not to mention how difficult it would be to continue to keep Ramia a secret."

"This is different," I argued.

"I'm not sure the High Council would see it like that."

"Then let me speak to Leylana, she will understand."

"She may be royalty, but that won't hold any sway when it comes to the security of our world."

"But this is Bennie we're talking about," I said, pleadingly. I wasn't prepared to let some stupid law prevent me from getting the treatment my best friend needed.

"I understand Sophie, I know how much she means to you."

"Okay then, how come Toby and I are allowed in Ramia? We've both received medical treatment since we've been there," I said, recalling the two occasions I had been to the doctors and the medical check-up Toby had had shortly after arriving back at the palace after he'd been rescued.

"That's different. Toby is heir to the Dinaran throne and you are related to him."

"Well then, I'll get the drugs and bring them back to her," I said, suggesting the next best course of action.

"Our drugs are very powerful, the dosing needs to be exact and they need to be administered by someone who knows what they are doing. You could kill her."

"You're medically trained, you can do it."

"I'm a vet, not a doctor."

"I thought I'd be able to count on you Ahran."

"Hey, that's not fair," he said, taking his eyes off the road. "Besides, it may not be drugs she needs. There are a range of therapies that may be more suited to the disease she has."

"But Bennie is going to *die*. Please at least speak to the King, surely he can persuade the High Council.*"

He paused. "I have already spoken to him," he replied, shaking his head to indicate the outcome of their conversation.

"Try again," I begged.

He sighed deeply. "Okay, I'll see what I can do."

I had to be satisfied with this for the time being.

"Can I phone her?" I'm not sure what I wanted to say, but I needed to say something, to hear her voice. I couldn't believe I had thought that she and Ahran were having an affair, I felt like such a numskull. And there was me thinking that the change in her appearance was because she had been over doing it, possibly with my boyfriend. Oh God! And I had been so short with her after she had gone out of her way to help us. I felt so terrible, miserable and scared.

Ahran pulled out the phone from inside his jacket pocket and handed it to me.

I called her.

"Ahran?" she said after it had rung a few times.

"It's me."

"Hi Sophie. Are you in France?" she said as if nothing was wrong. My heart went out to her, she was being so brave.

"Bennie. I know," I said, simply.

She didn't reply immediately. I wanted to cry, to scream and throw myself about at the unfairness of it all. I was angry. Angry because she hadn't told me sooner, angry because this was Bennie, my best friend, angry because I wasn't able to do what I wanted to do and take her to Ramia. In those few moments of silence I faced the very real prospect that there would be a time when Bennie would no longer be here.

"I'm sorry," she said, eventually.

"Don't be ridiculous," I said, my voice breaking and forgiving her immediately. "I wish you had told me sooner."

"I tried so many times, but I couldn't find the right words. I guess there was a part of me that was in denial."

"I could have been there for you, come to the hospital with you."

"I know how much you hate those places."

I felt so bad that in spite of everything she was going through she was trying to protect me. "You're such a div," I said affectionately. "And I was so horrible to you earlier." I felt like a completely heartless, selfish cow.

"Yeah, what was all that about?"

"I'm sorry Ben, please just forget it." I was too embarrassed to voice what I had really suspected then. "I knew something was wrong, but you wouldn't talk to me and you never seemed to have time for us anymore. I thought you had moved on with your life and we were drifting apart."

"I know what it must have seemed like, but the treatment knocked me for six. I felt so tired all the time. At least now I'm on some new steroids and I feel like I've got a bit more energy."

"Oh Bennie, I don't know what to do or say," I said, feeling completely helpless.

"You don't know how good it is to finally be talking to you. I was hoping that once my treatment had finished I would be able to tell you all about it and say that there was no need to worry because I was cured, but hey, life's a bitch!"

By this time, tears were streaming down my face. She was being so strong, so brave.

"I wish I was there with you," I said choked and half contemplating asking Ahran to turn around. But what good would I be to her if we were caught and put in prison?

"Everything is such a mess," I said forlornly.

"Maybe once you are back at Toby's grandparents I can come and visit."

"We'll work something out. One way or another we will get to see each other." I wasn't quite sure how I was going to make this happen, but I was damned well going to come up with something.

"Have you been staying at your parent's?" I couldn't

imagine how they were coping. She was their only child and it had been such a battle to have her.

"Yeah."

"How are they?"

"Dad can't look me in the eyes. It's like he blames me for not looking after myself, but mum's been a rock."

I was thankful that as insufferable as her mother could be at times, she had at least rallied around and been a support. She was part of that war generation who in times of crisis rolled up their sleeves and just got on with it. This experience must have been helping her to stay in one piece even though she must have felt like her world was falling apart.

"I'm glad to hear that. For a moment, I thought you were on drugs!" I said, recalling my first suspicion that she was an addict.

"I am, just not the kind you were thinking of."

"Oh Ben, I wish I could give you a hug."

"Now there's no need for that sort of thing," she said with a little chuckle.

I laughed in return. Bennie had never been big on affection.

"Well, you're damn well going to get one when I see you whether you like it or not."

"Okay, seeing as it's you."

"Look, we're going to get Toby to safety and then I'll call you and we can talk about how we can get together."

"Okay hun, I'll wait to hear."

"Oh, and thank you," I said.

"What for?"

"For everything you have done for us, it was probably the last thing you needed."

"To be honest, it was good to have the distraction. I may have aided and abetted, but it's not as if they'd send a dying woman to prison."

"Oh God Ben, don't," I said, not knowing how she could be so fatalistic.

"Look, I'll call you," I said, not wanting to hang the phone up.

"Do what you need to do, I'll be here."

"Love you lots."

"Love you too. Bye Sophe."

She hung up.

Ahran put his hand on my knee and I sobbed into my hands.

"Hey, Sophie please don't cry. We'll try and come up with something."

"Please do everything you can," I begged.

He nodded reassuringly.

Ahran's phone rang in my lap. I picked it up to look at the screen expecting to see Bennie's number.

"It's the palace." I put it on loud speaker.

"Hello?"

"Sophie, its Halsan. Are you all okay?"

"Bearing up," I said, not able to say we were fine because I felt anything but fine.

"Where are you? Are you near the portal?"

"About another hour to go," Ahran answered.

"Don't go through it," Halsan warned.

"Why? What's the problem?" I asked.

"We have reason to believe it has malfunctioned. Engineers are working on it as we speak."

I had been in Ramia for two years and I had never heard of a portal going wrong.

"What's wrong with it?" Ahran said, pre-empting my question.

"We're not sure, but the last person to use it has not returned."

"Oh my God, that's terrible! What do you think has happened?" I asked.

"We don't know yet, a full investigation is being carried out."

"Okay, so where does that leave us?" Ahran said.

"I'll send you Evo Salanda's number, he is our agent in Paris. He will make sure you have everything you need and somewhere safe to stay until the repairs have been made."

"How long will that take?" I asked, not at all happy about staying here any longer than we had planned.

"I'm not sure. I will contact you as soon as it has been made safe."

"Please hurry," I pleaded.

"Believe me Sophie, I want you all back as quickly as possible."

He hung up.

Evo Salanda, I recognised the name, he was the guy I'd danced with at Elaya's wedding. "I'll phone Evo," I said, looking at the number that had just come through in a message.

"No, don't."

I looked across at him. "Why not?"

"I have a friend who will help us."

"But the King said to go to him." I felt slightly irritated that Ahran wanted to deviate from the plan.

"I'm not going to Salanda," he said, adamantly.

"But…"

"Raoul will help us." Ahran said, leaving me no room to argue.

Toby stirred in the back. "Are we there yet?"

"Nearly sweetheart," I said, turning around. "Are you okay?"

"I need a drink," he replied.

I handed him a bottle of water that I'd taken from the minibar back at the hotel.

Ahran was on the phone speaking Ramian and after what sounded like a fairly jolly conversation he put the phone down.

"All set. Raoul has an apartment we can use."

"Great!" I guess I didn't care too much about who helped us as long as we had somewhere safe to go for a few hours.

THANKS TO THE PARISIAN TRAFFIC, it was another two hours before we pulled up outside a creamy-grey, stone, Parisian town house overlooking the Jardin du Luxembourg. It was much like other Parisian townhouses, five stories high, four windows wide with moderately elaborate iron railings at each large window to allow for their opening on a warm day without any unsuspecting voyeur tumbling out onto the pavement below. All the houses along the street were similar although no two were the same. We stepped out of the car and I wondered for a moment how these streets had been built. Did all these houses go up together or were they built in this higgledy-piggledy fashion, filling in the gaps as and when the Parisian citizens felt like it?

"Raoul and his girlfriend won't be back until tomorrow," Ahran said, breaking my contemplation of Paris' town planning and hauling me back to the present. "We have his apartment overnight should the repair on the portal take longer than expected."

I looked up and down the street, it was relatively quiet. The odd moped buzzed by, carrying its suitably stylish driver who, other than wearing a simple crash hat, saw no need to wear any other form of protective gear. It was clearly far more important to show off their designer clothes. All over Paris there were mopeds such as these, like swarthy little drones bombilating around leaving a not unpleasant trail of exhaust fumes, cigarette smoke and expensive French cologne.

"Which one is it?" Toby asked, as we got out of the car and looking up at the numerous floors.

"It's the one on the fourth floor."

Ahran pressed the buzzer for the ground floor apartment.

"Allo?" A woman's voice replied.

"Bon jour. Je suis Ahran Elessar, un ami de Raoul Coochan."

"Ah oui! Oui, oui entrez." And one of the double wooden front doors clicked open. I took a last look up and down the street, mercifully no one seemed interested in who we were or what we were doing and I relaxed a little.

It was a hazy, warm Parisian day and the contrast in temperature inside compared to outside was stark. I instinctively rubbed my arms and waited for my eyes to acclimatise to the darkness of the inner vestibule. We were met by a stout French woman who looked to be in her sixties and wore the typical black apparel of a Catholic widow. She had clearly been briefed about our arrival and was pleasant if not effervescent in her welcome.

"Bonjour! Je suis Madame Girez. Suivez-moi," she said as she gripped the wooden handrail and began to mount the stairs. By the time we arrived at the door to Raoul's apartment Madame Girez was out of breath, a sign of her advancing years or perhaps too much good food and French wine.

She took out a bunch of keys from the pocket of her cardigan and unlocked the door. "Eh, voila," she said breathlessly, pushing the door open.

"Merci Madame," Ahran said as we entered the apartment leaving the gloomy battleship grey stairwell behind us. She handed Ahran the key and bid us farewell.

"Wow!" I exclaimed. The entrance hall led into a large, airy lounge with high ceilings typical of regency architecture. I ran my hand along the back of the two-seater chaise that stood in a group with two other distinctly French chairs. There was an imposing cream marble fireplace and a large chandelier was suspended from the ceiling. Long, heavy drapes hung at the windows held back by ornate tie-backs and a deep pile rug luxuriated on the parquet floor. Every wall was adorned with a beautiful picture, some were modern, but some must have dated back several hundred years at a guess. It was expensive, exquisitely French and entirely beautiful.

"What does Raoul do for a living?" I asked nosily.

"He's an art dealer."

"That figures," I said, more than a little impressed as my eyes settled on a portrait of a beautiful woman, her hair piled high on her head and her eyes willing me to indulge in whatever wicked pleasures she had in mind. I'd had visions of being holed up in some dingy, basement apartment, but this was high end Parisian accommodation the likes of which only the rich and famous usually got to experience. I suppose I was used to the trappings of Ramian royal life, but there was something about Parisian design that was a class above everything else.

"Please be careful Toby," I warned as he skidded excitedly around the apartment.

"This is sur-weet!" he said, joining us after exploring the other rooms.

I shook my head at him in despair. He'd been back on Earth less than a week and already sounded like a youth on the streets.

"Well, what do we do now?" I said, turning to Ahran.

"We wait. Are you hungry?" he said, walking into the kitchen and opening the fridge door. I knew it wouldn't be long before the subject of food was mentioned.

I felt a little uneasy about poking around somebody else's kitchen, particularly the fridge, you can tell a lot about a person by looking at the contents of their fridge;

somehow it felt too intimate, like peering through a bedroom window.

"Maybe we should order something in?" I suggested.

"Raoul said to help ourselves," Ahran replied, preoccupied by a selection of cheeses and not in the least embarrassed about creating a smorgasbord from Raoul's leftovers.

Toby looked over at what Ahran was doing. "I'm starving."

I sighed, giving in to my own pangs of hunger. "I'll get some plates," I said as I started to open and shut cupboard doors.

We settled down to what turned out to be quite a spread and washed it down with a glass of Bordeaux.

"We should leave him something for the food and wine," I said, wiping my mouth on a napkin.

"He wouldn't take it," Ahran replied. "He knows how many times I saved his arse!" he chuckled.

"Were you in the army together?" I asked.

"No, school. The times I covered for him when he used to sneak out from the dorm to meet a girl."

"Didn't you used to do that?" I said, intrigued to find out more about Ahran's adolescence.

"Of course I did," he said unapologetically. "But I never got caught!"

I laughed. "Thank God Toby isn't at boarding school."

At this point both Toby and Ahran looked a little sheepish.

"What?" I said, looking from one to the other.

"Paps said I will be going to board at the beginning of next year."

I could see Toby bracing himself for what was coming next.

"Did you know about this?" I said, rounding on Ahran.

He shrugged. "He can't have a tutor forever Sophie, he's missing out."

"He seems to be coping perfectly well," I said, not wanting to admit there was an element of truth in what Ahran was saying. "Boarding school?! Is there not some-where local he can go?"

"Nowhere that is good enough for the heir to the Dinaran throne."

"Well, I can't see Leylana agreeing to this," I said, name dropping my number one ally when it came to anything to do with Toby.

"She knows it's in Toby's best interest to go to Stallards."

"Stallards?" I said, raising my eyebrows.

"It's where Tagan and I went, where my father and Halsan went. It's where all the boys in our family go."

"Where is it?"

"Giron."

"Giron! But that's bloody miles away."

"He'll be back in the holidays."

Toby had stayed very quiet during mine and Ahran's exchange.

"And what do you think about this?" I said, turning back to him.

He shrugged. "We might not even get back to Ramia," he said as if this might appease me.

My anger quickly dissipated at his forlorn expression.

"Yes, we will," I said, not particularly feeling the conviction with which I said it, we hadn't heard a dicky bird from the palace over the last couple of hours. "Won't we Ahran?" I said, needing him to back me up.

"Of course we will. This is just a minor glitch."

It wasn't the first time Toby had shown how much he loved living in Ramia and how little he seemed to care for being on Earth. I felt bad. Bad for Katie and bad for him wanting very little to do with his Sapien heritage.

This had brought an end to our conversation about Toby's ongoing education, but if we did ever get back to Ramia it would be one of the first things I was going to bring up with the King, that was, after I'd asked for help with Bennie. I had learned to stand up to Halsan over the last two years and I had every right to be involved in the conversations about Toby's future.

I picked up the dishes just as the door buzzer went.

13

I looked at Ahran as if to say *Who could that be?*

He shrugged and went to look out of the window to see who it was.

Ahran swore.

The buzzer buzzed again for a longer burst this time.

"Who is it?"

"It's bloody Salanda," he said.

"How did he know we were here?"

Ahran shook his head. "My phone must have been tracked."

"Are you going to let him in, he seems to be leaning on the buzzer?" I said, beginning to tire of the sound.

Ahran reluctantly pressed the door release and within seconds there was a knock at the door.

Evo Salanda was just as handsome as I remembered and wore a dark, extremely well-tailored evening suit and tie. He was clean shaven and smelled of expensive cologne. If it hadn't been for the Parisian beauty on his arm and the fact that I loved Ahran more than life itself, I may well have done exactly what his *come to bed* eyes were suggesting.

"Ahran. Good to see you again." He spoke in English. When I had met him at the wedding I had assumed he just had a Ramian accent, but there was a definite Parisian lilt.

Ahran shook his outstretched hand.

"Ah and the lovely Sophie, your beautiful English rose," he said, before kissing me on both cheeks. I had no idea why Ahran found him so objectionable, he seemed nothing but a perfect gentleman to me.

We walked into the living room. "This is my girlfriend Mimi," he said, introducing his stunning companion whose brunette hair was swept back in a sleek bun and who wore a black broderie anglaise cocktail dress which clung to her perfectly proportioned, if a bit on the skinny side, figure.

"Bonsoir," she said, holding out her fingertips for a fashionably, minimal contact, French handshake.

"And where is Toby?" Evo asked, looking over our shoulders.

Toby was sat at the breakfast bar in the kitchen drawing Ramian fighter planes, his latest obsession.

"Toby," I called. "There is someone who would like to see you."

"Who is it?" he said, entering the room.

"This is Evo Salanda, he is a friend of…" I was about to say 'A friend of Ahran's', but it was clear to see that Ahran saw him as anything but, so I finished by saying "Your grandfather's. He was at Elaya's wedding."

Evo bowed respectfully towards Toby.

Bowing to someone of Toby's position was common

practice and it was something Toby and I both secretly laughed at, although Toby nodded Evo's acknowledgement like a seasoned pro.

"You look just like your father," Evo said.

"So I am told," Toby said, unsurprised by Evo's observation, many people had said the same thing.

Evo's gaze lingered on Toby, he seemed a little awestruck.

Mimi sashayed across to one of the windows and opened it, saying, "Do you mind?" and lit up before anyone had a chance to answer her. I wanted to say, "Well, yes actually I do," but didn't want to appear the ungracious host in someone else's apartment.

Ahran raised his eyebrows at Evo.

"Mimi knows about the er…sensitivity of our situation," Evo said, responding to Ahran's unspoken question as he eyed Evo's girlfriend somewhat disapprovingly. I guessed that Ahran was more concerned about anyone knowing our whereabouts than any issue he had with her smoking a cigarette. I had to wonder whether she knew anything about Ramia because it would have been careless of me to ask.

"We are just off out to dinner. I was expecting your call, but when I didn't hear from you I thought you might have come here. Raoul must be doing well for himself," Evo said, as he surveyed the luxurious apartment.

"What is it you want?" Ahran asked rather sharply.

Evo didn't rise to Ahran's clipped question, but reached into his inside jacket pocket and pulled out a brown envelope.

"It would be unwise for you to use any credit cards so I

have been instructed to make sure you have some money. You chose not to come to me," he said a little prickly, "So I thought I would do the honourable thing and bring it to you," he said, finishing in a more light-hearted tone.

Ahran took the envelope. "Thanks," he said grudgingly.

An awkward silence fell and Evo shifted uncomfortably. "Well, it was lovely to see you all again. We would love to stay for a drink," he said, even though no drink had been offered, "But our dinner party will be waiting."

Mimi joined him at the door. "I am sorry to hear your journey has been delayed," Evo said, turning to me. He kissed me again on each cheek and turned to Ahran.

"Is Elaya well?" Evo asked.

Someone paying less attention could have easily missed the flicker of emotion that followed his question.

"Yes, she is well."

"That's good," he replied and there it was again, it was a look of hurt and disappointment and then it was gone. He smiled and turned to Toby. "Prince Saleth it has been an honour to meet you properly, I didn't get the chance at the wedding."

Toby nodded. "And you."

"Goodbye and have a safe trip back." Evo and his girl-friend walked out into the stairwell.

"Goodbye Salanda,"

I said goodbye too and Ahran closed the door behind them.

"Why don't you like him?" I asked, following Ahran back into the living room.

"It's a long story," Ahran said, evading my question.

"We seem to have some time on our hands," I said, throwing my hands in the air and looking around hopelessly at our luxurious half-way house. Evo seemed perfectly charming, I really didn't see what Ahran's problem was with him.

"Not now," he said dismissively. "Now let's have a look at these pictures," he said to Toby and walked into the kitchen, leaving me feeling puzzled. I remembered that at Elaya's wedding Ahran had implied Evo was work shy, but that was hardly reason enough to condemn a man.

LATER THAT EVENING, I lay in bed and decided to broach the subject of Evo Salanda again. "I thought Evo was a real gentleman."

"Hmmm?" Ahran said, whipping his shirt over his head.

Faced with Ahran's beautiful torso, I momentarily lost concentration. "I said, I thought Evo was a gentleman," I repeated, once I had remembered the thread of our conversation. "Why don't you like him? You said he likes to live the high life, but that's hardly a punishable offence."

"I don't trust him."

"So what was the long story you were going to tell me?"

He threw me a look of exasperation.

"I'd like to know," I urged, it wasn't like Ahran to take a dislike to someone.

He sighed when he realised I wasn't going to let it go. "Tagan and I were at school with him, he was a real computer whizz and then we were in the army together."

"So why would that make you not trust him?" I asked, struggling to understand what he was saying, or rather, not saying.

"He let Tagan down."

Ahran pulled the covers back and climbed in next to me.

"How?"

Ahran ran the back of his hand down my cheek. "I can think of better things to do than talk about Evo Salanda," he said with a seductive gleam in his eye. He ran his thumb over my lip, it was obvious he had no interest in the topic of conversation.

I leaned up on one elbow and tucked the covers around me not so easily deterred. "Well, it seems whatever wrongs he committed, he has made up for them now. It was very kind of him to bring us that money."

Ahran made a disapproving noise in the back of his throat. "We could have survived without it," he said, his words muffled against my neck as he began to kiss his way down to my shoulder.

"He seemed rather taken with Toby, and he asked after Elaya."

Ahran halted his seduction.

"What is it with you and Evo?"

"I just think that maybe you're being a little hard on him when he actually came out of his way to help us this evening."

He eyed me suspiciously. "He's a good-looking guy. Should I be worried about your interest in him?"

"Don't be ridiculous," I said, feeling a slight blush stain my cheeks.

Ahran looked at me for a moment clearly deciding whether it was prudent to go on and say more.

He sighed and sat up, abandoning his seduction. "Evo and Elaya were betrothed," he said.

"Really?" I said, surprised by this. I suddenly remembered a conversation I'd had with Elaya about her not choosing to settle for the man her parents had chosen for her.

"But she was in love with Tigor."

He nodded.

"Poor Evo."

Ahran gave a humourless snort. "Don't feel sorry for him, it was Evo and his men who left Tagan unprotected before he was killed."

Okay, so now we were getting to the bottom of why Ahran didn't like Evo.

"He should have been there to cover, but the cowardly bastard fled the outpost at the first sign of trouble." Ahran was struggling to keep his voice steady. "He later told an inquest that he had returned to base to send a message that we were in need of reinforcements, but I know for a fact that he never made it to base. He let Tagan down and his actions cost Tagan his life."

"I'm sorry to hear that," I said, feeling a little stupid that I had inadvertently fallen for Evo's charm.

"Yeah, well," he said, swinging his legs over the side of the bed and putting his face in his hands. I felt terrible that I had pushed it so much that I had caused him pain.

I knelt up and kissed him on the shoulder. "I'm sorry. I know how much you miss Tagan." Evo was quickly forgotten on my part, all I wanted to do was comfort Ahran, take away his pain, but Tagan was gone and there was nothing I could do about that. All I could do was offer him my understanding and help him take his mind off it.

I ran my hands over his shoulders and kissed him gently on the back of the neck. I inhaled his scent, it was faded cologne and that smell of him which I adored more than any other smell in the world. It was comforting and arousing at the same time. I trailed kisses across his shoulders and he rolled his head back.

I pressed myself to his back and ran my hands around him, over his chest and down over his abdomen. He groaned in anticipation once he knew where I was heading. The raw sound of it hit me in the pit of my stomach like a glorious little firework spreading hundreds of hot sparks igniting the blood in my veins.

I took him into my hand and ran my hand down his length.

"Ah, Sophie!" he growled.

I smiled against his shoulder and began a smooth rhythm up and down. He was hard and hot in my hand and the feel of it served only to heighten my own arousal. Feeling bolstered by the effect I was having on him, I climbed off the bed and settled between his legs.

I took him in my mouth. In previous relationships, I had always shied away from oral sex finding it a rather unsavoury experience, but with Ahran it was different. To know that I was giving him pleasure in this way was an empowering experience. I sucked and licked until he throbbed in my mouth. He quickly withdrew. I had fully intended on allowing him to take his own pleasure and fore-going mine, but he had other plans.

He pulled me up his body and turned me a little roughly onto my back. His mouth came crushing down onto mine, his tongue owned me as it plunged into my mouth and served as a promise of what he was about to do to another, more intimate part of my body.

Usually, he was a gentle and patient lover, but there was something different about our lovemaking tonight. There was a roughness, an urgency. It was like he was staking his claim, making it known that in no uncertain terms I was his. Maybe it was the whole Salanda thing and in my ignorance, by defending Evo I had made him jealous. Or maybe some good hard lovemaking was what he needed to take his mind off the memory of the excruciating loss of his best friend brought about by Evo's visit and my questioning. Whatever it was, it was animalistic, it suited the moment and I loved it.

"Ahh!" I cried out when he entered me and I dug my nails into his shoulders as he began to thrust hard and fast. I wrapped my legs around him drawing him into me as far as he could go. Every time he touched my core it was a step closer to that moment when the sensation was finally too much and I gave myself to him unreservedly and with so much love that I thought if it had lasted a moment longer I would have surely shattered into a million pieces of sheer pleasure and joy.

He came quickly after me, his rhythm changing slightly to a hard thrust, pause, another thrust, then pause, until his climax was over and he collapsed on top of me all sweaty and spent.

I giggled. "What did I do to deserve that?"

"Did I hurt you?" he asked, lifting himself off me, his voice full of concern.

"No, don't," I said, pulling him back on top of me. "Stay there." I loved the feel of him on top of me.

I trailed my fingertips up and down his back. "No, you didn't hurt me, I enjoyed it."

Ahran took his weight onto his elbows. "I lost control Sophie and I shouldn't have. I'm sorry."

"Don't apologise, I loved every second of it."

"Are you sure?"

"I'm sure, I'm sure."

He rolled onto his back taking me with him. "I love you Sophie McAllister," he said, kissing me tenderly as if to prove that his momentary lapse of control was a thing of the past.

"And I love you Ahran Elessar. I know if it really came to it you wouldn't hurt me."

"I forget sometimes how delicate you are."

I frowned at him. "I'm tougher than I look," I said, a little affronted.

"I know you're tough," he said with a chuckle. "You are the strongest woman I know," he added, changing his meaning slightly and suddenly turning very earnest.

"And you haven't seen me bench press yet," I said jokily, purposely misunderstanding his thread. I planted a kiss squarely on his lips before rolling off him. I settled into the crook of his arm and laced my fingers with his. His compliment made me absurdly happy.

THE FOLLOWING MORNING, I left Ahran to sleep and got up to have a shower. A little later Toby joined me in the kitchen. "What do you want for breakfast Tobes?" I asked, perusing the limited array of breakfast options.

If we had been on holiday I could have sent Ahran down to the local boulangerie for some fresh croissants or a warm baguette and some pain au raisin, but sadly, we were not, and had to settle for some kind of French All Bran or a chocolatey curly cereal I didn't recognise.

"That one," Toby said, predictably pointing to the chocolatey confection and a poor excuse for a healthy breakfast cereal. Anything with a green cartoon crocodile on the front of the box contained within it something of dubious nutritional value in my experience.

"Okay," I agreed reluctantly, "But there is no fresh milk, just UHT."

"What's UHT?"

"Long-life milk."

He nodded and shrugged seemingly none the wiser.

I poured myself a small bowl of the All Bran and padded over to the floor-to-ceiling window in the living room to take in the view of the park whilst I ate my breakfast. It was a warm, bright, sunny morning and I stood with my eyes closed and my face turned towards the sun, for a moment I was transported to Ramia with its warm sunshine and crystal clear fresh air, until thoughts of Bennie swiftly brought me back to reality accompanied by a painful lurch of my heart. The sooner we got back to Ramia the sooner I could discuss Bennie's case with the King. I knew Ahran would do his best for me, but I wasn't above pleading if it meant my best friend would be treated. I didn't care how, I would personally pay for the drugs and a private doctor to attend to Bennie to administer them if I wasn't allowed to take her to Ramia. Ahran would support me, I was sure of it.

He came out of the bedroom, freshly washed and shaved.

"Any news?" I asked hopefully.

He shook his head. "I've just spoken to the palace, the engineers are still working on the portal, it's complicated as you can imagine. It might be that they have to open up a new one."

"But that could take another week."

"It is what it is," he said, shrugging helplessly. "I'm ravenous, what's for breakfast?" he said, changing the subject.

"Smoked salmon and scrambled egg or a fry up with all the trimmings," I said, sarcastically.

For a split second, he looked hopeful.

"I'm kidding; slightly stale All Bran or Choco Crocos."

He grimaced and headed into the kitchen.

I took a mouthful of cereal and turned my attention to the outside world again. It was hot behind the glass, so I opened one of the French doors for some air and was greeted by the bustling sound of the city street below. I could hear the reversing alarm of a delivery vehicle. There was a road sweeper whirring along the gutter and a number of workmen in overalls, idly hanging around.

Huh! Parisian workmen obviously have the same work ethic as workmen at home, I thought to myself whilst spooning another mouthful of cereal into my mouth.

"What's so interesting out there?" Ahran asked as he joined me at the window with his own bowl of cereal.

"Just marvelling at how workmen work very hard at doing nothing," I replied.

Ahran chuckled and took a look for himself.

Suddenly he stood very still.

14

"What is it?" I said, peering out.

Ahran pulled me away from the window so abruptly that I spilt the milk in my bowl.

"We need to get out of here," he said, deadly quiet. "Those aren't workmen. Get into the kitchen."

I couldn't quite believe what he was saying, the guys down on the street looked like your average workmen to me. "Are you sure?" Admittedly they weren't engaged in any *work* as such, but that was typical behaviour, wasn't it?

"Workmen don't usually wear earpieces. They are staking us out."

He grabbed my arm and we ran into the kitchen where Toby was sat, putting the finishing touches to his fighter plane masterpiece.

Ahran threw up the sash window.

Toby looked up from his drawing and I hesitated for a moment.

"Now!" Ahran insisted, gesturing towards the window.

I trusted Ahran and knew we had no choice but to try
and escape, I could only assume that within seconds there
would be men hammering at our door and I wasn't about to
hang about to find out who they were.

"You first Sophie."

He helped me out of the window and I stood on the
metal fire escape waiting for them to join me. I swallowed
and tried not to look down. I had no head for heights and we
were four stories up. Toby climbed out the window like an
agile cat followed by Ahran who closed the window
behind him.

"Follow me."

I pressed myself against the wall doing as Ahran
instructed. The fire escape had not been well maintained
and there was a ladder missing between us and the floor
below.

"We're going up, okay?" Ahran said, checking I was
cool with this.

I was not, but I was in no position to argue. I looked up
to where he was suggesting, there was no more fire escape
above us, just a lead drain-pipe leading up to the roof.

"I can piggy-back you up if you want," he offered,
reading my hesitation as having cold feet.

"No, I think I can manage," I said, trying to work out a
route up.

"Put your foot onto that bracket, grab that ledge and pull
yourself up," he said, giving me some guidance.

I nodded. It was climb up onto the roof or be captured
and this time it wasn't just me, Toby and Ahran were in the
equation. I couldn't let them down.

I took a deep breath and stretched up to put my foot onto the bracket Ahran had pointed out. I pulled myself up and reached for the ledge. Ahran pushed me up as far as he could reach and it gave me enough momentum to be able to place my left foot onto the upper frame of the kitchen window. I was then able to bring my right foot up to another bracket and scrambled up onto the flat roof of a fifth-floor dormer window. From there I could lever myself up onto the lead roof of the building. I was panting from the exertion and ventured a glance below to see Toby taking the same route and looking like some world climbing champion. Ahran followed suit.

"This way," he said as he began to walk along the gentle slope of the roof.

"How did they know we were here?"

"It wouldn't have been Raoul," he replied.

"Evo then?"

"He may be a coward, but I wouldn't have said he was a traitor."

His answer left me feeling stumped.

There was probably a spectacular view from our vantage point, but I could only focus on the few feet in front of me. Even though the facade of these townhouses were some-what uniform the roofline was considerably more irregular. It wasn't until we were about halfway along the roof of the neighbouring townhouse that I heard some shouting coming from below. I didn't care whether anyone had noticed we were up there, all I could do was place one foot in front of the other. In an attempt to move more quickly, I lowered my centre of gravity, but my foot slipped and I gasped.

"Are you okay Auntie Sophie?" Toby asked.

"Y…yes, I'm fine," I fibbed.

Ahran took hold of my hand and I welcomed his support. I was petrified that one false move and I would be curtains.

We came to a gap in the roof line. I looked down at the street below and felt myself sway with vertigo. Ahran held me steady.

"We're going to jump this okay?" he said, sounding like a paramedic trying to reassure a road traffic accident victim. All I could think was that if I misjudged this I would *be that* road traffic victim, except there would be no surviving this one.

Ahran turned his attention to Toby. "You okay with this?"

Toby nodded, not looking anywhere near as terrified as I felt.

"Run as fast as you can and jump," Ahran coached. "It's a flat roof on the other side, it should be a safe enough landing."

I needed him to sound more certain than that. "Ahran, I'm not sure Toby should do this." I couldn't bear the thought of him risking his life. "Surely, there's another way."

"I can do it Auntie Sophie," Toby said bravely.

"He's right Sophie, Toby is just as capable of jumping this gap as I am."

I nodded, finally giving my consent and hoping Katie wasn't up above watching any of this. She would *kill* me!

Toby took a few steps backwards. I closed my eyes feeling like I might throw up.

"After three. One…two…three!" Ahran cried.

It was torturous. I couldn't look and yet I wanted to make sure he'd made it safely.

I covered my face with my hands and heard Toby's footsteps as he sprinted towards the gap. Suddenly time stood still. My whole body tensed as I waited to hear him land on the other side. But I heard nothing except the ominous sound of a siren blaring from the street below. I opened my eyes in panic to see Toby grinning at me from the building on the other side. I nearly fainted with relief. He must have jumped it so cleanly and landed so lightly that he'd barely made a sound.

"Our turn," Ahran prompted.

In my rejoicing, I had momentarily forgotten that I had yet to jump. "I think you are over-estimating my capabilities," I said, nervously.

"I'll hold your hand and we'll do it together."

I closed my eyes briefly in an attempt to calm my nerves. It made no difference.

Ahran started to back up. "When I say jump, jump!"

I'd done some mad things since knowing Ahran; leaping off a high speed train probably being the maddest, but jumping from one building to another fifty feet up came a close second.

I ran as fast as I could towards the gap.

"*Jump!*" Ahran shouted, and against my every instinct I did.

A greater force than the one I used to launch myself

propelled me across the gap and we easily made the distance between the two buildings. I should have had more confidence in Ahran's strength. Jumping that distance was a walk in the park for him.

"Okay?" he asked.

"Never better," I said with only a hint of sarcasm. The adrenaline was pumping and despite feeling scared out of my wits I felt exhilarated.

"Good girl!" He grabbed my hand and we continued along the roofline, jumping over several rows of chimney pots.

"There," Ahran cried, pointing to an open dormer window.

Toby led the way clearly less bothered about climbing through an open window than I was. How was the poor unsuspecting person going to react when three people climbed into their fifth storey bedroom window?

Fortunately, the occupants were early risers, the bed, although unmade, was empty.

We raced through the room and down the stairs only to meet a middle-aged gentleman in his pyjamas coming out of the galley kitchen.

"Eh?!" the man cried in surprise as he clocked the three of us.

"Pardon!" I said by way of an apology as we ran past him towards his front door. A flurry of angry French words followed us and if I'd had time to turn around I'm sure I would have found him standing there red-faced, angrily flailing his arms about like a Frenchman who had just found three uninvited strangers running through his flat.

His voice echoed down the stairwell until the door slammed.

We ran down the stairs as fast as we could and reached the vestibule on the ground floor.

"This way," Ahran said, leading us to a door into the rear courtyard. It was overshadowed by the surrounding buildings and not an overly pleasant place to sit if you had the time. Someone had tried to make an effort with some planters and a table and chairs. Ahran tried a couple of the doors which were locked and the adrenaline I had felt began to give way to rising panic. The third door he tried, opened. We went through it into an almost identical entrance hall to the one we had just been through. I couldn't quite get my bearings, but if my internal compass was correct, we were about to enter a street that was perpendicular to the one Raoul's flat was on and a couple of blocks along.

Ahran cracked the front door open to look along the street. I guessed he was using all his heightened senses to gauge whether the coast was clear. All I heard was another siren caterwauling down the street.

"Okay, let's go!"

We walked out into the morning sunshine and turned left away from the main street. We walked as fast as we could, trying to not look too suspicious; not an easy feat when trying to put as much distance between yourselves and those who we assumed were still in pursuit of us.

"Toby, bend down and pretend to tie your shoelace," Ahran said. He grabbed me and pulled me into a doorway his mouth crashing down onto mine. Not one to shrink away from Ahran's affection, I responded and caught sight of the black car that was about to pass us, it was an unmarked police car with a blue flashing light on the dashboard.

We pulled apart. "You taste good!" he whispered seductively. My nerves were a tight as piano wires, but Ahran seemed to be enjoying the danger. He was outwardly calm, cool and collected, the only thing that gave him away was the slightly feverish look in his eyes. I'd seen the same look on Elaya's face when we had escaped from Bazeera's castle. I could quite happily live without this level of excitement, but they seemed to thrive on it.

We carried on down the street. "What now?" I asked.

"I know someone else who will help us," Ahran replied.

"Who?" I asked, struggling to keep up.

"My old mentor, Saul, he lives on the other side of Paris."

Ahran often talked about Saul and thought a lot of him, but I didn't relish the thought of travelling through the city. I felt exposed knowing that our whereabouts was no longer secret and that somebody was after us. I looked around nervously feeling like everyone we passed knew who we were. It was a horrible feeling, like even the walls of the buildings had eyes and ears.

"Are you okay Tobes?" I asked, doubting my own state of mind more than his.

"I'm good," he said with a grin. If I wasn't mistaken, he had that same look of excitement in his eyes that I had seen in Ahran's moments earlier. So it was just me that felt scared witless then?

"Come on, we need to catch that bus," Ahran said,

sprinting towards the single decker that had just pulled up at the nearest bus stop.

We caught it just in time. "We haven't got any money," I said breathlessly.

Ahran pulled out a wad of notes form his back pocket, he'd obviously removed them from the envelope Evo had brought us the previous evening and winked at me.

I smiled, grateful for his foresight.

Ahran bought our tickets and we sat down towards the back of the bus. Having escaped from under the noses of whom I could only assume were either the French police or MI5, we had a moment's respite. I took in a deep breath.

Ahran held my hand and gave me a reassuring kiss on the knuckles.

"This is cool," Toby said, swinging around in his seat with excitement. "I've never been to Paris. Oh look! That's the Eiffel Tower," he said, pointing to France's most iconic landmark.

I couldn't help but be affected by his enthusiasm and allowed myself a moment to enjoy one of my most favourite cities.

"Can we go up it?" he asked hopefully, although I could see he already knew what the answer would be.

"We'll come back one day," I said. Maybe he hadn't entirely written off Earth after all.

The bus wound its way through the Parisian traffic for about fifteen minutes. "This is where we need to get off," Ahran said as we approached the area I recognised to be Les Invalides. We got off the bus and walked to the nearest Métro.

"Isn't it a bit risky going on the underground?" I asked, keeping pace with him.

"As long as we are careful, we'll be okay. It's the quickest way to get to Porte de Clichy."

Two policemen strolled past and I tried not to stare at the truncheons and guns that hung from their belts. I glanced up at one of them who, unusually for a Frenchman, had red hair under his standard issue side cap. Fortunately, they were deep in conversation and didn't seem to pay us any attention.

We took an indirect route to the ticket machines and I could only assume Ahran was doing his best to avoid the CCTV cameras. We bought our tickets and headed for the train.

Down on the platform it was hot and extremely crowded. I could hear shouting coming from the other end and I was being jostled by the crowd to my left who were having to make way for whoever it was trying to get through.

I caught a glimpse of red hair and realised it was the two policemen we had passed earlier.

Ahran grabbed my arm and pushed Toby in front of us, forcing a way through to the front of the platform where the underground train was just about to come to a halt.

"Arretez!" One of the policemen shouted.

I hoped for a second it was a case of mistaken identity, but I could see they were locked in on Ahran who, standing a good head and shoulder above the majority of the people in the crowd, was easy to spot.

The door of the train stopped just a little out of our reach and we had to elbow our way through to get to the open doors.

The policemen were at a distinct disadvantage being several rows of people back, but they had the arm of the law on their side and people were grudgingly moving out of their way.

We moved forward with the throng of people and got onto the train.

I could see the faces of the two policemen now and they called out again. "Arretez! Police!"

The warning alarm that the doors were about to close sounded and the red-haired policeman barged the final few feet to the edge of the platform. He would have succeeded in jumping on the train if it hadn't been for a small child who stepped in his path and his mother who reached out an arm to pull him back towards her. The doors slid shut and the policeman hit the glass with his fist in frustration, making me jump.

The train pulled away leaving him stood there, foiled by the swift efficiency of the underground train.

I squeezed Ahran's hand and gave Toby a tight-lipped smile. The people around us who had witnessed what had just happened were eyeing us with a degree of suspicion. I shrugged at them in an attempt to convey that I had no idea what all *that* was about.

"They will be waiting at the next station. We need to get off this train and try and lose them," Ahran said into my ear. We were squashed together like sardines and there was a pervading smell of hot bodies.

I nodded, fully aware that we were like sitting ducks if we stayed, but wondering how we were going to do that.

All too quickly, the train pulled into the next station, and I looked up at Ahran who was obviously assessing the level of risk as the train slowed. There were two sets of policemen standing at the back of the platform as far as I could see, and they were surveying the incoming carriages. It was likely that the only advantage we had was that they didn't know where we were on the train.

"Hold Toby's hand. Keep your head down and follow me," Ahran instructed.

At times like these there was no room for any form of courteousness and Ahran barged his way through the hordes, who to be fair were showing us little in return as they fought their way onto the train. I tried to pick out the policemen I had seen just now and saw that they had stopped a man who was almost as tall as Ahran.

"They've stopped somebody else," I said.

"I know, follow me."

We stuck to the edge of the platform and did our best to be as inconspicuous as possible. It was a beautiful late summer's day and the tourists were out in their droves. Fortunately, it was this heaving mass of sightseers that gave us the cover we needed. We made it off the platform and kept pace with the people who were walking in the same direction until we reached one of the main arteries of the Métro. A quick glance at the signs above and Ahran took us to the right for a train heading to *La Defense*.

Suddenly Ahran stopped us abruptly and with our backs to the ever-moving flow of people, two more police officers rushed passed, unaware of the three tourists who were seemingly absorbed in the notice on the wall. My heart pounded as we waited. The police headed in the direction we had just come from and as soon as the coast was clear, we picked up pace and walked onto the train that was standing rather conveniently at the nearest platform. This train wasn't quite as busy, although it was still standing room only. We changed twice more until we were on the *Pontoise* line having happily avoided any more run-ins with the French gendarmerie.

"Which station are we heading to again?" I asked, swaying to the movement of the train and relieved we were no longer under any immediate threat.

"Porte de Clichy," Ahran answered.

I'd not heard of the place.

We managed to get a seat on the last leg of our journey and sat there in silence. I felt shaken. I glanced at the orange digital display on the side of the carriage, it was still early. We had been a cat's whisker away from the police on more than one occasion over the last forty minutes, although it had seemed like hours. I couldn't have been more pleased to see the blue and white tiled sign *Pte de Clichy* on the wall of our destination a short while later.

"I can't wait for you to meet Saul," Ahran said with the usual amount of affection he showed whenever he talked about the man who had once been his mentor. I marvelled at how quickly Ahran was able to switch from highly trained soldier to someone who was excited about visiting an old friend without the slightest hint of anxiety or strain. I, on the other hand, felt positively rattled.

We walked up the stairs and out into the sunshine. Porte de Clichy was a typical Parisian suburb. The buildings here weren't quite as grand as those in the centre of Paris, but they were still three or four stories high with shutters at the windows. We stopped at a 'Boulangerie et Patisserie' at the end of the street, and knowing Ahran so well, thought we were getting something to eat, but instead he pressed the buzzer by the wooden door adjacent to the shop.

"'Allo?"

Ahran spoke in Ramian.

"Ahran!" Came the excited reply, followed by a flurry of Ramian.

The door clicked and we made our way up to the third floor where Saul was waiting for us.

The two men embraced before introductions were made.

"This is my girlfriend Sophie McAllister," Ahran said in English, "And Tagan's son Toby."

Saul looked like he was the cat that had got the cream. "What an honour it is to finally meet you," he said and bowed in front of Toby.

It was difficult to say how old this kindly-looking man was, he was older than Halsan, about the same height, but thicker around the waist. He had grey hair, a tidy beard and warm smiling eyes.

"And Sophie," he said, embracing me. "So, this is your beautiful Sapien."

I liked him immediately.

15

"Come in, come in," he said hospitably. "To what do I owe this great pleasure? What brings you to Paris?"

We stepped inside his apartment which was far more modest than Raoul's to find that there were books everywhere. They not only lined the walls, but were stacked in piles on the floor, in fact there was a book on pretty much every surface. Saul was clearly a scholar and I strained my eyes to try and read some of the titles. There were titles in many different languages, but some were in English and ranged from ancient history to geology, modern day film to medieval kingship, there didn't seem to be a topic that had been spared.

"Take a seat," Saul said, rushing to clear books and newspapers from the worn armchairs dotted around the room. "If I had known I was about to receive visitors, I would have tidied the place up," he said, sounding a little embarrassed.

"I'm sorry for the lack of warning, but we didn't have time to call ahead," Ahran said.

"No matter. Sit, sit," he said, gesturing towards the now empty chairs.

I glanced at the title of the open book that was face down on a table next to where Saul must have been sitting, *Memoirs of an Islamist Concubine*. The old devil! His tastes were certainly eclectic.

"Why do I sense you are in trouble?" Saul said guardedly.

"Because we are," Ahran said with a snort.

"Let me get you a drink and you can tell me all about it. Tea, Coffee?"

We gave him our orders and Ahran followed him into the kitchen as they began to converse in Ramian.

"What are they saying?" I whispered to Toby.

"Uncle Ahran is telling him what's happened." Toby got up and started to read some of the book titles on the nearest bookshelf. "This guy must like reading," he said in awe. "What's a Conker-bine?" he asked, looking at the book I'd noticed earlier.

"A con-cubine," I corrected, "Is er...usually a woman who er...has relationships with men she isn't married to," I said delicately.

Toby looked suitably unimpressed. "Oh." He picked up a small telescope from the windowsill and tried to adjust it so that it would focus.

"Toby! Put it down!" I said, fearful that he might break it.

"Oh, that's alright," Saul said, coming back into the

room with a tray of cups and saucers. "Let the boy play, he can't do any harm." He seemed to find Toby's inquisitiveness endearing.

"From what Ahran has told me it would seem you've had quite a time of it recently," Saul said, passing me a cup and saucer.

"Er, yes. We're pretty good at getting ourselves into scrapes."

"Indeed." He put two heaped teaspoons of sugar in his own cup and stirred.

"You have quite a collection of books here," I remarked.

He nodded in agreement. "Yes, you could say that. Need something to keep me occupied in my old age. We don't have the same books in Ramia that you have here, and I can't abide reading on a screen. Somehow the printed word has more integrity, don't you think?"

As much as I loved my Kindle, he had a point.

"I understand you've known Ahran a long time?" I said, conversationally.

"Since he was small. Did Ahran tell you that I was Tagan's mentor and by default Ahran's too?"

"Yes, he did mention it."

"I suppose I was like the Ramian equivalent of a governess," he said, searching for the right analogy.

I think he was unaware that I was not overly familiar with the job description of a governess. Ramians seemed to forget the discrepancy in their longevity in relation to mine, in terms of the last century I had only experience of the last three decades, whilst I would wager Saul had been around since the late 19th Century, he couldn't have been much younger than Grammour, Toby's great-grandmother. There was also the small issue of having been born into a working-class family, I had little experience of the trappings of the upper class, let alone alien, royal life.

"What do you mean 'By default you were Ahran's mentor too?' I said, seeking further clarification.

"I think he means that as a result of having such a preoc-cupied father, I spent a good deal of my time at the palace as a child, but he's too polite to say it," Ahran said, offering an explanation.

"The King was a good father, but by the nature of his role, he couldn't spend the time he wanted to with his son so he employed a mentor, a surrogate father if you like." I noted that he made no comment about Ahran's father. He chuckled. "I got to do all the fun things without any of the responsibility."

"Saul was an anthropologist before he joined the royal household and has a sense of adventure that would inspire the most sedentary pre-adolescent," Ahran added. "He taught us how to fish, how to build a raft, how to identify birds of prey in flight, we even made explosives using schoolboy chemistry."

Saul laughed, "I nearly lost my job when we blew up the summer house!"

I laughed too. "No way!"

"Can we do that Uncle Ahran?" Toby asked hopefully.

"I don't think your grandmother would be very pleased and besides, I'm not sure the royal budget would stretch to another one!"

He was right, the summer house in the palace grounds

was beautiful and huge, it probably deserved its own postcode.

We all laughed. It was so refreshing to laugh about something. The last week had been a dark period during which there had been little to laugh about. For the time being I felt safe. I was with the two people I loved most and felt I could make a friend of Saul. Ahran clearly loved this man and it was good to see him happy and relaxed in his company. And so, it was there that we happily wiled away the next few hours, whilst Saul regaled us with some of the many adventures he had been on.

LATER THAT EVENING, after we had eaten, Ahran received a call from the palace.

"What is it?" I asked when he'd hung up, the look on his face worried me.

"They are having trouble fixing the portal, something to do with unstable frequencies. It could be a few more days."

"A few days? I thought we would be on our way in a few hours!" I complained.

"We've got two options; we can lay low or travel to the nearest portal in Germany."

"Let's head to Germany then." I preferred the thought of keeping moving compared to staying put.

"If the British government have notified the French authorities, they will have notified all European borders," Saul interjected. "If you want my advice, lay low, don't put yourselves at any unnecessary risk."

I frowned at Ahran.

"He's right. We were lucky travelling to France, we had an opportune window where we were able to travel before our identities were discovered. Now our faces will be all over the news networks and we will not be able to travel so easily."

I hung my head and sighed heavily. "Why is everything always so bloody difficult?!"

"You are more than welcome to stay here tonight, although I would advise you to move on tomorrow," Saul said. "Tagan stayed with me on a number of occasions during his time on Earth, and it didn't take long for British agencies to come knocking on my door after he disappeared off their radar. I have moved since then, but they may well find me and come looking." He took a sip of his coffee thoughtfully. "Come to think of it, Tagan had a cabin, in the Vosges Mountains about a four-hour drive from here. As far as I'm aware no-one has been there since his death, but it is completely off the beaten track and would be a safe place for you to stay."

A four-hour drive was nothing compared to some of the distances we had travelled in Ramia, and if it was as remote as Saul said it was, it sounded like an ideal place for us to stay.

"I know it," Ahran said. "I stayed there once. You are right, it is in the middle of nowhere. It is unlikely they would find us there."

Saul nodded. "I think it's your only option until the portal is ready. You can have my car, it was serviced recently and should get you there safely."

"We can't take your car Saul," Ahran protested.

"Of course you can, I hardly use it."

"But…," I said about to raise my own objections.

Saul raised his hand. "I will hear no more of it," he said, silencing our objections.

"Thank you," Ahran said sincerely.

"It's very kind of you," I added.

"Good! That's settled. Now who's for a glass of *Sgrac?*"

I wrinkled my nose. "Not for me thanks, but I'll have a glass of wine if you have one." I'd had *Sgrac,* or translated; Devil's Blood, before. It was a Ramian homebrew made out of a native flower similar to gorse, but instead of bright yellow it was lime green which looked as innocuous as Green Tea, but would have you under the table after one glass. Ramians weren't big drinkers, but they were rather partial to a drop of it.

Toby had gone very quiet. He had been looking through Saul's telescope and every now and then claimed he had spotted some astronomical point of interest, but the excitement of the day had obviously caught up with him because he was now gently snoring, his head resting on his arm across the back of the seat by the window.

"Would you like to put him to bed?" Saul suggested.

"I'll carry him," Ahran said and scooped him up into his arms. "Where shall I put him?"

"Follow me, I'll show you," Saul said. I went with them to one of the bedrooms and tucked Toby in. I returned to the sitting room where Saul had poured a glass of red wine for me.

"Cheers!" I said, raising my glass.

"Hatcheena!" Saul and Ahran said at the same time.

I settled onto Saul's two-seater sofa whilst Saul and Ahran sat in the two armchairs opposite. It was nice to be distracted from our current situation and I began to relax. "Saul, you must have some juicy stories to tell me about Ahran as a boy," I said, giving Ahran a little wink.

"As a matter of fact I do, Sophie," he replied, clearly relishing the opportunity to share some of Ahran's childhood antics with me.

"Wait here. I may even have a photo or two."

"Oh no!" Ahran groaned.

"Excellent!" I said, enjoying Ahran's embarrassment.

"You have no idea what you have let yourself in for," Ahran threatened.

Saul left the room and returned with a small leather suitcase. "Now, let me see what I have," he said, sitting down and balancing the case on his knees.

I sat forward on the edge of my seat and peered into the case. In it was a leather notebook, what looked like some form of e-reader and a small collection of artefacts; some interesting crystals, a small box, a number of fossils, feathers and a penknife among other trinkets and treasures. Ahran, not able to contain his curiosity, got up from his seat to have a look at the contents of Saul's case. He picked up the penknife and smiled.

"I can't believe you kept this," Ahran said, turning the small pearlescent handled object over in his hand. "I loved this knife, it belonged to Tagan, but he gave it to me when we were nine," he explained. "Many a stick has been whittled with this," he said, pulling out the blade and running his finger along the edge.

"It got you into trouble once or twice if my memory serves me correctly," Saul said.

"Ooh, do tell," I said, encouragingly and tucked my foot under my bottom, keen to hear more.

Saul smiled at the memory. "The Queen had just had one of the palace gardens re-landscaped in memory of Halsan's father and had two, rare, five-hundred-year-old trees, which were a particularly slow growing variety, imported from Salesk. They were planted at the entrance to this garden which had become her pride and joy, but it wasn't until the grand opening that she discovered Ahran had carved his initials into one of them."

"Nooo!" I said, covering my mouth with my hand. I knew the trees he spoke of and was fully aware of how much Leylana loved this particular part of the palace garden.

"I was banned from visiting for a month. It was the longest month of my life!" Ahran said, clearly re-living his forced exile.

"Oh, poor you!" I said, touching his arm, knowing how hard it would have been for his nine-year-old self to be apart from Tagan and his Auntie and Uncle for that long.

"It taught me a lesson if nothing else," he said wistfully.

"What's this?" I said, reaching into the case and picking up what looked like an e-reader.

"That's an old photo album I keep meaning to have remastered into 3D," Saul said.

"How do I switch it on?" I asked, looking for the on/off switch.

Saul placed his palm on the screen and it sprung to life. "There are lots of stills and I think there is even some movie footage of the boys."

"What do I do?" I said, my finger hovering over the screen, unfamiliar with the interface.

"If you tap here you can look at individual pictures, or swipe your finger across the screen to start a picture show."

I touched one of the thumbnail sized pictures and two grinning, tanned boys, an arm slung around each other's shoulders, filled the screen. There was no mistaking who was who.

"How old were you here?" I asked Ahran.

He looked over my shoulder. "About ten."

I scrutinised the picture. Their lean torsos were tanned and bare. Ahran had almost white blonde hair that flopped over his eyes and Tagan had a mop of brown curls. It could have been Toby standing there.

"Wow! Look at how gorgeous you both were," I remarked. They looked so robust and healthy. The blue of Ahran's eyes stood out, just as mesmerising in his immature face as they were now.

The next picture was of both of them riding horses, with a slightly more youthful looking Leylana, also on horseback.

"I didn't know you rode," I said, noticing how comfortable he looked on a horse.

"I don't," he said, contradictorily.

"You look pretty competent to me," I said, examining the picture.

"It was obviously one of the rare moments when I wasn't being tanked off with or dumped on the ground. Horses and I are like oil and water, we don't mix."

"But you are so good with animals, especially cows," I said, recalling how gentle he was with the young heifers calving for the first time. They seemed to lose that wild-eyed look caused by the fear and pain of birthing whenever he was near. I often teased him that he should go into midwifery, he had a wonderful way with the bovine expectant mothers.

"That's because I don't have to ride them! There's nothing natural about sitting astride a large, four-legged animal with a mind of its own."

"You just haven't found the right horse."

"There is no such thing," he said, sounding unconvinced.

"How old were you in this one?" I asked, pointing to a picture of Ahran.

He peered at it. "Sixteen, it was taken at one of our end of year celebration ceremonies."

At the risk of sounding like a complete cougar, he looked seriously hot even at sixteen.

We continued to look at the photos together with either Saul or Ahran providing the commentary. Ahran pointed at a photo of all three of them, stood with what looked like some kind of tribal folk. "Do you remember this Saul?"

"Ah, yes. Our visit to the Hidden People."

I'd heard of them before, in fact I had met one at

Seraphia when we had fled from the palace after the cyber attack a couple of years ago. A shiver came over me as I thought about Thanuja who had supposedly been able to see into my future. I had almost forgotten about her and her visions.

"They are very shy and elusive and rarely let the likes of us into their world. It was a great honour for them to accept us into their village. Did you know that they are an ancient race who are believed to have inhabited Ramia before it was colonised by Sapiens many thousands of years ago?" Saul said.

"Yes, I have heard something like this." I handed Saul the tablet. "Can I see one of the movies?"

Saul scrolled through and tapped the screen a couple of times. The sound of rushing water burst out of the device.

"This was on one of our camping trips," he said with a smile. "Those boys were always dancing on the edge of trouble."

"No change there then," I said, referring to the tight spots we'd been in since Ahran and I had met.

Saul handed me the tablet and I began to watch the film clip.

"They were about twelve," Saul said, pre-empting my next question.

Ahran stood on a rock in the middle of a fast-flowing river, beckoning to Tagan who was on the opposite river bank and about to follow him over a series of rocks that were dotted amongst the white froth. The water looked like it was being whipped up underneath by an invisible giant whisk. They were struggling to hear each other over the noise, but both their faces were bright with adventure. And then Tagan began to leap from one rock to the next.

I gasped. "Weren't you worried about them?" I asked Saul, thinking he was being rather careless allowing them to do this. One slip and they would be in the violently swirling water.

"They were strong swimmers," he replied unperturbed.

I continued to watch, feeling distinctly uneasy, but fascinated by the footage of the young Ahran and especially Tagan whom I'd never had the chance to meet.

Two more leaps and Tagan was standing on the same rock as Ahran. They were both laughing until Ahran did exactly what I feared; slipped and fell into the water. "Oh no!" I said, clamping my hand over my mouth. I couldn't help but wonder why Saul was still filming and wasn't making any attempt to rescue him.

Ahran came to the surface and began to swim towards the riverbank with long powerful strokes. Tagan made his way to the other side and was ready to pull him out by the time his cousin reached the bank.

Of course, I needn't have worried, they were super-human and had the strength to make it across a dangerous river when your average human would have drowned. These people seemed so normal, it was easy to forget their abilities, the same rules just didn't apply. To a Ramian it was nothing to leap from one building to another or to swim across a river with a current that even an adrenaline-fuelled white-water kayaker would think twice about. To them it was child's play and all part of a fun afternoon out camping.

I handed the tablet back. "I don't think my nerves can take any more."

Saul chuckled. "They were certainly happy days," he said, nostalgically.

Ahran had gone quiet.

I took his hand and gave it a squeeze. "You okay?" I asked.

Ahran nodded. "I'm fine, just brings back a lot of memories."

I gave him an understanding smile.

Saul closed down the e-reader after we had looked through all the photos. "We had some fun didn't we?" Saul said, clearly remembering his time with Tagan and Ahran with great affection.

"I can see that." I yawned. "Thank you Saul, that was fascinating, but I think it's time I went to bed."

"I'll be there shortly," Ahran said.

I stood up. "Ok, night then."

"Goodnight Sophie," Saul said.

I poked my head around Toby's door to find he was sleeping soundly and then went into the bathroom to wash my face. I managed to locate some toothpaste without rummaging around too deeply in Saul's bathroom cabinet and with no toothbrush, did the best I could with the tip of my finger. In the bedroom Saul had shown us earlier, there were yet more books and the room smelled unused, but the sheets were clean and I quickly undressed, slid into bed and lay their waiting. Ahran and Saul's voices and frequent laughter filtered down the corridor. It made me smile and I felt happy for them both. If their easy way with one another was any measure, they clearly loved each other very much and it warmed my heart to know that Ahran had had Saul in his life as a boy to do all those things he missed out on as a result of having a father who was far more interested in his career than in his family. The minutes ticked by and it wasn't long before I realised that Ahran wasn't coming to bed anytime soon. As much as I wanted the warmth of his arms around me, I couldn't begrudge him time with Saul, from what I could gather, it had been several years since they had seen each other and they had memories to share, laughter to laugh and grief for the loss of Tagan to share. I switched off the bedside lamp and must have fallen asleep quickly.

I awoke to a loud crash that had me sitting up in the dark and my heart beating hard and loud. My semi-conscious brain tried to make sense of where I was and what was happening until another bang and a jolt of the bed made me realise that Ahran was drunk!

I switched on the lamp to find him trying to grope for something that would steady him whilst he tried to take off his shoes. After a couple of attempts, he gave up and fell onto the bed like a Redwood that had just succumbed to the lumberjack's saw.

"Hey, sweetie. Are you okay?" I said quietly, suppressing a laugh at his clumsiness. I had never seen Ahran inebriated, he rarely drank.

He replied in slurred Ramian and I could make no sense of what he was saying, so I just took his shoes off and helped him out of his jeans. He was babbling on about something or other and mentioned Tagan's name a couple of times.

"Ahran darling, it's Sophie."

A broad grin stretched across his face and he reached for my hand as if he had only just realised I was there. "Ah, Sophie."

He sat up and tried to train his eyes on me before turning very serious. "I lurve you Soff-ee," he said, his accent made stronger by the alcohol. He kissed my knuckles.

"I lurve you sooo much." And then as if something had suddenly occurred to him, he clambered over the bed and all but fell off the other side.

"Ahran, for God's sake," I said, trying to grab him.

"Sfine," he said. "I'm fine." He sat up grinning.

"You idiot!" I said, laughing.

"Shush! I got sometzing to say and for you I will do it za Eartz way." He concentrated very hard and managed to kneel. It suddenly occurred to me what he was doing.

He took my hand and I began to shake my head. "Ahran, no, don't do this now."

He frowned and put his finger to his lips whilst he composed himself.

I watched him half amused, half horrified that he was about to propose to me sozzled and in his underpants.

He looked up with a glassy expression, swaying.

"Ahran, just get into bed," I said, patting the space beside me.

He swiped the air like he was swatting away some bothersome fly. "I need to do eet now."

I sighed knowing I wasn't going to be able to deter him and sat there waiting for him to get on with it.

"I've lurved you from za moment I met you." He placed one hand over his heart and continued. "You own my hurt and my soul. Will you do me za greatest hon-oor and be my wayf."

I sat there and looked at his heart-stopping face, unable to hide my smile. Of course I wanted to marry him; he was my everything, but I wanted him to propose to me when he was at least compos mentis. The clothes? I could take or leave.

"No, I will not be your *wayf*," I replied, shaking my head. "Now for the love of God, will you *please* get into bed?"

He looked at me with a hurt expression.

"What?" I said unapologetically. "You can ask me again when you're sober. Now get into bed!"

Like a repentant puppy, he clambered back onto the bed. "You break my hurt Soff-ee and zen you reep it out of my chest."

"Yes, yes," I said, holding open the covers after he struggled to find the end of the sheets.

In the next minute, he was fast asleep and snoring like a train.

16

————————

"Please stop that drilling in my head," Ahran mumbled the next morning. He was face down, spread-eagle on the bed, his eyes closed and with a pained expression on his face. I had come to moments before and sat up on an elbow to look at him properly to assess the damage.

"I see you picked a fight with a bottle of *Scragc* and came off worse," I said with a chuckle.

"I haven't felt like this since I was in my twenties," Ahran complained. "That stuff is evil!" he said as if he had played no part in putting the glass to his lips.

"I guess it lives up to its name."

He nodded and stopped abruptly. "Aych! Il malura!"

"Of course it hurts!" I said, understanding his Ramian much better this morning. "You must have been drinking that stuff for hours."

"Saul and I had a lot of catching up to do," he said against the pillow.

I kissed the top of his head. "I'll get you a strong coffee." I got out of bed and turned my nose up at putting the same clothes on for the fourth day running. "We will have to get some new clothes at some point."

"Mmmm?" he said, not really listening.

"I'll get you that coffee," I said, shaking my head in despair. Ahran being hungover hadn't really been in our game plan and it made me feel a little nervous to think that potentially it made us more vulnerable.

At some point in the night he had stripped completely naked and his tight buttocks, which were a few shades lighter than the rest of him, were proudly bared along with his sculpted back and thighs. Fighting the urge to bite his bottom, I quickly left the room and checked on Toby and proceeded to walk smugly to the kitchen hangover free.

I guessed Saul was in a similar condition so I made him a coffee too and myself a cup of tea. I knocked gently on his bedroom door. "I've brought you a cup of coffee and some painkillers, shall I leave them out here?"

"One minute," came the response.

Saul came to the door still fully clothed, he'd obviously passed out on his bed in much the same way as Ahran had. "Thought you might need these," I said, offering him a drink on the tray and some ibuprofen I'd found in one of the kitchen cabinets.

"Sophie, you are a child of the angels," he said, appreciatively.

"Did you have a nice evening catching up?"

"Yes, we did, thank you."

He looked a little green and I could see that he was

struggling to stand there, not in any fit state to hold much of a conversation.

"I'll go and give these to Ahran," I said, excusing myself.

He managed a smile before closing his bedroom door to retreat to his bed.

Ahran had not moved a muscle by the time I returned. After Saul's warning that it probably wasn't safe for us to stay with him for too long, I was beginning to feel a little anxious that we should be on our way and heading for the Vosges Mountains where we could lose ourselves for a few days.

"Wakey, wakey! Your coffee's here," I said, placing it on the bedside, "And some headache tablets."

I opened the shutters in the hope that the morning sun might do a better job of rousing him than I was. A muffled protest came from under the pillow he'd just placed over his head.

I lifted the corner of the pillow. "I've brought you some water too."

"Hmph."

I settled back to drink my tea and there was a gentle knock on the door.

I threw some covers over Ahran's bare bottom.

"Come in," I answered.

Toby came in fully dressed.

"What's up with Uncle Ahran?" he asked, eyeing Ahran's prostrate form.

"Uncle Ahran has a hangover," I said, disapprovingly.

"I thought we would be leaving soon."

"We will be. Would you like to go and get a large ice-cold bucket of water?"

"You wouldn't dare?" Came a muffled voice from under the pillow.

"I spotted some ice in the freezer," I said, winking at Toby.

I could see the glee in Toby's eyes as he turned around to do what I had asked.

My threat did the trick as the gorgeous, slumbering, hungover beast that was my superhuman boyfriend, roused himself like a bear with a sore head.

He sat up and squinted. "I used to like you guys," he said with a grimace.

I laughed. "In all seriousness, we do need to be on our way."

"I know," he said after draining the glass of water I had brought him. "Just give me a minute," he said, shifting to lean against the headboard.

I finished my tea. "I'll get Toby some breakfast, by which time you'll be up." It was more of an order than a question.

With his head resting on the headboard and his eyes closed, Ahran did a half-hearted Boy Scout salute.

In the kitchen, I found some bread to toast and some jam in the fridge.

"Where are we going today?" Toby said with his mouth full.

I frowned at him, but let it go. "We're heading to the

Vosges Mountains. Your dad used to stay there. Apparently, it's in the middle of nowhere and we should be safe until the portal is ready."

Toby nodded. He was far too comfortable with the idea of being on the run than any ten-year-old should have been.

As we were finishing our breakfast, Saul appeared in the doorway, looking a little brighter than earlier.

"Did you sleep well?" he asked as cheerfully as his headache would allow.

"Yes, thank you. I hope you don't mind, but we helped ourselves to some breakfast," I said, feeling a little embarrassed.

"Not at all, make yourselves at home. I'm not sure there is much to choose from," he said, apologetically. "I can go downstairs and get some fresh bread and pastries?"

"Thank you, but I think we should be on our way."

Ahran joined us in the kitchen, fully dressed and looking like he was just about in the land of the living. I handed him some jam loaded toast.

"Are you nearly ready?" he asked.

I nodded. "Yep."

Saul started to rummage around in one of the kitchen drawers and then shut it, his search obviously proving fruitless.

"Go down to the garages behind this building, its garage *1b* and I'll join you down there once I've found the key," he said distractedly, looking in a pot on the windowsill. "I know it's here somewhere."

Toby, Ahran and I made our way down to the entrance

hall and left the building by the rear exit. We located the correct garage and waited for Saul.

"I'll drive," I said.

Ahran didn't put up much resistance. He and Saul must have drunk a lot last night, Ramians didn't tend to have hangovers for long on account of their fast metabolism, but Ahran still seemed to be suffering.

Saul appeared and walked across the small parking lot carrying a paper carrier bag and the small leather case he had brought out last night.

"I found the keys, they were in a coat pocket," he said and opened the garage. "She's no show stopper, but she'll get you to where you need to go." He reversed the car out of the garage and left the engine idling to say goodbye to us.

I gave him a hug. "Thank you for everything, I'm not sure what we would have done without you."

"Please, it was the least I could do. Hopefully we will meet again soon."

"You must come and visit us in Ramia."

"I would love to!"

After Saul gave us a piece of paper with directions to Tagan's hideout, he and Ahran embraced and clapped each other on the back.

"And you, young man," Saul said, offering Toby his hand. "It has been a pleasure and an honour to meet you. I shall follow your future with great interest."

He handed Toby the leather case. "I want you to have this, it contains memories of your father."

Toby took the case. "Oh wow! Thank you," he said, beaming at Saul.

"Okay, let's hit the road," I said, not keen to hang around any longer.

"Here, I picked up some pastries and drinks for you on my way down." Saul handed Ahran the bag.

He took a quick look inside.

"Why is there a bottle of *Scragc* in here*?*" Ahran asked, briefly turning an interesting shade of green.

"I saw it on the kitchen side, I don't think I could ever drink another drop again."

Ahran handed me the bag, clearly thinking that it was far too soon for him to be faced with it as well. "Er, thanks."

We said our final goodbyes and waved to the kind, gentle man that had been so important to Ahran in his formative years.

I drove and headed west out of Paris. Toby and Ahran tucked into the pastries and we sat in comfortable silence for a while. Staying at Saul's had provided a welcome respite from our current predicament and my nerves felt considerably less jangled. It wasn't long before my mind wandered back to Ahran's proposal last night. I wanted to marry Ahran more than anything, but I wanted him to be absolutely sure about marrying me. After meeting Saul, it would be easy to think that Ahran's father was no longer important, but as much as Ahran loved Saul, Driscan Elessar was still there in the background and whether Ahran wanted to admit it or not, there was a part of him that wanted his father to be proud of him. I couldn't help thinking that if he married me it would be the final nail in the coffin as far as their relationship was concerned.

"Do you remember what you said to me last night?" I

asked, my heart picking up tempo in anticipation of his answer.

"I don't even remember how I got to bed!" he said, shaking his head. "I'm sorry. Was it something bad?"

"No, no, not at all. It doesn't matter." I could feel stupid tears stinging my eyes. I don't know why my heart had lurched hopefully because I was fully aware at the time that it was the alcohol talking. My eyes returned to the road and I took a moment or two to compose myself.

"Tobes, can you pass me one of those drinks," Ahran asked.

He drained the can and rested his head on the headrest and groaned. "What was I thinking getting drunk last night? How could I have protected us? I was putting us all at risk.

I smiled and looked across at him. "Hey, no-one found us, don't be too hard on yourself. It was good to see you and Saul enjoying each other's company. You think a lot of him, don't you?"

"I do," he said sincerely.

"Have you heard anything about the portal this morning?" I asked, hopeful that maybe we didn't need to be making this road trip after all.

Ahran lifted his hips to reach into his back pocket. "Ratcha!" he exclaimed, making me jump.

"What is it?

"I've left my phone at Saul's!"

"Oh, Ahran! We've been on the road for half an hour!"

"I know; I can't believe I've left it. This is why I don't drink, it scrambles my brain!" He turned in his seat towards me. "We've got to go back for it, otherwise the palace has no way of contacting us."

I gave an exasperated sigh. "Where do you think you left it?"

"I'm not sure. It must have fallen out of my pocket when I was getting undressed last night."

"Can't we ask the palace to contact Saul or Evo? They can call us and let us know whether it is safe to travel."

"But there's no phone at the cabin, we would have to go into the town to call them. Besides, being without a phone would leave us vulnerable. We've got to go back for it."

"*Jesus Ahran!*" I said, losing my temper and abruptly pulled off the motorway at the exit we were just about to pass. I shot down a side street to turn around. "The longer we stay in Paris, the greater the risk to our lives."

"I know. I won't hang about," he promised.

Once we were heading back in the direction of Saul's, I put my foot on the accelerator, not just because I wanted to get back as quickly as we could, but because I was quietly seething, it was unlike Ahran to be so careless.

I could feel his eyes on me.

"What?" I snapped.

"You're driving twenty kilometres over the speed limit."

I knew that we couldn't afford to be stopped by the police. So I reluctantly eased off the gas and drove the thirty painstaking minutes back to Saul's apartment.

We pulled up in the parking lot we had left only an hour before.

"I'll be as quick as I can," Ahran said, getting out of the car.

I nodded, he still wasn't forgiven. Toby and I sat in the car. I looked in the rear-view mirror nervously, hoping that no one had witnessed our arrival and waited. And waited.

I looked at the clock on the dashboard, five minutes passed and there was still no sign of Ahran.

17

I watched the seconds tick laboriously by.

"Uncle Ahran's taking a long time," Toby said.

"I know." My palms were growing sweaty and my heart had started to beat faster.

I sat there contemplating what to do. All sorts of horrific scenarios played out in my head.

"Come on," I said, making a decision and not wanting to risk leaving Toby in the car by himself.

With no weapon to protect us, I felt scared and vulnerable. Scared not just for our own safety, but absolutely petrified about what might have happened to Ahran. We made our way to the back door of the building and as luck would have it a young woman, who had just pulled up, was about to let herself in. "Bonjour!" she sing-songed. "Qui est-ce que vous voulez?"

"Er…Saul Montan."

"Ah, oui," she said and held the door open for us.

We followed her in and she disappeared up the stairs. I

nervously scanned the foyer and all was calm. Toby and I walked the three flights of stairs up to Saul's apartment. We reached his front door. There was no sign of a forced entry, in fact the door was ajar. I took it as a bad sign and felt a surge of adrenaline.

"Stay here," I whispered to Toby. "If you hear me scream, run as fast as you can."

Toby nodded, looking pale faced and scared.

I drew in a deep breath and pushed the door wider, tip-toeing down the hallway to the lounge where we had spent such a pleasant evening the night before. My heart was beating so fast I could feel my pulse. I had no idea what I was about to face and as I entered the room it took a moment for me to comprehend the scene before me. The place had been completely ransacked, Saul was sat glassy eyed in his armchair with a dark red, almost perfectly circular bullet wound in his forehead. He was clearly dead and for one hideous, gut-wrenching moment I thought Ahran was too. He was knelt at Saul's feet, his forehead resting on the old man's thigh and holding his hand. Ahran turned towards me and for a split second I saw the raw pain and anguish on his face before he masked it. It was horrible to see Saul staring unseeingly in death, but the relief that Ahran was alive made me almost buckle at the knees and I reached for the door frame to steady myself.

"What happened?" I asked.

It seemed like my arrival had brought him out of his trance and he stood up quickly.

"We need to get out of here," he said emotionlessly and steered me back down the corridor. He went into the bedroom we had stayed in and I followed him in. It had been turned over much like the rest of the apartment.

"Where could my phone be?" he said, surveying the mayhem.

We started to search for it, and then suddenly Ahran stilled. I followed his line of vision. He knelt down and ripped up one of the floorboards. It was then that I spotted the gun in his waistband for the first time.

"Where did you get that from?" I said.

"What?"

"The gun."

He reached under the floor and pulled out his phone covered in dust and cobwebs. It was obviously slim line enough to have fallen down a gap between two of the floorboards. He blew on it.

"Saul gave it to me last night, and maybe if he hadn't he wouldn't be sat dead in that chair," he said as emotion flickered across his face once more.

"Don't blame yourself Ahran."

"But I do," he said as he stood up. "Where's Toby?" he asked, bringing our conversation to an end.

"He's out there," I said, pointing to the front door. I had begun to shake like a leaf.

"Come on!"

We greeted Toby wordlessly, who thankfully was still waiting by the front door, looking petrified. He held onto his questions as we ran down the stairs to the car.

Toby sat in the back, I sat in the passenger seat and Ahran climbed into the driver's seat, his hangover forgotten. Mindful of not drawing attention to ourselves, Ahran drove out of the parking lot as fast as the urban speed limit would allow. I was so scared I could almost taste my own blood as it pounded through my veins.

I glanced anxiously at Ahran, whose jaw muscle was working overtime. I had known him long enough to know that underneath the expressionless mask he was angry and hurting. I touched his arm to try and offer him some comfort.

"Please don't," he said.

I didn't know what to do or say, all I wanted to do was put my arms around him to try and help ease his pain, but he clearly didn't want it. So, I fixed my eyes on the windscreen trying to piece together what had just happened.

Had French or British agents shot Saul dead? I couldn't believe that either governments would do such a thing. Why would they kill Saul? Had our presence caused his death? What would they get out of murdering Saul and what had they been looking for? So many questions and I couldn't think of one feasible answer for any of them. I turned around and placed a hand on Toby's knee. He looked just how I felt, absolutely terrified.

"It's alright love, we're out of there now." It was lame reassurance, but it was all I could muster.

I noticed Ahran repeatedly glance in the rear-view mirror, his knuckles whitening as he gripped the steering wheel more tightly.

"What's the matter?" I asked.

"We are being followed," he said quietly, and stepped on the gas.

I pulled down the sun visor and looked in the vanity mirror to see if I could see who it was.

We'd pulled onto a dual carriageway and I was horrified to see a black car with blacked out windows, weaving in and out of the traffic behind us.

"Are your seatbelts on?" Ahran asked, ominously.

"Yes," Toby and I replied, our answers colliding in the air.

"Who do you think it is?" I said.

"I don't know, but I'm not sure I really want to find out."

Ahran slowed the car and pulled over into the outside lane. There was an exit up ahead and I could see that the black car was gaining on us. We were almost at the green plastic bollard indicating where to exit.

"Hold on!" he shouted as he jerked the car to the right and pulled off onto the slip road at the very last second. I shrieked as my seatbelt took the strain and bit into my chest. How we missed the bollard I do not know. Ahran sped up down the slipway and I glanced in the mirror again to see if we had shaken off our pursuers.

Ahran's quick manoeuvre had obviously taken them by surprise because they swerved off the main highway and clipped the bollard with the front left wing of their car, sending them into a barely controlled sequence of swerves, slowing them up, but not stopping their pursuit.

Taking the advantage this had given us, Ahran put his foot to the floor, his adherence to the speed limit vanishing as we entered the roundabout at the end of the slip road at breakneck speed. There was a blaring of horns and a screech of brakes as the oncoming traffic took the necessary precautions to stop from crashing into us. I gripped the door handle and tried to brace myself in my seat, but I was thrown from left to right as Ahran wound his way through the traffic.

"Toby, are you okay?" I shrieked.

"Yes, I'm fine."

We jumped some lights and narrowly missed a delivery lorry which temporarily obscured the black car from our view. We were entering a built-up area, travelling at God knows what speed. Ahran took a sharp turn left.

"Can you still see the car?"

I turned around and caught a glimpse of our pursuers, whose sights were clearly still locked onto us. "It's not working, we're not losing them," I cried.

Ahran pushed the thousand-litre engine of Saul's little hatchback to its limits.

"Watch that couple!" I said as a guy grabbed his wife's coat to prevent her from stepping out in front of us.

"I've got this under control, you just tell me what the car behind us is doing."

"Oh God Ahran! Please be careful!" I grabbed the door handle again as we took a sharp right, which caused the tyres to screech alarmingly on the tarmac. We were heading down more of a residential street and I just prayed that there were no children out playing because if one were to step out in front of us, even with Ahran's superhuman reflexes, it wouldn't stand a chance.

Ahran took another turn, bringing us out onto the main road through whichever town we were in. We crossed the flow of traffic to the other side and turned down another side street. I was horrified to see that not only was the black car still hot on our tail, but it was gaining on us.

"By the way that guy is driving, I'd hazard a guess he's not Sapien."

"So you don't think its British or French agents?" I asked.

"No, I'm pretty sure our friends back there are Ramian."

This piece of information had just upped the danger stakes infinitely and I wasn't sure I could feel any more terrified.

Up ahead was a level crossing and I sent up a silent prayer asking for the tracks to be clear because there was no sign of Ahran slowing down. I hastily looked from left to right; there was no train in sight, just some track engineers in orange jackets who had seen us coming and had jumped out of the way. No sooner were we over it, the black car came into view. The road was straight and the black car was able to pick up speed. It was a faster, more powerful car than Saul's and was now no more than fifty metres away.

"They're getting closer," Toby cried in panic.

Another left turn and we hit a dead end. It was a residential neighbourhood and it had been impossible to see that the train track swept around pretty sharply to the right. In front of us were jagged edge railings, a raised bank and the train track on top of it about four metres above the level of the road. We were trapped.

"Oh Shit!" I said, realising that there was no way out of this one.

The black car turned into the street and slowed to a halt behind us.

"Get down both of you!" Ahran yelled as shots were fired at the car.

I crouched down into the footwell of the passenger seat and held myself in a tight ball, hoping that Toby was doing the same. There was a loud crack followed by the sound of glass shattering and I was reminded of the time we were fired at by lasers. A small light aircraft had lifted us to safety then, but now, there was no such method of escape. We were cornered and our only hope was Ahran's skill as a marksman. I stole a glance at him, he was crouching low, but intermittently firing shots out of the back window.

A bullet ricocheted off the door frame somewhere near my head which made me squeeze into a tighter ball. I put my hands over my ears as the sound of every shot vibrated through my chest. I willed Toby to be safe.

"Aiych!" Ahran cried as I became sickeningly aware that he had been shot.

"Ahran!" I screamed and without thinking began to climb out of my hiding place.

"Stay down!" he commanded.

I began to shake with ice-cold fear. I heard two more shots and then nothing.

I'm not really sure what happened in the moments that followed, maybe I passed out, maybe I was actually blinded by fear, but it was a while before I could move. I sat up my muscles screaming in protest at being held so tightly in one position for what had seemed like a lifetime. Ahran sat in the driver's seat, breathing hard, his right hand pressing against the left side of his chest.

"Is…is it over?" I said, my teeth chattering. I couldn't tell how seriously he had been injured.

He gave me a curt nod.

"Are you okay?"

"I'll probably live."

I needed him to be more certain than that. "Let me take a look."

"Just drive," he said between gritted teeth.

I nodded. "Toby, are you alright?"

"Yes, I'm okay," he said, coming out of his hiding place and brushing off the shattered glass from the rear window.

I felt faint with relief and turned my attention back to Ahran. The colour had drained from his face.

"We need to get you to a hospital," I said, trying to take command of the situation.

Ahran shook his head. "Just get into the driver's seat," he said, his voice pained.

I yanked open the passenger door and made my way around to the driver's side. I glanced at the black car with morbid curiosity and saw one body on the ground behind the open passenger door and the outline of the driver slumped over the steering wheel.

Ahran got out and went around to the passenger's side and I climbed into the driver's seat. I tried not to notice how much discomfort he was in and turned the key in the ignition as the sound of a siren came from somewhere in the distance. My strength was returning and I marvelled at how your body was able to respond when presented with a life or death situation. The car behind us was blocking our exit, but I thought I could probably squeeze past it if I mounted the pavement. I threw the car into reverse and hit the gas. We bumped up onto the curb and Ahran cried out.

"I'm sorry," I said, forgetting that he could probably feel every lump and bump in the road. I steered past the black car, not wanting to see the bodies of the two men whose gun skills were no match for Ahran's. I threw the car into reverse and it screamed down to the end of the street until I was able to swing round and drive away from the sanguineous scene behind us.

"Where do I go?" I said, squinting to try and read the signs ahead.

"Away from the siren, it's coming from that direction," he said, pointing to the right.

I took a left and relied on my sense of direction to try and get us back out onto the main road. By some small miracle, I found a way back towards the main high street at the other end of town.

"There," Ahran said, unable to point, but nodding his head towards the sign for the motorway.

The blood was oozing between the fingers of his right hand and was beginning to dry in long streaks down his arm, like the tentacles of a bloody octopus. His t-shirt was soaked. "We need to stem the bleeding." I glanced at Toby in the rear-view mirror. "Toby, give Ahran your hoodie."

He took off his sweater and offered it to Ahran.

"Can you fold it," Ahran said, the pain evident in his voice.

Toby did as he said and passed it to him.

I looked across to check that Ahran was still conscious

and he must have caught the expression on my face. "Just keep driving," he said.

I concentrated on the road ahead, trying not to think about how badly he was injured. It wasn't long before we were back on the motorway and heading west.

The wind howled through the broken rear windscreen and it was cold in spite of the warm sunshine. I stole another glance at Ahran. His head was resting on the headrest, his eyes closed and my heart went out to him. Not only had he saved our lives *again*, but he'd lost a dear friend and narrowly missed being killed himself. I could only assume that those bastards who had been chasing us had also been responsible for Saul's death and I felt a wracking sense of guilt that we had brought this upon the kindly old man. Although, I couldn't help but glean a small sense of satisfaction knowing that they had come to their own sticky end.

Who they were and what they had been after was still a mystery, maybe if we had searched their car we would have found some answers, but we didn't have the luxury of time. All we could do now was drive.

18

"We need to do something about that window?" I said, anxious that we might be pulled over for having a gaping hole in the back of our car and more than a little concerned that Toby was surrounded by glass.

Ahran nodded. He was holding himself rigid and I could tell he was in a great deal of pain.

"Someone needs to look at your shoulder," I said, wincing as he tried to make himself more comfortable.

"You can look at it when we get to the cabin."

"What can I do?" I asked. I wasn't particularly squeamish, but I feared he was over estimating my first aid skills.

"I think the bullet is still in there and you need to get it out."

"You must be joking!" I said, with a humourless snort.

"Do I look like I am laughing?" There was pain etched into every line of his face.

"I can't dig a bullet out of your shoulder," I said, trying

to convince him that his suggestion was ludicrous. "Let me drive you to a hospital, we can make up some story like… like you accidentally pulled the trigger whilst you were cleaning your gun."

He looked at me with a healthy dose of scepticism. "I was cleaning a loaded gun?"

I shrugged. "I don't know, something like that, people do some pretty stupid things sometimes."

He shook his head. "We can't risk it. What if they reported it? And what if they took some blood?"

"Then… they would see… you aren't Sapien," I said as the penny dropped.

"I'll do it!" Toby said from the back.

I laughed at his enthusiasm.

"Thanks, *chechna*, but I think I'll take a rain check on that," Ahran said.

I caught Toby's shrug in the rear-view mirror as if to say *Please yourself.*

"I'll guide you through it, I've done it before," Ahran said.

"You've dug a bullet out of yourself before?" I asked incredulously.

"Not myself, but I have removed shrapnel from another soldier's leg."

I grimaced at the thought.

"Battlefield surgery isn't rocket science. If you get something alien under your skin, you've got to get it out."

I snorted. "I know an alien that's got under my skin, and I'm quite happy for him to stay there."

Ahran smiled for the first time since we'd left Saul's.

"You'll be fine. We just need to get some basic supplies."

Once we were clear of Paris, we pulled off the motorway and found a backwater village shop. It was an unusual shopping list: antiseptic, some dressings, a sewing kit, a manicure set, heavy duty black bags, painkillers and some duct tape. Whilst I was there, I also picked up some food to see us through the next couple of days, and at the last minute bought some candles and matches. I'd got the impression the cabin was pretty basic.

I cleared the glass out from the back of the car as best as I could and Toby helped me make a more than half decent attempt at patching up the rear windscreen.

"There," I said, as we got back into the car. "It won't feel like we're…" The words stuck in my throat as I noticed Ahran sitting motionless with his eyes closed and looking even paler.

"Ahran?"

"Still here," he said, without opening his eyes.

"God, you frightened me for a minute!"

"Can you pass me that bottle of *Scragc*?"

"I thought you'd sworn never to touch the stuff again," I said, handing it to him.

"Needs must," he said, opening the bottle and raising it in cheers before taking a swig.

"It's okay auntie Sophie, battlefield surgeons used to make people drink alcohol when there were no anaesthetics," Toby said authoritatively. "Uncle Ahran knows what he's doing." In the last couple of hours Ahran's hero status had increased exponentially in my nephew's eyes.

Ahran's lips curled up in a smile and I rolled my eyes. "We have painkillers," I said testily. I wasn't happy that as the designated surgeon I faced the prospect of operating on a drunk! Ahran was seemingly oblivious to the nerves I felt about being the next Florence Nightingale and took another swig.

"Okay, let's get to this cabin so we can get this over with," I said, turning on the ignition.

We re-joined the motorway and drove for another couple of hours before reaching the Vosges Mountains by late afternoon. After a couple of wrong turns and a steep climb we were bumping along an unused track. Saul's car was not built for this kind of terrain and Ahran silently withstood the pain every bump must have caused him. At one point, Toby and I had to shift a small tree that had fallen across our path and eventually we made it to our safe house, a small log cabin set in a clearing.

"Park around the back," Ahran advised.

There was no drive to speak of, but a carpet of pine litter the surrounding trees had generously shed, allowing us to drive across it without leaving any tracks.

"Grab the bags Toby, I'll help Ahran out of the car."

I tried to help him, but he insisted he could manage. It clearly took a considerable amount of willpower to remove himself from the vehicle, but with my arm around his waist I did my best to support him as we walked to the front door.

"It's locked," I announced after trying the door handle.

"The key should be under a stone below the decking at that end," he said, indicating with a nod of his head.

Sure enough, when I reached in I found a grapefruit

sized stone and underneath it was the key. "Let's get you inside," I said and pushed open the door into the cool darkness of the cabin.

"Help me open the shutters Tobes," I said, and we set about opening up the room. With more light we were able to see the standard of our accommodation. The main living area had a fireplace with a worn leather sofa and an armchair at one end, a small open plan kitchen with a utilitarian wooden table and chairs at the other. There were two doors leading off the main room which led to the bedrooms, but there was a distinct lack of bathroom. Everything was covered with a thick layer of dust and an intricate network of cobwebs.

"Okay," I said, looking around not sure where to start. "Where do we get water from?" I asked.

"There's a well out the back," Ahran replied as he sat down on one of the kitchen chairs. I could tell he was in pain, but he hadn't utter one word of complaint.

I searched through the cupboards and found a bucket under the sink. "I'll get some water. Toby you come with me and collect some wood."

I tried not to think about the task ahead and got on with the job of filling the bucket with water from the well. I left Toby scouring the surrounding area for firewood and went back into the cabin. There was some old linen in one of the bedrooms, which I tore into strips and I found an assortment of bowls in one of the kitchen cupboards. I poured some of the water into each of the bowls, pulled my sleeves up and set about scrubbing the table as hard as I could.

"You okay sweetie," I said, when I had finished. Ahran

had been sitting there quietly, every now and again taking a swig of *Sgrac*.

"Just thankful I have my old friend," he said in a slightly slurry voice and holding up the bottle.

I needed to crack on, it would be no good if he passed out. I emptied the contents of the shopping bags on the kitchen side and put the scissors and the small metal nail file into an enamel bowl that had become a makeshift steriliser. I placed the bowl on the table next to Ahran and picked up the small emergency sewing kit which consisted of a needle, two pins and a choice of white, black or brown thread; it was no better than the kind you would find in a middle of the range Christmas cracker and I took out the needle eyeing it dubiously.

"It will do well enough," Ahran said, encouragingly.

So far, I had managed to carry out my tasks with almost emotionlessly, but the time where I was actually going to have to cut in to Ahran's shoulder with the rudimentary tools I had gathered drew nearer, and my hands began to shake as I tried to thread the needle. After several attempts, I finally succeeded and put the needle and thread in with everything else in the enamel bowl. I poured some more antiseptic into another of the bowls and opened a roll of cotton wool with my teeth.

"Okay, nearly there," I said as I scrubbed my hands in some of the water I had reserved for this purpose. "It's not the most sterile of operating theatres," I said apologetically, looking down at the worn surface of the table. "But it will have to do."

"Fortunately, I have a strong constitution," Ahran replied.

I eyed him doubtfully, he had consumed nearly half of what was left of the bottle of Sgrac. "You're going to need it in a few minutes," I said, as I picked up the scissors ready to cut his shirt off him.

I took a deep breath. "Ready?"

He nodded.

I tried to pull the t-shirt away from the wound but it had stuck to the skin with dried blood. He tensed as I managed to ease it free and proceeded to cut it off him. "Sorry, is that hurting?" I asked, suddenly not feeling so brave and knowing I hadn't missed my vocation by not becoming a nurse.

He shook his head as if to say *Its fine go ahead.*

I surveyed the injury, dismayed to see the entry point of the bullet was alarmingly close to his heart. I tried not to think about what would have happened if it had been only a few centimetres lower. I felt decidedly sick as I gingerly dabbed the area with antiseptic.

"You can be a bit firmer than that," Ahran said.

"I don't want to hurt you."

"Sweetheart, it already hurts."

"Okay, so where do I start?" I said, standing back and holding my hands up like I'd seen surgeons do on the T.V.

"I can feel the bullet grating against my collarbone," he said after swigging freely from the bottle in his hands. "It can't be too deep. Use the file to see if you can feel it."

I prevaricated at his suggestion, this went against all my instincts and I stood motionless.

"Sophie, I'm not getting any younger here," he said in a strained voice.

"Yes, no, I mean, right." I picked up the file and took a deep breath as my hand hovered over the wound. My stomach was in knots and although I willed my hand to push it into his chest, the message didn't quite reach my fingertips.

"I can't do this," I said, pulling away.

"Yes, you can," he said patiently.

I blew out a big breath.

"The sooner you do it the better," he added.

"I know, I know," I said testily. "Believe it or not sticking a nail file into the chest of the man I love isn't particularly high on my bucket list."

"If you don't, I will have to do it myself."

This was enough for me not to delay any further.

"Okay, I'm going to do it," I said, more to myself than for the purposes of providing any kind of running commentary.

I stood between Ahran's legs and placing my left hand on the other side of his chest, for balance, I pushed the end of the file into the wound with a less than steady hand. He growled and I hesitated.

"Keep going," he said between clenched teeth.

I felt sick, but pushed it in further until the file made contact with something and Ahran flinched.

"I'm so sorry!" I said, quickly withdrawing the file from the wound. The blade had disturbed the already trau-matised tissue and blood started to ooze in a steady trickle. I dabbed it with some more antiseptic soaked cotton wool and could feel myself breaking out in a sweat. "I think that was it."

"You need to get the file behind the bullet and ease it out."

I nodded and Ahran drank deeply from the bottle in his hand. I watched his throat constrict several times and then he picked up Toby's blood-stained hoodie.

"Ready?" he said.

I nodded. He held a mouthful of hoodie between his teeth and I resumed my position in front of him.

I pushed the file in and angled it to the right. I felt the blade grate against the bullet again. I stilled before easing it in further, trying to do it as cleanly as possible without wiggling it around too much. Ahran sat as steady as a rock.

"Ok sweetie, you're doing really well," I said, soothingly. I felt more in control knowing what I had to do.

At the point where I thought I had come to the end of the bullet, I pushed the file a little further to try and get behind it to ease it towards me.

Ahran growled through the cloth between his teeth.

"I'm so sorry," I said and hesitated.

Ahran shook his head, as if to say don't stop, carry on.

I changed the angle of the file slightly and felt the resistance provided by the bullet.

"I've got it." I continued the pressure, pushing the handle of the file away from me.

Ahran made another sound deep in his throat, but I continued until I could see the end of the bullet break the surface. A fraction more and I was able to take hold of the end of it with my left thumb and forefinger and pulled it out.

Ahran let out another groan.

I dropped the bullet into one of the bowls, plugged the hole in his chest with a handful of cotton wool and took a moment to catch my breath. I'm pretty sure I had been holding it throughout the whole procedure.

"Are you okay?" I asked.

He nodded without saying anything, looking ashen. I kissed his forehead. "I'm so proud of you!"

My hands were coated with his sticky blood. "Do you think you can hold this whilst I wash my hands?" I said, indicating towards the wadding I was holding to stem the bleeding.

His hand replaced mine and I went over to the sink to clean myself up in preparation to sew the wound.

I returned to the patient and picked up the needle and thread. "Okay, ready?"

He nodded.

After five minutes of careful stitching I stepped back to review my work. The white thread had created an inch-long welt that stood proud of the surrounding skin, but it was neat and had stopped the bleeding.

"I think soldier, that's a wrap!" I said, feeling satisfied with my work.

"You are a good woman," Ahran said with a slightly glassy eyed expression.

I took the nearly empty bottle of homebrew out of his grasp, held his face in my hands and planted a kiss firmly on his lips.

"You are amazing," I said.

He gave me a lop-sided grin and swayed slightly in his

seat. I think I loved him more in that moment than I ever had.

"And I see the *Scragc* has done its job," I said with a chuckle, feeling a little teary with emotion.

I dressed the wound and made a sling out of the remaining linen. "Now, you need to rest!" I said, doing my best impression of a formidable hospital matron.

He nodded woozily and I left him whilst I made up the small double bed with the bedding I'd found. I helped him out of the chair and into bed so he could recover from his surgery and sleep off the alcohol. I could only hope that when he woke up his headache would take his mind off the pain in his chest. I gave him a kiss and left him to sleep, glad that ordeal was over.

Having returned from collecting fire wood, Toby was lighting matches in the kitchen and attempting to light the wood he'd put in the stove.

"Hey, hey, hold on a minute," I said, seizing the matches from him, concerned to see the discarded ones had been dropped carelessly on the wooden floor. "Hasn't anyone ever taught you to lay a fire?" I asked, peering into the stove.

"I thought the wood was dry enough," he said a little defensively. No ten-year-old boy liked to have his pyrotechnical skills questioned.

"No, it won't light like that. Can you see any paper anywhere?"

"Here," Toby said, picking out a faded newspaper from the basket next to the fireplace at the other end of the room.

I set about laying the fire again and it was soon blazing away.

"There," I said, dusting off my hands. I stood for a moment watching the flames. "Well, at least now we can make a cup of tea." I filled the kettle and put it on the stove.

"Do you mind giving me a hand to get this place ship-shape?"

I had always made Toby help out with the chores at home, but having servants meant that he hadn't had to lift a finger over the last couple of years. Fortunately, he was a willing boy and together we whipped the small cabin into shape.

When I went in to check on Ahran he was sleeping like a baby, so I left some painkillers by his bed, made a cup of tea and joined Toby on the sofa. "I'll get us something to eat shortly, I just need a minute," I said, closing my eyes, it had proven to be another difficult day. Ahran's wound could very easily have been fatal and without the clinical standards of a modern day operating theatre, it still could be. What would I do then? It was too much to contemplate a world without him in it. I began to wonder whether there was somebody up there who had it in for me, surely it was enough to lose my parents and my sister? I couldn't possibly lose Ahran as well. No, the surgery had been a success and as Ahran had said, he had a strong constitution.

19

I must have eventually dozed off because I woke up to the sound of the door slamming. I jumped up disorientated and ran to the door, throwing it open not really sure what I was doing. Toby was walking back from the car with Saul's case in his hand. He looked up at me in surprise.

"Please don't do that to me," I said as my heart rate began to normalise.

"Do what?" he asked.

"Disappear!" After what had happened lately my nerves were in tatters.

"I was just getting the case Saul gave me, my father's diary is in it and I want to read it."

I smiled and held open the door for him. "I'm so pleased you have it. It was really kind of Saul to give it to you."

It was getting dark, but I managed to light the two old gas lamps that were in the cabin and left Toby on the sofa with his father's diary to get on with preparing dinner—a campfire affair of pasta and some tinned Bolognese. I re-stoked the fire and once the stove was hot enough, put a pan of water on before emptying the sauce into another.

"Is there any food? I'm starving," Ahran said, coming out of the bedroom a little while later, the white linen of the makeshift sling standing out against his bare chest.

"Hey, you. How are you feeling?" I asked.

He tilted his head from side to side as if to assess his current condition.

"A bit sore and my head is pounding, but I'll live," he said, coming over to plant a kiss on my forehead.

Seeing him so bright allayed my earlier fears and enabled me to breathe a little more easily.

"I found some old clothes in the ottoman in the bedroom, they must have been Tagan's," I said, pointing to the shirt, jeans and sweater I had laid over the back of the sofa. "Dinner won't be long."

He picked up the clothes and went back into the bedroom to get changed.

"I've been reading my father's diary," Toby said once we had sat down to eat.

"It's weird. When I read it, it's like I can hear dad's voice."

I smiled at him sympathetically. If only Toby had had the chance to meet Tagan, he only had what people told him and pictures to go on. But at least now, he had his personal diary, it was another small way he could connect with his father. I had always found it strange whenever I came across hand-written notes of Katie's. Somehow it was like she was speaking to me from the grave. It brought a mixture of emotions, on the one hand a sense of comfort, on the other a prickly sense of injustice. How is it that those indelible marks of ink survive, mocking the weakness of flesh, blood and bones by living on, in some cases, forever? There was a part of me that wished that everything a person had written or created dissolved at their death because then it wouldn't catch you when you were least expecting it, bringing back all the feelings of loss and emptiness.

"What is it?" Ahran asked, pulling me away from my thoughts.

"Oh, nothing really. I was just thinking how good it is that Toby has something of Tagan's. Particularly his diary."

"You're right. There is something about the handwritten word, it brings a person to life."

"That's just what I was thinking!"

"Tagan has been talking about how much he'd like to see Earth and Ramia come together in peace," Toby said, speaking as if he had only just spoken to him and illustrating mine and Ahran's point.

"He was very passionate about it," Ahran explained. "He often shared his thoughts on war, about how futile it was. He believed we should focus our energies on making peace. He was a reluctant soldier towards the end of his military career, he had seen all too often the pain and suffering that conflict brings."

"He talks about some of the people he met on his travels," Toby informed us. "He said that the British Prime Minister was very nice and confessed that he had a weakness for Pot Noodle, but told Tagan not to tell his wife, because she was an excellent cook and a *'mangenere'*. What's a *mangenere?"*

"She likes good food," Ahran translated. "But…is quite…particular?" he said, unsure he had translated it accurately.

"She was a food snob?" I offered.

"Yes, that's it!" Ahran said.

"How funny?! I wonder how on earth he got to meet with world leaders and people of influence?" I said.

"Tagan had the gift of the blab," Ahran said.

"You mean gab!" I said, chuckling at yet another of Ahran's misquotes.

Ahran shrugged as if to say, *Hey! I'm foreign…but lovable.*

I smiled at him and squeezed his knee under the table.

Toby got up from the table and retrieved the diary from the kitchen side. "There's something in here that I don't understand," Toby said, pointing to a passage in the diary and showing it to Ahran.

Ahran smiled. "It's a secret language Tagan and I devised. We used it when we didn't want any of the adults around us to understand what we were saying."

"Oh cool! Will you teach me it?" Toby said enthusiastically.

"Of course I will. As Tagan's son, its only right that I should pass it on to you."

I could see this pleased Toby no end. He put the diary down and continued to eat thoughtfully. "He also said that the King of Bahrain bit his fingernails and made a funny joke about if he was as rich as he was believed to be then surely he could have paid someone to have bitten them for him!"

I chuckled. "So, all vital information in the name of inter-world peace."

"Not really," Toby said, taking me literally, "But it's funny."

Ahran and I chuckled.

"Your father had a good sense of humour and could charm the birds onto their knees."

"Out of the trees!" I said, rolling my eyes.

"I know, I know, just wanted to check you were listening," Ahran said, laughing.

I gave him a jab in the ribs.

"Aiych!" he said.

I dropped my fork. "Oh God, I'm so sorry," I said, fearing I had caused him further injury.

He gave me a lop-sided grin. "Other side," he said and gave me a wink.

I shook my head at him and narrowed my eyes. He was obviously feeling better. I couldn't help thinking Saul had not fared so well. "What do you think the guys who killed Saul were after?"

Ahran gave a one-shouldered shrug. "Your guess is as good as mine."

"Saul's dead?" Toby asked, looking mortified. I'd forgotten he wasn't aware of what had happened back at Saul's flat.

I put my hand on his shoulder. "Yes sweetheart, I'm afraid he is."

"Was it Bazeera?" he asked.

"We don't know who it was, but Ahran seems to think that they were almost certainly Ramian."

"I bet it was her, she hates us, doesn't she?"

"Please don't worry about it, it really isn't your problem."

"As future King of Dinara, I think it is my problem," he said, defiantly.

I could be forgiven for thinking that at ten Toby was still a child, but he seemed older than his years. Physically, he was nearly as tall as me and with a strong athletic build. Over the last two years he seemed to be maturing quicker than I had expected. Not that I was any expert on ten-year-old boys, but he could interpret situations and grasp concepts that went beyond his tender years. I was pretty sure it had to be something to do with his Ramian DNA, he was growing up fast, and sooner or later I was going to have to come to terms with that.

We finished our dessert and I washed up whilst Toby dried.

"I found a pack of cards in the drawer over there," Toby said, yawning. "Can you teach me how to play?" he said, when we had finished.

"There'll be no card games for you tonight young man, future King or not, you need your sleep and its bed time."

The usual groans of protest followed until he finally gave in and took himself off to bed. I followed him in a short while after, to say goodnight.

I sat on his bed. "You okay?" I asked, missing his curls that, at moments like these, I would often sweep an errant one away from his eyes.

He nodded. "My father loved Earth."

"So it would seem," I said.

"Do you think Ramia and Earth will ever become allies?"

"Now *that's* the million-dollar question!"

"When I first came back to Earth I hated being here, it reminded me of how much I miss mum."

"I know what you mean, sweetie."

"Especially when I went to Auntie Audrey's."

I nodded.

"I don't like the thought of never being able to come back here though."

For a moment, I thought about my friends and especially Bennie. Our most recent drama had meant that I had briefly forgotten the battle Bennie was having and the thought that I might lose her hit me hard.

I fought back the tears. "Nor I."

"Maybe one day I could carry on what my father started."

I took a deep breath. "One day you are going to be a great King; you will be able to do whatever you want."

He seemed satisfied with my answer.

"Don't worry Auntie Sophie, we're going to be alright."

I chuckled at his confidence. "I know we are love. Now you need to get some sleep."

He wriggled down under his duvet and I kissed him on the cheek.

"Goodnight your highness."

Toby laughed. "Goodnight."

I found Ahran sat on the top step of the veranda at the front of the cabin, looking up at the stars.

"What do you see?" I asked, sitting down next to him and following his gaze.

"A lot of twinkly lights in the sky?" he offered.

I laughed. "And there was me thinking that you were some astronomy expert."

"I'm expert in many things," he said suggestively. "But astronomy isn't one of them."

"You Ramians are such a let-down!" I said jokily.

"I was actually thinking about Saul," he said, turning more serious.

I sat down next to him, put my arm around him and rested my head on his good shoulder.

"I can't believe he's…dead," he continued. "I used to console myself as a child that it didn't matter how bad my father was because I always had Saul to turn to and now… now he's gone." There was a note of disbelief in his voice.

"Life can be so cruel," I said quietly, wishing I could take away some of his pain.

He took a deep breath and let out a single sob, no tears, just one heart-wrenching, hit-you-in-the-pit-of-the-stomach sob.

My heart broke for him. "Oh. Sweetheart."

What could I say? I was all too familiar with that cycle of grief. The disbelief, the denial, the anger and then eventually acceptance. It was a rough journey and I didn't wish it on anyone, let alone this big, brave, strong man I was holding in my arms and whom I loved more than life itself. I kissed his shoulder. We sat for some time, there was no need for words, they were of little comfort, all I could do was hold him and offer him my support and understanding.

"If I had just…" he said, eventually.

"*If* is a harsh, punishing word," I said, interrupting him before he could finish his sentence. "It serves no purpose."

He sighed. "You're right."

"We work with the information we have at the time. You had no idea his life was in that much danger."

"No I didn't," he said regretfully.

"Thankfully none of us know what's around the corner. We have to squeeze out whatever good we can find in every situation we find ourselves in." This was how I had tried to live my life since being in Ramia, since being with Ahran and by and large I had succeeded. It wasn't like Ahran had given me the strength because I'd had to find that within myself, but he had been my rock, always there if I needed his quiet support. Just as I had tried to be his.

"I couldn't agree with you more. Come here," he said, pulling me onto his lap.

"I don't want to hurt you," I said, frightened to lean back.

"You won't," he said, adjusting my position so that I was clear of his wound and gave me a lingering kiss where my neck joined my left shoulder.

"Are you sniffing me?" I asked, turning towards him.

"Yes, I am. How is it that after three days on the run you still smell like a summer meadow?" he said.

"Are you implying I've not washed?" I said, taking offence.

He laughed. "No, I'm just saying you always smell so

nice." He pulled away a fraction and the atmosphere between us changed. He paused for a moment and we sat there in silence. Even though the night sky was doing its best to impress us with its spectacular display; like a numinous, static firework show, its majesty was quickly forgotten, as the universe suddenly shrunk to consist only of us.

"Turn around so I can see you," he said. I shifted my position so I was still sat on his lap, but facing him, my knees either side of his hips.

"I love you so completely Sophie…"

"And I…" But he didn't let me finish and pressed his finger to my lips stifling the words I was about to say. "Let me speak," he said softly.

I did as he asked and watched his beautiful features settle into an expression of concentration as if what he was about to say mattered a great deal to him. I felt a warm glow at his words of love.

A smile touched the edge of his lips. "I think I loved you from the moment I first saw you."

I chuckled. "And I thought you were some serial killer about to claim your next victim."

"Love has been known to blossom in the most unlikely circumstances you know," he said with a chuckle.

I laughed too, feeling more than a little drunk from happiness at the prospect of what I suspected he was about to say.

"Now shh," he said. "You're distracting me."

"Sorry," I said, and wriggled my bottom into a more comfortable position.

"And you can stop that," he said. "Otherwise all I want to say will be forgotten."

"Ok, no wriggling, just listening."

"We've been through so much together."

I nodded, not wanting to interrupt and delay him any further.

"So much more than your average couple."

I wanted to say there was nothing average about our relationship or him for that matter, but I held my tongue.

"You are so beautiful," he said, stroking my cheek. "I thought I would never feel the kind of love that I feel for you."

Emotion began to wash over me as I sat there listening to his sweet confession.

"I want to protect you, cherish you and love you until my last dying breath." I saw confirmation of everything he was saying in the cool, endless depths of his eyes.

He paused for a moment and took a deep breath. "Sophie McAllister, will you marry me?"

This time he was proposing to me sober, at least I think he was after sleeping off the remainder of the *Sgrac*. He was really, actually *proposing* to me. I could hardly believe it. I nodded and shakily answered the most ridiculous question he had ever asked me. "Nothing would make me happier."

He looked relieved as if there had been a chance I might say no. His mouth plundered mine until eventually he pulled away breathlessly.

"I have this," he said excitedly and struggled to pull whatever it was out of his jean pocket.

After some straining and wriggling, he freed the object

and placed it in my palm. It was a small, beautiful, jade pebble with a perfect hole through the middle.

I extended my hand to study it, "It's beautiful!"

"I found it on the farm, the colour is an exact match of your eyes," he said. "I've been carrying it around for weeks waiting for the perfect moment to ask you to marry me."

My heart sung, but I was too choked for words.

"We don't have engagement rings in Ramia," he said, slightly apologetically, "But I thought that maybe you could wear it on your necklace."

I laughed through my tears. "It's perfect!"

"Back home jade represents beauty and wisdom, it's believed that it protects the wearer from negativity and evil."

"Sounds like something I could do with," I said with a chuckle. "It's a lovely sentiment, I love it!"

I threw my arms around his neck and under the stars kissed him in a way that I couldn't express in words.

20

"Are you comfortable," he said, kissing the top of my head sometime later. I was lying in the crook of his arm on a makeshift bed we had created out of cushions and blankets on the deck. The night was cool, but our skin was heated.

"Surprisingly so," I said. "How's your shoulder?"

"It's fine," he replied.

"You wouldn't tell me if it wasn't, would you?"

"Nope."

"Well after the way you just made love to me, you would never know you'd been shot earlier today."

"You can't keep a good man down Sophie."

I laughed at his attempt at arrogance.

"To tell you the truth," he said conspiratorially. "I knew that if I told you it aches a bit, you wouldn't have let me near that body of yours."

"I knew it! Ahran Elessar, you are a bluffer and a cheat!"

"I'll say anything to get you into bed."

I smiled. As if I needed any tempting?!

"Do you think if we practice enough we might have children one day?" I asked wistfully and pulled the blanket over my shoulder. It was a hopeless question, but it was out before I had a chance to stop it. I so desperately wanted some reassurance that we would have kids of our own.

"Sophie, please don't torture yourself."

I leaned up onto my elbow. "I know, but I can't help thinking that if Katie and Tagan managed it, we at least have a chance, don't we?"

He shook his head slowly. There have been Ramians on Earth for decades, centuries even and there have only ever been two children born to Ramian/Sapien parents. "It just isn't worth getting your hopes up."

"So you want to marry a woman you can't have children with?" I said angrily as if it was all his fault.

"Hey," he said, tilting my chin towards him. "All I know is that I want to marry *you*, and if that means we don't have kids, then so be it. We are meant to be together Sophie."

I thought about this for a moment. Would the fact that we couldn't have children be a deal-breaker for me? Hell no! I had never really believed in fate, but Ahran was right, we were meant to be together and we would just have to build a life that didn't feature children in it. I was lucky enough to have Toby and if that was as close as I was going to get to motherhood then I had every reason to be thankful.

"You're right," I said with a sigh. "What's important is us."

Losing Saul had been a devastating blow for Ahran and my heart broke for him when I heard his restless dreams as he wrestled with his loss that night. I had held him in my arms trying to comfort him and he had wrapped himself around me so tightly as if I was his only chance of survival. His nightmares eventually passed and he settled into a less fitful sleep and I must have drifted off a short while after. I awoke the following morning to shards of light coming through the shutters and I nestled into him with a contented smile on my face. As hard as yesterday had been it had ended in the most perfect way. I touched the jade pebble at my neck, I could hardly believe that we were actually engaged and I couldn't have felt any happier.

Ahran stirred.

"Hey, sweetie," I said, softly. "How are you feeling?"

"Sore," he said, telling me the truth this time.

"I'll get you some painkillers," I said and went to get out of bed.

An arm snaked under the covers and prevented me from moving any further.

"Not before I've had a kiss."

I willingly obliged and then insisted I fulfil my nursing duties by getting him some painkillers. Giving him the correct dose was a difficult thing, I was pretty sure an average adult measure wouldn't be enough, so I risked doubling the dose which he said he had done before and had lived to fight another day. Somehow, now that we were engaged he was even more precious to me. I couldn't fathom why, but I just felt different, like we were two halves of the same whole. Not just boyfriend and girlfriend, but one and the same. It was a wonderful feeling, but scary, I had even more to lose now. I stopped that thought in its tracks. I wasn't about to let the old negativity ruin my morning so after I had washed and dressed, I laid the table for breakfast and set about stoking the stove. There was something grounding about making fire and putting it to good use, like I was somehow tuning into my ancestors who had done the very same thing to provide for their families.

I hummed my way around the kitchen and put some croissants in the stove. Toby appeared at the doorway.

"Morning sweetheart. Are you ready for some breakfast?' I asked.

"Yeah," he said absentmindedly, preoccupied with what he was holding in his hand.

"What's that?" I asked.

"I don't know. It fell out of the sleeve of my dad's journal."

I rinsed my hands. "Let me have a look," I said, wiping my hands on my jeans.

"It looks like a memory card of some sort." I took it from him to examine it more closely.

Ahran came into the kitchen, no doubt lured by the smell of our breakfast.

"Look at this, Toby has just found it in Tagan's journal."

"It's a memory card," he said, confirming my initial thoughts.

"What do you think is on it?" I asked.

"I don't know, let's have a look," Ahran said, pulling his

phone out of his back pocket. He slipped the card into a hidden socket in the side of his phone. I had no idea it had such a capability.

"It looks like some kind of government files," he said, peering at the screen.

"What kind of files?" I craned to have a look.

He scrolled through them. "Co-ordinates, names, addresses. I wouldn't mind betting all pretty sensitive information." He opened up another file.

"*Harenka!*" he exclaimed.

"What is it?"

"This one contains information about black ops."

"What are black ops?" Toby asked intrigued.

"They are secret operations which have been sanctioned by a government. They are usually highly dangerous or extremely politically sensitive. Leaking this kind of information could put those involved at great risk."

"But presumably, if this is Tagan's, this information is at least eleven years old."

"Yes, it probably is, but it doesn't mean it's any less sensitive." He ejected the disk from his phone and put it in his pocket.

"What is it?" I asked, looking at the expression on his face.

He went over to the kitchen sink and picked up the bullet I'd dug out of his shoulder that was still in a bowl on the side. "This is Ramian army standard issue," he said examining it. "This confirms that the people who chased us yesterday were Ramian. So why would they be interested in information about the British government?"

I shrugged, not sure where he was going with this.

"Maybe the people who were following us in the black car had nothing to do with Saul's death. Maybe it was the British government that killed him and ransacked his apartment." He paused for a moment. "Perhaps the reason MI5 are still interested in Tagan is not because they think he's a terrorist necessarily, but because he has this information," he said, retrieving the disk from his pocket. "The British government are trying to cover their tracks."

"So you think it was the British government that killed Saul?" I said.

Ahran nodded. "It's a possibility."

"Oh My God! Would they really do that?" I said, feeling totally let down by my fellow countrymen.

"It's happened before."

I stared at him wide-eyed, struggling to believe that the government could be that brutal. "So, that might solve one mystery, but why are there Ramians after us?"

"Toby could be right, it could be Bazeera?"

"But she's in prison," I pointed out.

"She still has loyal supporters."

I waved my hands dismissively. "I don't want to think about it. The sooner we get back to Ramia the better." I knew we were in trouble. I didn't want to be reminded of how much.

"Let's have breakfast," I said and went to the stove to take the croissants out.

"What are we doing today?" Toby asked once we were all sat at the table.

"We can't stray too far from here Tobes I'm afraid," I

said, reminding him that although we felt safe in the cabin, technically we were still on the run.

"There's a stream a little way up the mountain, I think it would be okay to go there."

I looked at him doubtfully, I had hoped that we might be able to avoid any drama today, lay low and bide our time until we were given the green light to head back to the portal.

"No one ever comes up here, we'll be fine," Ahran said, answering my worried expression. "Hey, Tobes. Fancy doing some fishing?"

Now fishing I could handle. Not that I was big into hooking fish out of the water until they suffocated, it always made me feel slightly claustrophobic as I watched them helplessly gasp for breath, but a quiet few hours spent on a river bank could be the perfect antidote to the last few days.

"We haven't got any rods," Toby said.

"I'll show you how to make one," Ahran said with an excited glint in his eye. Judging by the photos and film clips I had seen of Tagan and Ahran as boys, fishing was not only an occupation that Ahran was comfortable with, but one he was also good at. Now why did that not come as any surprise?

We finished our breakfast and I packed up a picnic for the day ahead. We found a great spot a little further up the mountain which had several deep pools, ideal for trout and pike Ahran assured us.

It was difficult for Ahran being one-handed, but with Toby's assistance they busied themselves with making some rods. I watched them for a bit and then asked Toby if he minded me reading his father's diary which he'd brought along with him. He'd spent most of the morning with his nose in it and I was intrigued to find out more about Tagan myself, I was also more than a little hopeful that there might be something about Katie in it. I settled back against a tree and began to flick through the diary, whilst Ahran and Toby tested their new rods.

It wasn't quite what I had been expecting. There were some diary entries, but there were also lots of hastily written notes, dates, names and addresses, itineraries for planned overseas trips, bullet pointed minutes of meetings, and agendas for appointments coming up. It was less of a memoir and more of a working document that tracked Tagan's movements in the year before he died. Some of it was in English and provided a window into what he was trying to achieve, much of it was in Ramian and lost on me. However, interspersed between the logistics of what must have proved to be a fascinating time for Tagan were personal entries which provided some commentary, little gems that gave me an insight into what was important to him, what was frustrating him and the gains he was making as he carried out his task of trying to glean as much infor-mation about Earth, its culture, its rulers and the way it was governed. It was like the *Hitchhiker's Guide To The Galaxy*, but this time the tables had been turned. *An Alien's Bird's Eye View of Earth* may have been a more fitting title.

I flicked forward to the autumn of that year, the time when I knew he had met Katie, and searched the pages for anything that might have related to her. I thumbed through the month of October.

Nothing. Nothing. Nothing.

Until a word jumped off the page and made me stop in my tracks. It was the name I had been looking for.

I'VE MET A GIRL. Katie. She's a Sapien.
Does it matter? Should it matter?
What the hell?! All work and no play…

I SCANNED through the next few entries. Stuff about meeting with some Lord, map grid references and notes on what looked like a telephone conversation with the Home Secretary's secretary. *Jeez Louise!* Tagan really hadn't been messing about.

And there was her name again.

I COULDN'T BE sure Katie was going to be there again. I'd sat at the bar like some pervert scrutinising every woman until she arrived with her friends. I bought her a drink and we talked for most of the night. Hell, she's so sweet! Beautiful. Straight-forward.

I LOOKED up from the diary unseeingly. He must have liked her if he had gone out of his way to wait for her. He was right. Katie always came across as sorted, somebody who knew what she wanted and for Tagan, it was obviously something that had attracted him to her.

I GAVE her my number and asked her to call me. I thought that maybe if I left it to her she would make the decision for me...

I called her.

Who can blame me? I just want to see her again. I'm taking her out to dinner. Shit! I'm nervous.

I SMILED. He was obviously worried about the Sapien thing, but he liked her. I silently congratulated Katie. I read the next few entries in the hope that her name would appear again. There were notes about a meeting to do with climate change in Brussels, names of people and organisations and a 'To do' list. In the margin, Tagan had scrawled '*Without our help Sapiens are screwed!*'

I paused for a moment. Did we really have no chance? Where were we going so wrong? And there was I thinking that people were finally getting the message about climate change, but the world was obviously in a far worse state than I had realised.

I carried on reading. On the list was a note to speak to a person who was obviously an environmental specialist back in Ramia and a reminder to speak to Halsan about how he could feed this information back to the people on Earth who needed to know. I turned the pages scanning for Katie's name again, but it was all about meetings, phonecalls and action plans. I felt deflated. For a moment, I had felt close to her, which I knew was a little ridiculous bearing in mind that I was only reading the notes of a man who had died nine years ago, but to just read his thoughts about her was comforting.

And then Ahran's name jumped out at me.

AHRAN CAME TODAY. It was good to see him. He's counting down the days until he leaves the Special Force. Can't say I blame him. I'm hoping I can persuade him to join me here. He'd make a bloody good ambassador. I took him to the club where I had met Katie, I was hoping I might bump into her again, but she wasn't there. Perhaps a good thing. I'm not sure he would understand the attraction of a Sapien girl.

I STOPPED READING. "Huh?! Bloody cheek! He certainly *does* understand the attraction of a Sapien girl!" I said to myself out loud.

ONLY 5 HOURS to dinner tonight…

I READ this line again and realised he was talking about his first date with Katie. It wasn't easy reading Tagan's disjointed scrawl. In spite of the important nature of what Tagan was doing on Earth, Katie had gotten under his skin. She had meant something to him and for me, that was an enormous relief. I hurriedly read on.

SHE LIKES ME. I've obviously still got it! The girl kissed me and without too much encouragement from me. Jesus! That kiss...

"AUNTIE SOPHIE! AUNTIE SOPHIE!"

I looked up from Tagan's diary slightly disorientated and not entirely sure where I was for a moment.

Toby was running towards me with something in his hands until it slipped out of his grasp and onto the ground. I had been so absorbed in what I had been reading that I had totally forgotten I was sitting on a mossy river bank. For the last ten minutes, I had been inside Tagan's head and I tried to shake the feeling that I was an uninvited voyeur. When he had made this log, he'd had no intention for the sister of his new-found love interest to read his innermost thoughts and I couldn't help but feel guilty.

"Ratcha!" Toby exclaimed as he bent down to pick something up.

"Toby!" I said, chastising his use of a Ramian swear word.

"Sorry," he said slightly breathlessly, but with a grin on his face, obviously hoping that I would be too impressed by what was in his hands to give him any further grief for the expletive he'd just let slip out.

"It's a trout!" He said excitedly.

I turned over the corner of the page I had been reading and placed it on the ground so that I could give Tagan some privacy for a moment and gave Toby my full attention.

I peered into his hands. "It's not very big," I said, without thinking.

Toby looked crestfallen, I think he had hoped that I would shower him with more praise than that.

"No, but it's only the first one I've caught," he said defensively.

Ahran joined us. "You should have seen the one that got away," he said, gesturing with his hands, his good arm extending out from his body about two foot away from his other hand that was anchored to his body by his sling and indicating the size of the river monster that had given them the slip.

Now, I was no fisherman, but I had heard how prone to exaggeration fishermen could be so I nodded, not entirely convinced by the yarn that was being spun.

"You should have seen it Auntie Sophie, it was massive!"

"And it got away you say?"

"Yeah, so annoying!" Toby said stubbing his toe into the ground with frustration.

"Shame."

Ahran winked at me and I wasn't about to cast any further doubt on a story that I'm sure would live on in Toby's mind. By the time he was a grandfather I'm sure the 'One That Got Away' would have grown by at least another foot.

"So, we get to eat tonight, after all," I said more in the vein that Toby had been hoping for.

"This is just the beginning, isn't it Uncle Ahran?" Toby said. "He's got this secret bait that will catch anything."

I looked up at Ahran inquiringly, wondering how on Earth he had acquired the Holy Grail of the fishing world. As far as I could remember, he'd been stuck in the same cabin as I had with a hole in his shoulder. "What is this secret bait?"

Ahran looked sheepish and before he could stop himself, he glanced at our picnic that I had painstakingly prepared earlier that morning.

"Ahhh-ran," I said suspiciously, and began to look through the picnic basket to find that the ham baguettes had been plundered. I grabbed a handful of moss and threw it at him, "That's our lunch!" I said, unable to hide my amusement at his audacity.

"Secret bait…my eye!" I was still chuckling and marvelling at Ahran's ability to say anything to Toby that he thought might impress him.

"Talking of lunch," he said as he dropped down beside me and after realising that leaning back on one elbow caused too much discomfort, gave up and sat cross-legged instead. "This fishing lark is a hungry old business."

Toby carefully laid his prize catch on the ground before settling down himself.

"Any kind of business is a *hungry old business* for you boys," I said as I began to unpack our food. I caught sight of the glassy-eyed stare of the fish.

"Toby, can you move that, it's looking at me." Anything dead gave me the heebie-jeebies.

We began to tuck into what was left of the ham baguettes.

"Have you been reading my father's diary?" Toby asked.

"I have." It then struck me whether it was appropriate for Toby to read Tagan's diary. "I think maybe I better read it first before you read any more."

"Why?" Toby asked.

"Um…because it is a diary written by an adult and there may be some things that aren't appropriate," I said, thinking back to the point where I had left it. I shot a glance at Ahran, who seemed vaguely amused. I had no idea how much detail Tagan would go into concerning his relationship with my sister, in fact, I questioned whether even *I* should be reading it.

"If it's that good, maybe I ought to read it," Ahran said.

I frowned at him disapprovingly.

"I think I have the right to read my father's diary," Toby said with a hint of indignation.

"And I think it's only right that you should, but I am going to have a quick scan of it first. I wouldn't want you to read anything that you might find distressing." I had already decided that I would skip anything more explicit. After all, Tagan may not have intended anyone to read it and I already felt like I had pried by reading as much as I had. But there was also another part of me that craved to hear more about Katie as well as a fascination with what Tagan had found out whilst on Earth.

"Okay, if you say so," Toby said reluctantly.

Once we had finished eating, Ahran and Toby resumed fishing and I picked up Tagan's diary once more.

There were more entries about places he'd been, people he'd met and new discoveries about Earth he had found, it made for uncomfortable reading at times. The more I read, the more I realised Tagan wrote his commentary about Earth often without judgement. If only Compton, my MI5 interrogator, had realised what an ally Tagan had been and how ludicrous it was to suggest that terrorism had been his motivation, if indeed that was what they thought. One could only imagine how much of a saviour of the world Tagan might have been had he not met such an untimely death. It made me consider how futile life could be and I wondered what could have been achieved throughout history had some people not died before their time. A cure for cancer? The answer to world peace? Who knew where we would be now?

I turned the page that I had been staring at for the last few minutes and a folded slip of paper fell into my lap. It had obviously not been disturbed for a long time because it had taken on that well-pressed nature, much like that of a flower head that had been placed between the pages of a book and been forgotten about.

I unfolded it and began to read.

My dear Tagan

WE HAVE GOT to know each other well over the last few months and I admire your compassion and robust intellect. If Helen and I had ever had a son, you would be the kind of son we would like to have had. Forgive my flattery, it is the ramblings of an old man coming to the end of his days, but I speak the truth and I make no apologies for it.

We have spent many an hour discussing the strengths and weaknesses of the British government and it has given me great pleasure to share my humble experience. There is something different about you Tagan, and I find your point of view quite refreshing. I have enjoyed our afternoons at the club immensely.

As you know, I am a man of status and have spent my life serving this country, there are few who are as loyal and enthusiastic in their support. However, there are some I am afraid to say, who are driven by greed and corruption.

A while ago I was entrusted with some information by a great friend of mine who shares our views. However, it has become somewhat of a burden in light of my failing health. This blasted illness is sapping my strength, and I feel sure it will take me sooner rather than later. I am, therefore, extremely worried that it might fall into the wrong hands when I am gone. It wasn't until we last met that I realised you might just present the solution. And so, accompanying this letter is a memory stick containing some extremely sensitive information. Why not just destroy it? I hear you ask. And I have certainly considered this, but this information needs to be shared at some point. I have found you to be an honest, like-minded man which is why I am passing it to you, for you to decide its fate. Destroy it, keep it or share it with whomever you believe should know about it, it is not a decision I am capable of making now.

There is little else for me to say other than I wish you all the best. One day you will make a great politician, I am sure of it.

FAREWELL TAGAN. Sadly, I think it is unlikely we will meet again. God bless!

E.D.

I SAT for a moment pondering the contents of the letter. Tagan had obviously made some friends and allies during his time on Earth, so much so that someone who was clearly high up in the British government was prepared to entrust state secrets with him. Ahran was now in possession of the mysterious memory stick. We had only briefly looked at its contents, but I would now encourage Ahran to scrutinise its contents more closely. Fortunately, for *E.D,* whoever he was, it had passed into the hands of someone who was equally principled, smart and compassionate and it was now down to Ahran to decide what to do with it.

I looked up and stretched out my back and neck. I had spent the last half an hour crouched over the diary. Ahran and Toby were sat side-by-side on the riverbank in silence, their eyes trained on the ends of each of their homemade fishing rods, looking like two highly focussed gnomes. I smiled and turned my attention back to the diary in the hope that I would find more snippets about Katie.

An entry caught my attention, it had no date or introduction, it simply said:

SHIT! I think she means something. When did that happen?

MY HEART LURCHED for my sister. Did she ever know that she was important to Tagan? The way she used to talk about him made me think she did, but the fact he never got in touch with her again was a bitter pill for her to swallow. I read the last few entries:

FATHER HAS SUMMONED ME. New intel. Bazeera's forces are preparing to attack our northern borders. Will she ever give up?!

THERE WAS ANOTHER 'TO DO' list like many others in the diary.

- *Contact Hans Schermer - Discuss European trade links*
- *Book flight to Helsinki*
- *Review American ambassador's papers*
- *Katie – Book table for dinner*

AND THEN THE FINAL ENTRY.

08.00 HOURS – Bazeera's forces attacked Bozava and have seized the town.

I TURNED the page and then the next. That was it. The last twenty or so pages were empty. I sat back feeling bitterly disappointed. Nothing more about Katie and nothing more about Tagan's life, his voice had gone silent. Of course, I knew the story from that point onwards. Tagan never got to have dinner with Katie and his final *To do* list was never ticked off. I felt a lump in my throat. Thank goodness Tagan was unaware of how this story ended. I looked up at Toby with tears in my eyes. At the time of Tagan's last entry he was already growing inside Katie, little did he know he would never get to meet his father.

21

Apart from feeling rather melancholic after reading Tagan's diary, it turned out to be a quiet, uneventful day and I enjoyed the reprieve from the drama of the last few days. The fishing expedition was a success and we had several fresh trout for our tea. We all went to bed that night, feeling the benefit of the tranquil surroundings and the mountain air.

The next morning, the ringing of Ahran's phone woke us up. He reached across to the bedside table and answered it in Ramian.

"What is it?" I asked when he'd put the phone down.

"The portal is finally safe," he replied.

"*Hallelujah*!"

"If we head off now we could be home by lunchtime."

"Oh God, I can't tell you how pleased I am to hear that!"

It didn't take long for us to get ourselves together and once we'd had a quick breakfast we shut up the cabin. I couldn't help but feel a pang as we left what had been our little safe haven for a while. I was coming away from it an engaged woman and it would always have a special place in my heart. I drove and Ahran helped navigate the mountain roads until we eventually reached the main highway that would take us back to Paris.

"Where is the portal exactly?" I asked

"It's in a cemetery in the Sacré Coeur area," Ahran said.

"In a cemetery?! I exclaimed, looking across at him dubiously. It sounded a little too gothic for my liking.

"A cemetery is a good place to have a portal," he argued. "They are quiet, away from CCTV cameras and its inhabitants aren't likely to share our secret."

I shivered in response. "Ooh, don't say that."

Ahran chuckled, "Cemeteries don't bother me, I find them quite therapeutic."

"Do you? I hate them. What if you come across a ghost?"

"I'm not afraid of the dead, if anything I'd ask them what I could do to help them with their passage. Ghosts are only souls with unfinished business."

I gave him a sideways look and grimaced. "You're weird."

He chuckled again. "The only thing that scares me is losing you," he said in a hushed tone.

My heart did a little somersault. "Well, you have nothing to fear on that score."

He winked and gave me a heart-stopping smile.

It was a conversation we'd had before and I marvelled again that there wasn't much that scared him. I had spent pretty much my whole life scared of something; the dark, school exams, losing the people I love, the future and ending up an old spinster with nothing but a grumpy old cat to keep me company at night. In spite of his issues with his father, Ahran was so grounded. He knew what he wanted out of life and he went after it, he never let anything hold him back. He was one of life's achievers, but he did it in such a quiet unassuming way. I was proud of what I had accomplished in terms of my own personal battles, but I knew I would never be as strong as Ahran.

"Auntie Sophie," Toby said, pulling me away from my thoughts. I'd decided that there was nothing in Tagan's diary that wasn't suitable for Toby and I'd given him full permission to read it. He'd had his nose stuck in it since we'd left the cabin.

"Did you read the bit where he says he believed that one day we could tell the world about Ramia and offer our help?"

Admittedly, much of it was in Ramian and I had skipped bits in my search for entries about Katie, so it wasn't surprising that I had missed such an important detail but I had gathered that it was Tagan's ultimate aim.

"Really?" I glanced at him in the rear-view mirror and he nodded.

"Do you think it was a good idea?" Toby asked.

"It was something your father was very passionate about," Ahran said, answering Toby's question. "I really believe he would have been the right person to have done it too."

"I can tell how important it was too him." Toby said, before pausing for a moment. "I think he was doing the right thing. I don't understand why some people back in Ramia want to break ties with Earth. I think that once people here get used to the idea, they wouldn't pose any threat. I think humans would be fascinated. Besides they don't have the technology to cause a problem in Ramia. A pact could be made that in return for help they would have to promise to respect Ramia and not cause any problems."

"Wow Tobes! You've really thought about this haven't you."

He shrugged. "I just think maybe dad was right to have done what he did."

I glanced at Ahran and he smiled at me.

"I think your dad would have been very proud of you," I said. It seemed Toby's attitude towards Earth was thawing.

THANKFULLY OUR JOURNEY to the portal was not hindered by any would-be assassins, the British government or the French gendarmerie. Going to the mountains had been a good idea, we had been able to lay low and not excite any unwanted interest. And now we were only minutes away from being in Ramia.

"You okay Tobes? You are very quiet."

He had put Tagan's diary back in the case and was staring absentmindedly out of the window. "Just looking forward to getting back home."

"Me too."

We parked on a side street just up from the main entrance.

"Do you know where it is exactly?" I asked, peering at the hundreds of graves and tombs behind the iron railings ahead of us.

"It's at the back of the cemetery marked by a large tomb with an angel on the top," Ahran said, looking up and down the street. The area was quiet. "Are you ready?"

"Just take me home," I said wearily.

We left Saul's car on the street, it's fate was now in the hands of the Parisien police, and would no doubt lead them to discover Saul's untimely end, if it hadn't been discovered already. I touched the bonnet of his car as a parting gesture to him and we crossed the street to the cemetery. We entered the gates of the sacrosanct area where loved ones had been laid to rest, some still remembered, but judging by the condition of some of the graves, many sadly forgotten. I held Ahran's hand and put my arm around Toby. "It's such a shame, I used to really like Paris," I said as we walked between the rows of headstones. "But after this trip it doesn't hold the same kind of appeal."

"One day it will be safe for us to return," Ahran said.

We made our way to the back of the cemetery. It was not a cold day, but somehow it felt cool, maybe it was just the feeling of being surrounded by the dead. "There's a tomb with an angel on top," Toby said, pointing to a large stone sarcophagus that was tucked away in a secluded corner at the end of an avenue of graves. Ahran had been right, it was a good place for a portal.

"That looks like it," Ahran said, confirming that it was indeed the tomb.

We were about twenty paces away when we hear a voice behind us.

"I was hoping I might see you here."

We turned around to find Evo Salanda standing in front of us and I felt Ahran bristle at my side.

"Salanda. What can we do for you?"

"I think you've done enough," he replied, still with a pleasant expression.

He was dressed impeccably in a steel grey suit, with a dark shirt and tie and his hands resting casually in his pockets. He was the picture of Parisian style and elegance.

"I'm not sure I understand you," Ahran said. His grip on my hand tightened and I could feel him coiling like a panther ready to pounce. I struggled to understand his reaction as he eased us backwards towards the tomb.

The smile slid from my face and I blinked at Evo. Was I reading the situation correctly? This was Evo Salanda the handsome, charming man who I had danced with at Elaya's wedding and who had helped us when we had first arrived in Paris. Why was Ahran acting like he was about to pull a gun on us?

"Don't take another step," Evo commanded and whipped his right hand out of his pocket, a small pistol in his grasp. He stood there with his left hand still in his pocket, his right wrist twisted so that the gun was on its side, pointing it at us almost casually. Apart from the addition of a weapon, his body language and his expression hadn't changed.

"You think you are so above it all, don't you Ahran," he said with a chuckle. There was an unsteadiness to his voice that gave a true reading of what he was really feeling. He wasn't angry, he was *seething*. I felt the cold fingers of fear tip-toe up my spine. Suddenly, he didn't look dangerous, he looked psychotic which was infinitely more alarming.

Ahran pulled me behind him and I tucked Toby behind me.

"I have no idea what you are talking about Salanda, but if you put the gun down we can talk this through."

"I don't want to talk anymore. I've had enough of you and your family. I've had enough of the way you have no respect for Ramia, for Ramian traditions. And I think it's about time to put an end to it." His expression twisted into an ugly snarl.

I glanced down and saw the outline of Ahran's gun under his shirt, it was tucked in the waistband of his jeans at the small of his back. I contemplated how I could get it without Evo noticing.

"You are going to have to give me more than that," Ahran said, shaking his head slightly.

Evo threw a glance at me. "You and that Sapien bitch," he spat. "If it hadn't been for you two, Elaya and I would still be together."

Ahran nodded as if the penny had suddenly dropped.

"Not to mention your bloody cousin who couldn't keep his dick in his trousers and spawned that little bastard," he said, nodding towards Toby.

I wanted to protect Toby from his words, but I knew one false move could have us all shot.

I was still gripping Ahran's hand behind his back, it wouldn't take much for him to seize the gun that was brushing his knuckles.

"If this is how you treat your fellow compatriots, maybe Elaya made the right choice."

I willed Ahran not to say anymore, Evo was already in a heightened state of emotion and it wasn't wise to antagonise him.

"If it hadn't been for you and Tagan pissing all over Ramian lore, Elaya wouldn't have followed suit. It should have been me she was marrying two weeks ago. Instead she married a weak blood who's not nearly good enough for her."

"And so you holding a gun to our heads means you are?" Ahran said pointedly.

Now it was beginning to make sense. By not choosing their parent's choices, Evo clearly thought Elaya and Ahran were setting a precedent by turning their backs on Ramian tradition. Tagan's betrothed had died so technically he hadn't turned his back on his culture, but he had fathered a child who was half Sapien and clearly this was something that Evo found equally distasteful.

"Your family are tainting Ramian blood and you are going to pay for it," he said.

I knew that some Ramians didn't have the highest respect for Sapiens, but this was the first time I had come across this kind of fanaticism. And to think I thought he was charming!

"Ok, so before you shoot us all," Ahran said. "Why did you accept your assignment here on Earth if you find the idea of an Earth/Ramian alliance so disgusting?"

Evo snorted humourlessly. "Because I'm trying to stop it you fucking idiot!"

I was getting to the point where I'd had enough of his foul mouth. If I had thought my aim was good enough I would have reached for the gun and shot him myself, but I couldn't risk him shooting Ahran first.

"And Mimi?" Ahran said, referring to Evo's French girl-friend. "It's okay for you to have a relationship with a Sapien?"

"She works for the government, she's useful and so a necessary lapse of judgement."

"So you think you can get away with shooting two of the heirs to the Ramian throne," Ahran said, trying a different tack.

"If it means I get rid of the threat to our world that you both represent then I think there would be many back in Ramia who would happily help me pull the trigger."

"And the King would see it in the same light?"

"He has been brainwashed by the likes of you, in time he would understand my reasons."

"I'm not sure he would thank you for killing his grand-son," Ahran argued.

"The King is a great man and with the right council around him we could put an end to this nonsense."

"And you are putting yourself forward for the job?" Ahran was clearly trying to stall him with more questions. He slowly let go of my hand and curled his fingers around the hidden gun.

The sound of my heart was pounding in my ears as I anticipated the next few moments.

Ahran inched us back further towards the tomb.

Evo pulled his other hand out of his pocket, and in it was what looked like a phone.

"You've got nowhere to run to," he said, holding up the device. "I can close the portal from here. The only way out of here for you my friends is with a bullet."

"So it's you who's been messing with the portal," Ahran said accusingly.

I remember Ahran telling me that Evo had been some kind of computer genius and rather inconveniently he had obviously worked out how to tamper with portal technology.

"If I control the portals, then what would be the point of an alliance with Earth," he said, sounding like a villain right out of a James Bond movie.

"I'm guessing you tipped off MI5?" Ahran surmised. "And that you are responsible for the black car that was hot on our tail?"

"Your assumptions would be correct," he said, looking rather pleased with himself

It would seem that we had underestimated Evo Salanda.

"Why not close the portal now?" Ahran asked.

I couldn't understand why he was suggesting Evo did this.

"It's such a drag opening a new one," he said, sounding bored. "Besides, once I've killed you, someone needs to go and tell the King the sad news."

Ahran whipped the gun out of his waistband and pointed it at Evo. "Take Toby and run!"

Now I understood, Ahran wanted to make sure it was still open for us to travel through. My instincts told me to stay with Ahran, but I grabbed Toby's hand and sprinted the five metres towards the tomb, marking the portal. Ahran was an excellent shot, all I could hope was that he would dispatch Evo before Evo shot any of us.

The question was, did we have enough time to get to it before Evo closed it? Toby stepped in, but I hesitated and looked back to check that Ahran was following us.

What happened next happened in slow motion. I turned to find him still with his back to us, making no attempt to follow. He and Evo were pointing their guns at each other neither of them moving. I'm not sure who fired the first shot, but I saw Evo's body crumple and in the same instance I witnessed Ahran absorb each one of Evo's bullets and fall lifelessly to the ground.

"Nooooo!" I screamed before I was sucked into a vacuum.

22

I spun and hurtled, hurtled and spun for what seemed like an eternity, unable to comprehend what I had just witnessed, my thoughts and emotions as tumultuous as the ride. And then the darkness swallowed me.

Gradually, I came around, lying on the ground and then proceeded to vomit so violently that I struggled to draw breath. And then it hit me; an excruciating nightmare, except that it was something more harrowing and more horrific than I could ever have imagined. *I had just witnessed Ahran's death!* I collapsed on the ground, falling once more into unconsciousness.

Sometime later, I came to, aware that someone was shaking my shoulders and speaking incomprehensibly. I struggled to focus on the blurry figure above me until the acrid smell of my own vomit acted like some form of repugnant smelling salts and dragged me unwillingly into consciousness. Somewhere in the dim recesses of my mind I debated whether to fight or just let whoever this dark figure was do whatever he wished. It took only a moment more to come to a decision; I didn't care what happened to me and turned my head wordlessly willing him to do his worst. Ahran was dead and the sooner I joined him the better.

The man threw me over his shoulder and I pummelled his back, not because I wanted him to put me down, but because he had spared me. I hit him as hard as I could for not being more evil or violent in his intentions.

My ears roared as the blood rushed through my head, and yet I welcomed it, the sound was helping to prevent any comprehensible thought from forming. If only I could block the terrible, hopeless, dragging sensation clawing at my stomach.

I was dimly aware that I'd been carried indoors and eventually was dropped into a chair, where two heavy-handed women stripped me of my clothes and dumped me in a bath. I was numbly compliant, in shock and unable to process what had happened in those last moments in Paris. I sat motionlessly whilst the women scrubbed me clean and it wasn't until I was out of the bath that I started to have flash-backs. Horrible, torturous, twisted images of Ahran convulsing as he was hit by each of Evo's bullets and then sinking to the ground; a scene that would scar and haunt me for the rest of my life. I refused to believe it. He can't be dead. He just *can't* be! But the vicious voice in my head insisted that no-one could have survived that, not even Ahran.

At that point, I didn't cry, I didn't feel pain, I didn't feel anything except the most peculiar hollow feeling as if someone had scooped out my insides like a pumpkin at

Halloween. In fact, it didn't feel like I was in my own body, it felt as if I was floating around somewhere near the ceiling, merely an observer, watching the women chatting as they worked, hardly acknowledging I was even there and carrying out their task with well-practiced efficiency.

Once they'd dressed me and I was escorted by a guard through the palace. I'm not sure whether it was the feeling of familiar surroundings or everything beginning to sink in, but suddenly it felt as if someone had flipped open the top of my head and had started to pour in all the feelings and emotions that watching Ahran's death had caused. By the time we arrived at Sulaan's office, I was a swirling mass of hurt and pain.

I stood in front of Sulaan as he eyed me with expectant enquiry and spoke Ramian.

"Ahran is dead," I said, feeling like the words were choking me.

"What do you mean, Ahran is dead?" he said, switching to English.

"Ahran was shot by Evo and now he's *dead*!" I said, grimacing at his obtuseness and losing all patience as the force of emotions began to build in intensity. Suddenly, I felt extremely agitated, like a battery that had been over-charged. Every atom in my body jiggled restlessly, trying in vain to discharge some of the energy that now threatened to have me thrashing around the room like some mad woman wrecking everything in her path.

"What are you talking about?" he persisted.

Every part of me was willing it not to be true, but the pain was resolutely seeping into every cell of my body.

Unfortunately for Sulaan, he was the first person to hear it, and all the fear and grief that I felt was compelling me to hurt him in the same way it was hurting me.

The door opened. It was Leylana.

The sight of the Queen, my dear friend and confidante, made me crumple to my knees and sob into my hands. I would have run to her and thrown my arms around her if the restless energy caused by the shock I had been feeling moments before, hadn't just sapped out of me like water down a drain. "Ahran is dead," I whispered. They were the three most painful words I had ever spoken.

She and Sulaan exchanged words, whilst I sat there in my misery, struggling to behave like someone who still had a grip on their sanity and wishing I had some kind of inbuilt self-destruct button I could press that would bring about my immediate demise.

"What do you mean Ahran is dead?" she said, echoing Sulaan's exact words.

I looked up. "Evo Salanda…shot him and now he's…" I just couldn't say it again.

Leylana looked at me quizzically, not at all convinced by what I was saying.

"Didn't you hear me? Ahran is dead!" I screamed, hoping the more I said it the more someone would shake me by the shoulders and tell me to come to my senses.

"I was sucked into the portal and couldn't go back to him and I…" I broke down, unable to say anymore.

"He's not dead," she replied, clearly in denial.

I understood her disbelief, I was having a hard enough

time believing it myself, but I wasn't sure whether I had the strength or the patience to explain it again.

"I have just spoken to him," she continued.

I looked up, not sure I'd heard her correctly. "What do you mean you've just spoken to him?" Had I got it all wrong? Had I just been given a grain of hope that he hadn't died and had somehow made it back to Ramia? Maybe he was being treated in hospital at this very moment.

Leylana made a phone call and I wiped my tears with the back of my hand.

I gripped the arm of the nearest chair, fearing I might faint and struggling to comprehend what was happening. "Can I have a glass of water please?"

Sulaan filled a glass and handed it to me. I drank deeply. Leylana waited whilst I composed myself. A few moments later, the door opened and I looked up regaining my senses in time to see Ahran walking through the door chatting and laughing with the man following him.

Words failed me as I stared at him. Perhaps I had been drugged and in my stupor had conjured up the sick daydream that had me witnessing his death, because here he was, stood before me, in all his glorious *aliveness* with no hint of an injury.

I stared at him for a moment or two and then ran to him, throwing myself into his arms. "I thought you were dead!" I cried, sobbing into his chest. He was like some miraculous apparition. How long had I been in the portal? It must have been days, weeks even, because Ahran was standing here, fit and strong; his gunshot wounds healed! I sent up a silent prayer thanking God for the strength of his Ramian constitution.

He patted my back lightly and then set me away from him.

"Sorry, do I know you?"

His question caught me off-guard.

I looked up into his face, his confused expression forcing me to take a step backward. "It's me…Sophie," I said, half expecting him to say *"Joke! Come here and give me a hug,"* and preparing myself to give him a right roasting for being so bloody insensitive.

I shook my head as if to dislodge the tiresome blockage that was preventing me from getting a handle on the situation. "Sweetheart, it's…me," I said, falteringly. It suddenly struck me that his hair was longer than it had been.

Ahran looked at me blankly and glanced over my shoulder at Leylana. I was overcome by an ice-cold fear as a horrible realisation began to dawn on me. "You don't know… who I am…do you?"

He shook his head. "No, I'm sorry, I don't."

I turned towards Leylana to seek her reassurance. "You do, don't you?"

"I'm sorry dear, but none of us know who you are." Suddenly, I felt like I was back in the portal with no grip on reality. What the *hell* was going on?!

I glanced at the man standing next to Ahran who was looking at me as blankly as everyone else. He was just as tall and athletically built, but his dark, brown hair wisped into the beginnings of what would have been curls if he'd allowed it to grow any longer. And then I looked into his eyes, realising I did know who he was after all.

"Ho-ly mo-ther of God," I whispered, fumbling for the chair and gaping at the living dead who had literally just walked through the door.

Tagan looked at me with what barely amounted to mild interest before speaking to Ahran.

"Are you feeling unwell?" Leylana said.

I tore my eyes from him and turned my attention to the Queen. "How is it that Tagan's alive?" I asked in utter disbelief.

"Who are you and how do you know anything about us?" Ahran asked, eyeing me with suspicion, his lack of recognition making my chest feel tight.

My eyes snapped back to him. "I…I'm…" I stuttered. I was trying to piece together what had happened, but my poor brain just wouldn't play ball. I glanced at Leylana and Sulaan and then at Ahran and Tagan, in an attempt to come up with a feasible explanation.

"Who has sent you? Who are you working for?" Sulaan asked, beginning to show his impatience.

"I don't work for anyone," I said, feeling panicked.

"How do you know about the portal?" Tagan asked.

"Ahran told me."

Tagan looked at Ahran who shrugged and said something in Ramian.

"You seem to know us all," Leylana said. "How is it that you know who we are?" Her tone was less sharp than Ahran's.

"Because you are my family, mine and Toby's family," I said, the tears beginning to stream silently down my cheeks.

"Where's Toby?" I asked as panic began to replace my confusion.

Leylana looked blank. "You are disorientated my dear." She turned to Sulaan. "Get the poor girl, something to eat and drink."

I gave a humourless snort. *How bloody typical?!* Trust a Ramian to think that food would sort this mess out!

"Look, I don't want anything to eat, I just want to go back." Maybe if I went through the portal again everything would be normal. But back in Paris, Ahran was dead. I closed my eyes to the pain and then opened them to see him standing in front of me. I had never felt so relieved, and yet so utterly confused.

All four of them began a somewhat heated discussion, which I could only assume was about me.

I had to buy myself some time. There was so much I needed to try and unravel.

"Actually, I'm not feeling too good. Maybe after some food and rest, things will be clearer," I said, when there was a lull in their conversation.

Sulaan looked like he was about to argue, but Leylana silenced him with her answer. And then he took hold of my elbow and began to steer me out of the room. I looked back at Ahran desperately, but the lack of recognition and suspicion in his eyes nearly killed me.

Followed by two armed guards, Sulaan and I walked through the palace to one of the guest suites. I contemplated whether to plead with him to take me back to the portal, but his expressionless countenance was all the indication I needed to know that I would be wasting my time. I had witnessed this implacable streak in him before. For the most part Sulaan was a pleasant, if not a jovial sort of person, and I knew he took his service to the royal household very seriously. There was nothing I could say or do that would make him disobey the Queen's orders.

"You are to stay here, until you are sent for," he said, before closing the door between us and locking it. I stared at the back of the door, momentarily paralysed as I listened to their footsteps fade away.

When all was silent, I began to restlessly pace the room, playing the last hour over and over in my mind, trying to come up with some reasonable explanation as to what had happened. Half of me was still in shock after witnessing Ahran's cold-blooded murder, the other half of me dared to feel relief, knowing that somehow, he seemed to be very much *alive*. I grabbed handfuls of hair at my temples in frustration, feeling like I wanted to pull it out at the roots. How could I not be thankful that he was living and breathing? But, how could I cope knowing he didn't have clue as to who I was?

"No, come on Sophie, this isn't really happening, wake-up, *wake-up!*" I said, shaking my arms restlessly. I waited for that moment when you come to from a horrible dream, flushed with relief that it was *only* a dream; a cruel mechanism of the subconscious mind sifting through one's biggest fears and life experiences. But nothing happened, I didn't wake up. I was already wide awake.

I began to violently shake and sank into a heap on the

floor. I'm not sure how long I stayed there, the sense of loss, fear and hopelessness incapacitated me to the point where I thought I might actually die from it. I'd heard of people dying from a broken heart, but my heart wasn't broken, it had been completely and utterly obliterated.

23

I was in such a state of shock that I hardly noticed a servant bring in a tray of food. The last thing I felt like doing was eating.

What the hell had happened and what in God's name was I going to do about it? Dying a slow painful death brought about by my own misery seemed infinitely preferable to carrying on, but as much as I willed it to happen it wasn't about to. Another option would be to finish myself off with the belt on the white fluffy dressing gown that no doubt was hanging on the back of the bathroom door. I grimaced at the thought. I had to focus on the fact that Ahran was alive and bizarrely, so was Tagan. I also had to find out what had happened to Toby. Maybe I should just try to get back to the portal. But there was no telling whether it would even be open and even if it was, I couldn't face the thought of seeing Ahran dead, nor risk encountering Evo again.

And so, as I deliberated, two explanations began to

present themselves. Had I stumbled into a parallel, *parallel* universe?

I shook my head. It seemed unlikely that they would also have portals to Earth and for there to be doubles of Ahran, Leylana and Sulaan. It was too crazy to even contemplate and yet the other possibility, was just as ridiculous.

I began to question my sanity. I stood up and paced the floor again. "I'm going mad," I said, clutching my head. "This time, I have well and truly gone mad!" I walked the length of the room. "It's all a figment of my imagination," I said, walking back again. "There's no such thing as *time travel*," I muttered and then I stopped dead as a thought occurred to me. "Oh God! Maybe Ramia doesn't even exist, maybe it has all just been the creation of an over-active, *psychotic* mind!" I started to feel like I might hyperventilate and sat down, putting my head between my knees, taking deep breaths and counting as I exhaled. Instinctively, my hand went to my neck in search of the pebble Ahran had given me to seal our engagement and my fingers came to rest on its smooth surface reassuring me that I hadn't lost all grip on reality.

This was ridiculous, the last two years had happened, Ramia was real and so was Ahran. Not to mention the love I felt for him, which was not only real, but life affirming and sanity saving! I hadn't gone mad. I sat up and slowly began to talk myself back down, trying to piece it all together.

As incomprehensible as it was, I had to look at the facts. No-one here knew me and they didn't seem to know who Toby was either. Tagan was alive, as was Ahran. Time travel was the most likely explanation. I laughed out loud. This was insane, stories may have been written about it, but nobody *actually* did it. Ramia might be ahead of Earth in lots of ways, but in the two years I had spent here, I had never heard of anyone travelling through time. It was a preposterous idea and yet here I was, seemingly in the past.

I reminded myself that there had been a time when the idea of travelling through a portal to another world where a race of super-humans existed, seemed equally outrageous. Since then I had not only found out my nephew was half alien, I had also fallen in love with one of them. If I couldn't accept the bizarre and extraordinary there was little hope for anyone else. The big question was, if indeed I had travelled back in time, how far had I gone?

I snorted, *God!* How many times had I wished I could travel to the past and right all the wrongs that had happened in my life? And then the next thought hit me like a lightning bolt and temporarily superseded all my other woes. "Katie!"

I sat up straighter and my heart beat faster. If I had time travelled, would she be alive and would I be able to see her again? I started to consider this impossible possibility and wanted to laugh and cry at the same time. I hadn't a clue how it could have happened, but if Tagan was alive, there was a distinct possibility Katie was too.

I began to daydream about what it would be like to have the chance to tell my sister I love her, argue with her, shop with her, tell her my deepest darkest secrets, all those things that most sisters take for granted and what I had been deprived of for the last three years. I hugged myself and laughed through the tears. And then another thought occurred to me; could I prevent her death? I was stunned by this realisation and it was some time before I was able to think coherently again.

My thoughts became more and more erratic. What did I know about time travel? Wasn't there some delicate time equilibrium that needed to be maintained? Would I have to be careful about what I said or did in case it detrimentally influenced the future? Who knew whether what I had said or done had not already changed things? I sighed, it was pointless worrying about it. If indeed I had travelled back in time, I would be a fool not to at least try and save my sister's life. The only problem was, I was in Ramia, locked in a room; a prisoner.

My mind fired one disconnected thought after another as I tried to make sense of everything and how I could exploit the possibilities that seemed to have presented themselves. There was so much to think about I could hardly process it all. If I managed to save Katie's life, what then? Was it at all possible that I could return to my own time? I had absolutely no idea, and spent the next hour wrangling with all the possible permutations of being trapped in a different time realm.

Just before one of the palace guards came to take me back to the Queen, I reached a realisation that gave me some comfort. I had been in difficult situations before, admittedly they weren't circumstances quite as catastrophic as these, but I knew I was stronger now. The last two years with Ahran had taught me so much. I no longer felt damaged by the loss and suffering that had so tainted my view of the future and sapped all my strength. Thanks to

Ahran I was a much better version of myself. I almost laughed at the irony. At one time my past had been something that had caused me so much pain and fear, and yet the time I had spent with Ahran, was now the only thing that gave me hope. I drew strength from it. He had made me a better person, more resilient, braver. I took a deep breath. I was scared out of my wits, but I would at least try to unravel this mess one stitch at a time.

I WAS COLLECTED by a guard who walked me back to Leylana's office, where she and Sulaan were waiting.

"I hope you have had a chance to rest," Leylana said from behind her desk.

I stood in front of her, wringing my hands with nervous anticipation. Sulaan stood behind her, his face, as usual, expressionless.

It was difficult coming to terms with the fact that the Queen and I were strangers. I took a deep breath and tried to put myself in the right head space. "Thank you my Lady, yes I did," I said, addressing her as a subject should.

"Take a seat." She gestured towards the chair in front of the desk.

"Thank you." There was no sign of Ahran and I felt my strength beginning to diminish as I sat down. *I can do this, I can do this*, I chanted to myself.

Her warm, chocolatey eyes surveyed me. "Let's start with your name," she said.

"It's, S…" I stopped myself. Something told me I shouldn't reveal my real identity.

I chose my mother's name. "It's Grace, my Lady."

"Please could you tell us how you know about our world Grace, and how it is that you have come here?"

I contemplated my answer. "I am not here to cause any trouble," I said, trying to keep my voice neutral. "But please believe me when I say that it is better for everyone that I say as little as possible."

"I think we are entitled to an explanation," she said patiently. "You coming here *uninvited*, is a serious matter and represents a risk to our world and its security. You should be thankful that my husband is away on business because I am not sure he would be so lenient."

"You have to believe me when I say I know better than anyone how important it is to keep your world secret, and I want to reassure you in any way I can, that I do not mean any harm." I took a deep breath. "Please could you tell me what the date is today?"

She threw a quizzical look at Sulaan before answering.

I sat there in a daze for a moment or two. *Jesus Christ!* It was more than a decade in the past! I could hardly believe it, I had indeed travelled back in time and Katie would still be alive.

Whilst I had been in my room I had come up with a plan, albeit a sketchy one. At first I had thought I would just try and call Katie to warn her of her death, but the desire to see her was so strong that I knew I had to somehow get back to Earth. I would then return to Ramia to do everything in my power to get back to my own time, preferably before Ahran had been shot. Of course, there were inherent weaknesses in this plan. Firstly, I had to get Leylana to agree to let me return to Earth. Secondly, I wasn't sure if having time travelled once, I wouldn't time travel again. And Thirdly, if I managed to do these things, I had no idea how I was going to return to the time I wanted to.

"I know I am not in any position to be making requests," I said with as much humility as I could muster, "But I would like to ask you to consider allowing me to travel to Earth. It really is a matter of life and death." My stomach was in knots and I struggled to think where Katie would have been eleven years ago. "Once I have tended to this urgent business, I will return to Ramia to answer all your questions."

"What is it that you need to do so urgently?" she asked.

"I…I can't tell you."

"I'm afraid I cannot allow you to leave the palace," she said with a hint of frustration.

"I beg you, please let me return to Earth, I cannot tell you how important it is."

"I'm not sure you understand the position you are in," Sulaan interjected.

Neither the Queen, nor Sulaan looked at all like they were about to agree to my demands and I began to feel the prickle of fear and desperation.

I stood up and gripped the edge of her desk. "You've got to let me go back," I pleaded.

Sulaan approached me and put a restraining hand on my arm. "Please… sit down!" he insisted.

I sat down on the verge of bursting into tears, but I knew I had a trump card. It was the one thing, over and above anything else that would persuade Leylana to agree to my demands.

"I have information about your son," I said.

This caught her off-guard. "My son?"

I nodded. Even though I was about to blackmail Leylana, my heart felt a little lighter knowing that after all the love and kindness she had shown me over the last two years, I could spare her grief.

"Yes," I replied.

Sulaan spoke to Leylana and they exchanged words. Eventually, Sulaan stepped back, silenced by whatever Leylana said to him and not looking at all happy.

"Please continue," she said.

"What if I were to tell you that I know of your son's death?"

Leylana's eyes widened. She clearly hadn't been expecting this.

"You are talking rubbish girl! What kind of...of...." She struggled for the word in English, "*Soottensayoor* are you?" She said, resorting to Ramian. I had rarely seen Leylana angry and I felt guilty for making her feel like this, but I held my nerve knowing that my intentions were for the best.

I leaned forward and looked directly into her eyes. "I will strike a deal with you," I said, ignoring her accusations and trying to keep the tremor out of my voice. "If you let me go back to Earth for a short while, no questions asked, I will return and give you information that will save your son from an early death."

Leylana stood up abruptly. "Take her back to her room!" she said, angrily.

"*Please* Leylana, I promise you, I'm telling the truth!"

She didn't answer and turned her back on me to look out of the window.

Sulaan grabbed my arm and I could no longer hold back the tears. "Your majesty *please!*" She didn't answer and I was frogmarched out of her office.

Once again, I was locked in my room, all my hopes and plans shattered. I slid down the door hopelessly.

I didn't touch the food that was brought to me some time later. I'm not sure I had ever felt more despairing. My plan had failed. Ahran may well be alive, but he was no longer mine. I had no way of getting in contact with Katie and I was stuck in a time I didn't belong in. I was stupid to think that I could try and blackmail Leylana into meeting my demands. Why would she? There was no reason to believe me, to them I was just a hopeless Sapien who had stumbled into their world. What more could I say? Should I tell her everything and risk impacting the future so much that if I was ever to return to my present, nothing would be the same?

I spent a restless night, stricken by my own misery, missing Ahran and Toby and unable to come up with anything that seemed like a way forward. I watched the sun rise and feared what the day may bring. If the King returned today, I would stand next to no chance of getting what I wanted. I had to try and win Leylana round, but after yesterday, I wasn't at all sure how I was going to do this. It was a desperate situation and I hit the pillow in frustration. I thought I was stronger, but it turns out that at the first hurdle without Ahran, I had crumpled. I cried more tears and pitifully mourned my loss, which was only made worse by the very real possibility that I probably would never see Toby again.

Eventually, as the sun began to rise and feeling exhausted and despairing, I got up, had a shower and wrapped myself in the dressing gown that hung on the bathroom door. I padded out to the table next to the window where my breakfast had been left. Feeling hopeless, I sat down and stared out at the familiar view, but not really taking any of it in. I was mindlessly watching two birds of prey dive-bombing each other when I heard the door click and then open.

I jumped up expecting to see Sulaan or a servant, but Leylana walked in and closed the door behind her. She was immaculately turned out, as usual, but looked as if she'd had about as much sleep as I'd had.

"Leylana," I said with surprise, forgetting we weren't on first named terms.

"I want to talk to you," she said with a slight abrasiveness I wasn't used to.

I tightened the belt at my waist, wishing now I had put some clothes on.

"Yes, yes of course."

"Take a seat." She gestured to the sofa next to her. "The King would be most displeased if he knew I was here."

Even though the Queen did pretty much as she pleased

in and around the royal household, it was not following protocol for her to come to the room of a prisoner, unaccompanied. If anything, she should have summonsed me to her office, but here she was and I dared to hope that this was a good sign.

Feeling unequipped for this meeting, I sat down and pulled together the hems of my gown.

Leylana remained standing. "I still have no idea who you are and why you are here," she began. "For all I know you could be a spy, a criminal, a *mad* woman," she said, throwing her hands up in the air and eyeing me as if she still wasn't sure she'd made the right decision to come here.

"I'm not here to cause trouble," I said, repeating the reassurances I had tried to give her yesterday.

"There is a part of me that thinks I should just go ahead and tell my husband about you."

I remained silent, willing her not to.

"But something stops me."

I breathed a little easier.

"I like to think I'm a good judge of character and I'd like to believe that you are not a bad person."

I closed my eyes briefly in relief and nodded.

"Are you a mother?" she asked.

"No, I am not," I said, shaking my head.

"Then maybe you would not understand what it feels like to be told that your son will die."

"I'm sorry," I said, watching a range of emotions chase across her features. At that moment in time I hated myself for causing her pain.

"I want to ask you a question," she said. "Woman to woman."

I nodded, encouraging her to continue. In that moment, I knew I loved Leylana. She was smart, emotionally intelligent and so in tune with people that she was able to operate on a different level when it came to her relationships with others. I was pretty certain she had spent a sleepless night agonising over what she should do. It would seem that now she was putting her royal duties and loyalties aside and speaking as a mother. How could she not try and find out more? It was my guess that she hadn't made a conscious decision to come here this morning because sense would have prevailed and told her otherwise, if I was not mistaken, she was operating on instinct—a mother's instinct, which dictated that above all else she was bound to love and protect her child.

If my feelings for Toby were any measure, I had some understanding of how she was feeling. Had I not protected him as if he were my own son?

She took a deep breath. "Why are you here?"

"I didn't mean to come here." I wasn't ready to share my theory just yet. "But I do have information that for both our sakes, I urge you not to ignore."

She sat next to me, which I took as an indication to continue and I began. "I know that Tagan is in the Ramian army and that you are at war with Bazeera of Morana."

"Anyone would know that," she said, still not fully prepared to trust me.

I ploughed on. "Your son takes his role in the army very seriously and he is a good and talented leader."

She nodded.

"Tagan and Ahran are great friends and have been since they were boys." I smiled. "I know that they used to worry you with their fearlessness and sense of adventure."

"Yes, they did," she said, wryly.

I felt she was beginning to thaw just a little.

"Ahran and Tagan had a secret language they used when they wanted to communicate with each other without anyone else knowing," I said, recalling what Ahran had told me about it and hoped that this inside knowledge would give me some credibility.

She gave me a half-smile, half-frown. "It was infuriating."

I felt like I was winning her over sentence by sentence and paused for a moment.

"How do you know all of this?" she asked

"I'm sorry, but I can't tell you just yet."

"You promised you would tell me information that would help me protect my son," she said, withdrawing a little.

"I will," I said, pausing briefly. Talking about Ahran was hurting, but I resigned myself to the thought that there was little I could do about him at that moment, all I could do was focus my energies on saving my sister. "But first you must let me return to Earth."

She stood up and walked to the window. I could only assume that she was debating whether to trust me as well as grappling with the need to protect Ramia and the desire to save her son's life.

After what seemed like forever, she turned around.

"Okay, I will let you return to Earth for one day with an armed guard."

"A day may not be long enough" I said without thinking.

"It's all I can offer you," she replied.

I knew she was taking a great risk by agreeing to this without consulting Halsan, but she had no choice other than to accept.

I took a deep breath. "Okay. Thank you." I began to think through my plan to find Katie. "Do you have a portal that goes to London?"

She nodded. "Yes, in the palace grounds."

I let out the breath I'd been holding. "Good. When can I leave?" I was beginning to feel more optimistic than I had a right to.

YULA, one of Leylana's personal bodyguards who, although short for Ramian standards, was power-packed and intimidating, walked me to the site of the portal. It was September, Katie would be at University and it was only a few weeks before she would meet Tagan. I had been wracking my brain to try and remember Katie's phone number, but it was no good, I couldn't remember any number from eleven years ago, not even my own. So I would just have to do my best and try and find her. I knew she would be here because the new term was underway and it was close to the time I went travelling. I was pretty sure I'd spent some time with her before I left.

My heart hammered as we approached the portal, not

only because my recent experience had made me more wary of portal travel, but because I was about to see my sister who, as far as I was concerned, had died three years ago. It was one of the strangest feelings I'd ever had. What would she think when she saw me? I was in actual fact eleven years older than the nearly eighteen-year-old she knew. My hair was certainly different; short and dark, not the long, blonde, braided hair of my student years, but did I look that much older? I liked to think that living in Ramia for the last two years had hindered the ageing process somewhat and I hoped I'd get away with it.

"After you," Yula said.

"Okay," I said, slightly breathless with nerves. Was this really happening? *You don't really think you can pull this off, do you?* "Oh, shut up!" I said, trying to silence the dissenting voice in my head.

Yula looked affronted.

"Oh sorry, not you." I smiled weakly.

I squeezed my eyes shut and my fists tight. I stepped into the portal and considered it a good sign that I didn't feel any of the hurtling and spinning I had experienced yesterday, only mild nausea, a sign of normal portal travel. That's if you could say any of this was *normal.*

We stepped out from behind a large beech tree and found our way onto a tarmac path. We were in a London park and it was a short while before I realised I'd been here before, it was Lincoln's Inn Fields park and was only a ten-minute walk to Embankment and Katie's faculty. My thoughts raced. The new academic year would be underway and the university was a good place to start.

We walked out onto the street and I could feel the clock ticking with every beat of my heart. I was inadequately dressed for the crisp, late September day, but was oblivious to the cold, thanks to the adrenaline that was pumping through my veins. It was a measured long shot coming here.

We reached the Arts and Humanities building and entered the foyer. I scanned the area hoping to see her. It was of course like looking for a needle in a haystack. I caught sight of a boy and a girl chatting next to a vending machine and my heart jumped into my throat. "Oh my God! It's her!" I said, not quite able to believe my luck. All the heartache of the last three years vanished in a heartbeat as I looked on at my sister who was stood just a few metres away from me living and breathing. I rushed over to her.

"Katie!" I said, touching her arm, feeling like my heart was about to burst.

She turned around and smiled.

I tried my very best to match the face in front of me to the face I loved so much, but failed miserably. I faltered as if I was about to faint. It wasn't her.

"I'm sorry, I thought you were someone else," I said, trying to pull myself together and on the verge of tears.

"No worries," the girl replied and turned back to the guy she was chatting to. With my track record, I was stupid to think I could be *that* lucky.

I approached the reception desk doing my best to recover from the worst possible case of mistaken identity.

"Oh, hi," I said as cheerily as I could to the receptionist who had just put the phone down.

She looked up at me with a smile. "Can I help you?"

"I hope so," I said, putting the disappointment of the girl at the vending machine not being Katie behind me and tried to sound charming yet vulnerable. "My sister is a student here and I need to get hold of her urgently. I've lost my phone and all my contacts with it and was wondering whether you could help."

I could see in her eyes what her answer would be, even before she'd said it.

"I'm sorry. We cannot give out our student's contact details. Data protection and all that," she said with a shrug.

"You don't understand. It's a family emergency and I need to speak to her urgently." I was beginning to lose my cool.

She shook her head. "I'm sorry, I really can't."

I took a deep breath. "Okay then, would you be able to phone her so that I could talk to her?" I would rather not have the conversation I was about to have with my beloved sister, whose death I had heart-wrenchingly mourned in the middle of this busy foyer, but if it was the only chance I had, then I would take it.

The receptionist thought about this for a moment. "I'll see what I can do," she said kindly. "What is her name?" She clicked the mouse of her computer several times.

"Katie McAllister. She's a History student here."

"How are you spelling McAllister?"

I spelt out our surname and tapped my fingers on the desk nervously.

"I can't see...oh, wait a minute Katie Anne McAllister?"

"Yes, that's her!"

The receptionist picked up the phone and dialled, passing the receiver to me.

The myriad of emotions I felt in those few seconds was almost more than I could bear. As I tried to think about what I would say I choked back the tears at the thought of *actually* speaking to her.

My hopes began to fade when I realised she wasn't answering. After two more rings the answerphone kicked in. The crushing disappointment paralysed me for a moment or two. *Jesus!* Was I going to have to warn my sister about her death in years to come in an *answerphone message*?

Her voicemail bleeped in my ear, I didn't have time to prevaricate, so I began to deliver my message regardless. "Er, Katie…it's me. This is going to sound completely random…" The receptionist was listening. I gave her a little smile and turned my back on her, lowering my voice slightly.

"There's something I need to tell you…God this is so hard." I took a deep breath. "Okay, it isn't going to make much sense, but promise me that no matter what happens you will do exactly as I say."

I proceeded to tell her that if her son, who she hadn't actually had yet, was invited to a birthday party on that November day, she wasn't to let him go. I kept it vague, but hopefully giving enough information so as to prevent the tragic events that had led to her death.

"So I guess, that's about it," I said, having delivered my cryptic, but hopefully life-saving message. I was reluctant to put the phone down. And then a thought struck me. I had been so wrapped up with the situation I had found myself in and exploiting it to save my sister that I hadn't even thought about my mother. She would still be alive too.

"There's one more thing," I said, putting the phone back to my ear. "Tell mum to go to the doctors and get her heart checked out." I knew I wasn't actually speaking to Katie, but just talking to her answerphone felt like I was connecting with her in some way.

"Oh, and…I love you." There was so much more I wanted to say, but I had to stick to my plan to not say more than I could get away with. I swallowed back the tears and handed the phone back to the receptionist.

"Are you okay?" she asked.

I shook my head, "No, I'm not, but thanks for your help."

I looked miserably at Yula and walked numbly out of the building. I had no idea whether what I had just done would work. My future was so uncertain that even if my sister did survive, there was no guarantee I would see her again. I sat on the steps outside the building and tried to gather my thoughts. I could spend the whole day chasing around London trying to find her to no avail. I scrubbed my face with my hands. "Arghhh!"

25

I sat there for some time thinking through my options. I had a day on Earth, I wasn't sure where Katie was and had no way of contacting her. Maybe I could go and visit my mother. I could be fairly certain she would be at the coffee shop, she never missed a day and she would have Katie's number. If I couldn't see Katie, maybe I could at least see my mum. Yes, that's what I would do, I would visit my mother.

Although the decisions had been made, I made no effort to move as the enormity of what I was about to do sunk in. My mother had died five years ago, her death had been a shock and there were days when I missed her, especially after Katie's death, but we had never been close, not helped by my mother's bouts of depression after my father's death. I guess this is what had made Katie and I so inseparable. However, there was a part of me that longed to see her, somebody who was my own flesh and blood, somebody I could call my own because at that moment in time I felt so dreadfully alone. I had nobody. I willed my tears to stay put and stood up determined not to waste this opportunity I never dreamed I would ever have.

"Yula," I smiled apologetically. "Could I go and see my mother? She is about an hour's train journey away?"

He shrugged. "All the Queen said was you have a day. It's up to you how you spend it."

Before I could stop myself, I hugged him and he responded like a stiff board, I don't think he'd been expecting my affection. "Thank you." In spite of his aloofness, I sensed he felt some pity for my plight.

"I don't suppose you have any money for the train fare?" I asked with a tight-lipped smile, realising that I had nothing.

"Leave it with me," he said. I can't say he smiled, but his expression definitely softened.

I SAT on the lunchtime train and watched the familiar Sussex countryside speed past. Yula was sitting next to me and for a time his large presence drew some interested stares, but as the journey progressed the few people who travelled with us began to mind their own business, their attention drawn back to their book or newspaper. It struck me that there was something different about the way the people on the train behaved, until I realised that there wasn't one person on their phone. It was easy to forget that there was a time when people weren't surgically attached to their smartphones. I smiled wryly to myself, it was difficult to tell whether modern technology had freed us or tethered us to this small, but demanding, electronic device. I knew I was as guilty as the next person for checking social media, my email, the news, the weather or any random Safari search that popped into my head, but I couldn't help thinking the worship of this little 21st century demi-god was getting out of hand and it concerned me to think where it all might end.

I sighed and looked back out the window. I only had a day, there was little I could do to save mankind from the plight of the smartphone so I turned my attention back to the reason for me making this trip and felt a surge of emotions. I had butterflies at the prospect of seeing my mother, which were mixed with a range of other emotions I hadn't felt since her death. They were the old feelings of rejection, helplessness and anger at a mother who all too often felt out of reach. Katie and I weren't neglected as children, our mother provided us with a roof over our heads and food on the table and even though we didn't feel the love of a mother in a way that should be the right of every child, she loved us as best she could.

Yula nudged me whilst adjusting his large frame in the train seat. "Sorry," he said.

He was a silent companion and I felt no need to try and make conversation. I smiled and returned to the silent chattering of my mind. I did my best not to dwell on the mess I was in and I made every effort not to think about Ahran or Toby. So much had happened in the last couple of years, things that were so extraordinary that if someone had come up to me with a crystal ball and had told me what was going to happen I would have laughed in their face. I, therefore, tried to comfort myself with the thought that the impossible was not necessarily always so impossible and this helped me cling to the hope that maybe by some miracle I would find my way back to Ahran and Toby. Even beginning to think how I might start, was enough to send me crazy, so I decided that I would take it hour by hour, exploit any opportunity I had and gather as much information as I could. After all, I didn't know what I didn't know and it was pointless throwing myself around in a frenzy of despair. I had a good brain, I would just have to be smart about how I went about things. And so, with only ten minutes left of our journey, it occurred to me that I had not only been given the opportunity to see my mother again, but this was one of those opportunities to be exploited. Could she shed some light on something that had been bothering me for some time? Her answer could have a significant bearing on my future.

YULA and I pulled up in a taxi outside the coffee shop, and I looked up at the store front. It had the old signage and paintwork and didn't look quite like my coffee shop, but then I guess it wasn't, it was my mother's. Yula paid the taxi driver and I got out of the car with my heart in my throat. I approached the front door not quite sure how to greet my mum and pushed on it. I was greeted by that old familiar smell of coffee and toast.

I scanned the place anticipating the first glimpse of my mother, but the only middle aged waitress I could see was the woman who had always been there for me, when my own mother had not. I groped for the back of a chair, my lungs feeling like the air had just been sucked out of them. I had been so wrapped up in how I would feel about seeing my mum, I had forgotten about Audrey. She was a sight for sore eyes.

She looked in my direction obviously having sensed someone had just walked through the door. It was a moment or two before I saw the recognition in her eyes. She finished taking the order from a vaguely familiar gentleman and came over to where I stood rooted to the spot.

With tears in my eyes, I threw my arms around her and hugged her tightly. She hugged me back before stepping away. "Your mum didn't tell me you were coming home. Aren't you going off on your travels in a day or two?"

Of course! I was about to go off travelling and I had decided to spend a few days with Katie before I left. The reason she wasn't at college was because she was with me. Or should I say, my eighteen-year-old self.

"Er, yes, I am, but I thought I would just make one last trip home to say goodbye and er…thought I'd bring my friend Yula with me to see my home town."

Audrey glanced at my companion clearly trying to draw some conclusion as to whether he might be more than just a friend. He looked exactly like who he was, a bodyguard. She had a puzzled expression on her face, but didn't push me any further.

"It's nice to meet you Yula," she said holding out her hand.

"And you ma'am," he replied, shaking her hand and bowing his head slightly.

"He's a friend from work who wanted to see what rural Sussex was like. He's er…Polish," I said, saying the first thing that came into my head.

Audrey nodded, clearly a little bemused by my unannounced visit and my bald-headed, beefcake of a companion. She smiled politely.

"You've changed your hair, I didn't recognise you at first."

My hand went to my hair self-consciously. "Oh yeah, I fancied a change," I replied. "Do you like it?" I marvelled at how I was discussing something as mundane as my hairstyle with my oldest and dearest friend, eleven years in the past.

She cocked her head to the side whilst trying to think of something tactful to say. "It's quite dark isn't it? I think I prefer it a little longer."

I couldn't have cared less what her thoughts about my hair was, after all that I had been through lately, it just felt incredible to be there with her and I stood with a silly grin on my face. She looked slightly confused by my behaviour.

"Sit down and I'll get you something to eat. Your mum has just popped out to the post office. Does she know you are coming?"

I shook my head. "No, it's a surprise." I temporarily forgot my troubles and felt like the kid at Christmas who had been given everything she had asked for.

I sat down at the nearest empty table and looked up at Audrey, still grinning like a Cheshire cat.

"Just wait there a minute," she said. "I'll just take this order through to Alice," she said distractedly.

Yula sat down and picked up the menu, his Ramian appetite had obviously got the better of him.

"This is my mother's coffee shop, well, mine and my mothers," I said by way of explanation. Yula nodded in a polite, but not overly interested way, before his attention returned to the menu. We sat and waited, my eyes flitting to the door every so often, feeling buzzed at the thought of seeing my mother.

"Right, so what can I get you?" Audrey said slightly breathlessly as she turned to a fresh sheet on her pad.

I ordered a toasted cheese sandwich and a mug of tea. Yula gave his order to Audrey, but I was distracted by the door opening and my mother walking in like some saintly figure from the bible who had been miraculously resurrected. She didn't notice me at first which afforded me a moment to watch her as she removed her coat and gloves. I remembered her green, large weave coat that she had picked up from a charity shop years ago, she loved it especially as it was Aquascutum and had picked it up for next to nothing. Seeing that coat triggered a stream of childhood memories as if someone was holding up a flip book and flashing a silent movie of my early life right in front of my eyes. The whole situation felt utterly surreal and a flood of emotions swept through me.

My mother walked towards me and did a double take when she realised I was sat in front of her. "Sophie?"

I glanced at Yula to see if he had noticed that she had called me Sophie and not Grace. He gave nothing away, so I turned my attention back to my mum who was still looking confused. Clearly my hairstyle was dramatic enough that even my own mother didn't recognise me.

I was rendered speechless. She looked just how I remembered her; her sandy blonde hair was a few shades lighter than her natural colour and styled in her usual, neat bob. She was trim for a woman in her early fifties, and wore her signature cashmere sweater, an a-line skirt, flesh colour tights and brown leather sensible shoes. I don't think I had ever seen her in trousers. No one could accuse her of being a fashion icon, if anything she reminded me of a Stepford wife. Her perfectly neat and well-turned out exterior did an excellent job of belying the black dog which I knew raged within her and sapped her of any emotion that could be spared for those around her. For a long time, I had been angry at her, I couldn't understand why she wasn't like other mothers, but now I realised that she had battled so hard just to keep her head above water. The day my father died precipitated years of depression. When she had a heart attack five years ago, I believed it was her heart's way of saying, *I give up! I'm just not strong enough to deal with this loss.*

I stood up and gave her a lingering hug, "Hi mum, I thought I would surprise you." She smelt just as I remembered and I felt tears sting my eyes.

"What brings you here? I thought you were spending some time with Katie before you leave," she said, pulling away. She seemed happy enough to see me. I can't say I felt that my existence had ever enriched her life, her mental illness had stripped her of any maternal feelings, but she cared for me well enough. Some mothers seek solace in their children after experiencing the loss of their partner, but my mother, for whatever reason, was unable to do this. Instead, Katie and I brought her some relief from her inner darkness not because we were somewhere to channel her love, but because we were more of a distraction.

I continued with my Just-Thought-I'd-Say-A-Last-Goodbye story. "Katie had some errands to run and I wasn't sure when I would see you again, so I thought I would pop back and say goodbye before I leave." I turned to Yula. "My friend here is from Poland and he's not been out of London yet, so I thought I'd kill two birds with one stone." I laughed nervously, it sounded all rather suspect. I shot Yula an apologetic look in the hope that he wouldn't contradict me.

My mother looked from me to him and nodded slowly, but seemed to accept my story.

"Well, it's nice to see you. Have you eaten?"

I stood staring at her not quite able to believe that she was standing there before me, living and breathing.

"Sophie?" she said waving her hand as if to break my trance.

"I, er, no Audrey is just getting us something."

My mother looked at the clock. "I'll join you, I haven't had anything since breakfast. Sit down."

I gathered myself together and we all took a seat at the nearest table.

"How's your sister?"

"Erm, fine," I said noncommittally.

"I thought you were shopping for sunglasses and a swimsuit with her today?"

"Oh yeah, we were, but she had some stuff to do."

Audrey brought us our drinks. "Can you manage on your own for a bit?" My mother asked.

"We are hardly rushed off our feet," Audrey replied, her eyes sweeping over the two other occupied tables. "You sit and enjoy your lunch with your daughter Grace, I'll be fine."

"Thanks, I'll have some of the soup," my mother said, before turning her attention to Yula. "Have…you…been…in…the…country…long?" she said slowly and loudly.

"Er, yes a little while," he said perfectly fluently.

"That's good then," she said, a little affronted that his English was better than she had assumed.

She turned her attention back to me.

"Will you be staying long, or is this a fleeting visit, because if you stay I'll have to make up the spare bed." I know she didn't mean to sound unwelcoming, but my mother had learnt to operate on more of a practical level.

"No, it's just a flying visit. Thanks anyway. Have you been busy mum?" I asked, enjoying having a normal conversation with her. She was just how I remembered and that was kind of comforting in a way. My mother may have had shortcomings, but I was thrilled to be sitting here having a benign conversation about business.

"Well, Monday is always pretty dead, but it keeps me out of mischief."

"Things haven't changed Mondays are still dead," I said,

recalling the slack period at the beginning of the week that I had experienced whilst running the business.

My mother gave me a funny look.

I shifted in my seat uncomfortably realising my mistake. Fortunately, Audrey brought us our lunch and I tried to ignore my little slip. I decided it was a good time to start making the most of this opportunity. I wished beyond anything that I had more than a day. I couldn't help wondering that if I had more time, would my mum and I have a chance of getting to know each other better?

I began a topic of conversation that I hoped she could shed some light on.

"There's been something I keep meaning to ask you," I said after swallowing a mouthful of my sandwich.

She looked over at me as she slurped a spoonful of soup. "What's that?"

"I'd like to find out more about my ancestors."

"Really? What's brought this on?"

"Oh I don't know," I said shrugging and trying to appear as nonchalant as I could. Little did she know that any information she could give me could help me to understand if Ahran and I had a chance of having a family. Of course, I wasn't really in a position to be considering a future with him, when at that moment in time he didn't have a clue who I was. But, I could hope; it was that hope that was preventing me from drowning in the depths of despair. Ahran proposing to me had been the most wonderful moment of my life, but it had brought fresh concerns about whether we would ever be able to have children. I hardly dared to believe that somehow I would find my way back to him, but if I ever did, I was counting on my mother being able to give me some information that might help explain why Katie was able to have a Ramian child. This might then help me to understand what my chances of having a child with Ahran were.

"I was just wondering whether there was anyone who stood out in our family history." It was my guess that there was a Ramian somewhere in my family tree and that I might be able to recognise who it was if they had demonstrated some extraordinary talent or were different in some way. I had reminded myself of the conversation I'd had with Bennie when she had taken it upon herself to do some research on who Ahran Elessar might have been. At the time, I had laughed at her conclusions, but now the idea of extraordinary people in history being Ramian didn't seem so far-fetched. If I could identify someone like that in my family, then I may have the answer I was looking for.

"I'm not sure what you mean," she said, looking puzzled.

"Is there anyone who stood out in their field, like an outstanding athlete or somebody who possessed a talent that set them above the rest?"

My mother thought about this for a moment. "Well, my uncle Henry was a talented Trombonist and used to regularly play at the Guildhall in town."

My great-uncle Henry had been a kindly old man and I remember going to one of his concerts, but he had suffered from polio as a child which had left him with a life-long limp so in spite of how musically talented he may have been, I don't think he was who I was looking for.

"But he wasn't really outstanding."

"He was well-known locally," my mother said, sounding slightly put out that I seemed less than impressed.

"No, I mean someone who was well known nationally or internationally."

My mother looked perplexed. "I can't think of anyone."

"A famous scientist or a commander in the army?"

"Well, there was your great-great grandfather who fought in the first world war."

"He died of influenza," I said, trying not to sound disappointed that I didn't come from a more robust family line.

"He did, but whilst he was in the army he led his regiment to victory, it wasn't until several years later that he died."

"It's got to be someone who didn't have an illness or die," I said.

"I'm sorry to break it to you Sophie, but we all die in the end," my mother said as if she was breaking some terrible news.

I shook my head in frustration. "I know that, mum. I would just be interested to know if there was anyone in our family who was celebrated for their achievements or there was something unusual about them, maybe someone who lived to well into their hundreds?" Of course, I wanted to say anyone who seemed superhuman, but I suspected my mother already thought I was acting strangely, I wasn't about to say anything that might make her question my sanity further.

"I'm sorry, but I can't think of anyone." She paused. "Although, there was your great-grandfather on your father's side who went out for a walk one day and never returned, he made the national press."

"Really?" Was she onto something here? Had he disappeared, never to be seen again because he had returned to Ramia?

I sat further forward in my seat. "Was there anything exceptional about him?"

"Your father used to say he was a brilliant artist, apparently he was much acclaimed. We went to an exhibition in London to see his work once, but I can't say it was my sort of thing. It was all that modern, abstract stuff. Critics say he was ahead of his time, but it left me a bit cold if I'm honest. I prefer paintings of actual things like landscapes and people."

I clapped my hands together. "That could be it!" Maybe the reason he was believed to be ahead of his time was because he was Ramian.

My mother stared at me for a moment. "What could be it? Why all these questions all of a sudden?"

"Oh, I'm just interested that's all. It's fun to think there might be someone remarkable in our family history, don't you think?" Admittedly, it was a fairly lame explanation. However, I couldn't help but be excited by the possibility that my great-grandfather could have been Ramian and perhaps it was because of him that Katie was able to conceive a Ramian child. Did it mean I could too? I felt a flash of hope.

"Is everything alright?" my mother asked.

I looked into her eyes, feeling like I was staring into the face of a ghost. Which to all intents and purposes I was. It wouldn't be long before I would have to leave. Tears prickled my eyes. "No, yes, I mean, it's nothing you should worry about."

"Are you in some sort of trouble? she asked.

"No, I'm fine," I said with a sigh. "Everything is fine."

And then I suddenly remembered something else I must do. "Have you been to the doctor lately mum?"

"The doctor? No, why?"

"Oh, its just er…a friend from school's mum had a heart attack last week. She was er…about your age." I cringed inwardly, she knew most of my friends at school and was bound to ask who it was.

"Who was that then? I haven't heard anything," she said, not disappointing me.

"It was someone in the year below."

"How awful?! Poor girl."

"Apparently, heart disease kills tens of thousands of women every year."

"I didn't realise it was that many," she said.

"Please promise me you'll go and have your heart checked out?"

"But I don't smoke or drink and I eat healthily."

"I'm sure you're fine, but it's just good to get these things checked."

"Yes, yes, okay then, I will." she said, clearly concerned that she may have been remiss by not doing this sooner.

"It is time we were getting back," Yula said, interrupting our conversation.

"We've got plenty of time haven't we?" I said, feeling panicky that he was hurrying me.

"We need to be back by six o'clock."

"Six o'clock? That's not a day."

Yula shrugged, "That is the time I was told."

"Sophie, are you sure everything is okay?" my mum asked. She looked between me and Yula, suddenly paying more attention to him than she had been. "Are you sure this is a friend of yours?" she said, eyeing him.

The last thing I wanted was to cause trouble and for Yula to report back unfavourably to the Queen. I needed her on my side if I had any chance of getting back to the present.

"Yes, don't worry mum. It's just a little joke between us," I said, trying to offer an explanation. "Just a few more minutes?" I said to Yula.

He nodded.

I stood up and and hugged my mother and she hugged me back.

"Are you sure you are going to be okay?"

"I'm absolutely fine, but clearly you are not. What's wrong?"

She pulled me away from her. "I'm worried about you."

I felt tears sting my eyes. "I'm fine, really I'm fine." The last thing I wanted was for her to worry about me. "I think it's finally hit home that I'm going to be away for a year," I said, trying to come up with an explanation for my distress.

My mum nodded seemingly relieved that it wasn't anything more serious. "Well, your sister and I will come and visit at some point, maybe we can meet up in Italy. I've always wanted to go to Italy."

I smiled a shaky smile and gave her another hug.

"That would be good."

"Don't be upset, you'll have so much fun. I'm always on the end of a phone."

I nodded.

I turned to Audrey who was walking towards us obviously having noticed that we were leaving.

"Bye Audes. It was good to see you." I gave her a hug too. "Don't ever work in here on your own, will you?" The last time I had seen Audrey was on a hospital bed after she had been attacked. I hoped that the precautions I was taking to protect Katie and my mum would mean Audrey would never be put in that position again, but it didn't do any harm to warn her.

"No, of course not dear."

"Well, I guess we ought to be going," I said, not wanting to move. I wondered whether I should give up any hope of going back to my former present and just stay here instead. I looked up at Yula who was beginning to look impatient. But, I would never be able to persuade him to leave me here and there was also the matter of my eighteen-year-old self floating around somewhere. What would happen if we were to meet?

"Goodbye then," I said and reluctantly turned to leave.

"Sophie?" my mother said before I had taken a step.

I turned back to her.

"You know that I love you, don't you." she said.

It was the first time she had ever said it. "I love you too mum."

I knew it would not have escaped Yula's notice that my mother had called me Sophie, but I chose not to raise the issue with him on our way back. We returned to the palace with seconds to spare and I was taken straight to Leylana's office.

"I trust you attended to your urgent business?" she said.

"Er, yes, thank you." I replied.

"Take a seat."

She sat down at her desk whilst Sulaan continued to hover behind her. "You don't look very happy," she said.

"Things didn't quite pan out as I had hoped."

"I'm sorry to hear that. Now, I believe you have something to tell me." There was a noticeable strain in her voice. I wanted to put my arms around her as I had done so many times before to comfort her and to feel her calm reassurance, but I knew I couldn't.

"Yes," I replied, knowing there was no easy way for me to say it. I wanted to save Tagan just as much as I wanted to save my sister, but in my haste to save her, I hadn't considered whether it was right to play God in this way. I began to feel increasingly uneasy about it.

"Could I have some water?" I asked, my mouth suddenly going dry.

Yula poured me a glass from the pitcher on the desk and handed it to me.

"What information do you have about my son?" Leylana said, clearly impatient for me to begin.

I took a deep breath. "This isn't easy." Like in my message to Katie, I was only going to tell her enough to save Tagan and no more. And then something occurred to me, if I successfully saved Tagan's life I needn't have gone to Earth to warn Katie. If he survived, then surely she would live. I brushed it off, there was no telling if any of what I was doing would change the course of history and I comforted myself with the thought that at least I was covering all my bases.

"Your son will be killed whilst on manoeuvres a few months from now."

Leylana hesitated and then laughed, looking relieved. "I'm sorry my dear, you are mistaken. I can happily say that my son is no longer in the army."

She stood up as if about to dismiss me.

"You are right and he is about to return to Earth to continue with his year of travelling."

I leaned forward in my chair. "Bazeera of Morana will launch a surprise attack on your western borders in a few months' time and because Tagan believes he owes it to his country... and his men," I added, "He will return to Dinara and together with Ahran, they will lead a crack force to try and defeat her army."

She knew as well as I did how loyal Tagan was, I also knew that they had received intelligence that Bazeera was up to something, but they didn't know what. I told her more and Sulaan noted it down.

When I had finished, she stared at me, looking very pale.

"I'm sorry, I don't mean to upset you."

"I can't say any of this makes much sense, but can I afford to not listen to you?"

I shook my head. "If you ignore it, your son will die." I knew she was listening and I wondered whether now would be a good time to ask for more help.

I took a sip of my water. "There is something else I need to tell you."

"Go on," she said.

I took another deep breath. "I came here through the portal, and for some unknown reason, I travelled back into the past. This is how I know about your son."

I searched her eyes for a reaction. She looked completely stunned, so I seized the advantage and continued. "I am stuck where I don't belong and I really need to return to my own time."

She glanced at Sulaan, I guess to seek some kind of reassurance that she had heard me correctly. He looked sceptical.

"I know it sounds crazy, but you have to believe me."

She shook her head. "If what you say is true, I'm afraid I cannot help you. You have obviously come from a place

where time travel is possible, but we have no such understanding of how to move through time."

I realised it was good of her to even entertain the idea. I
shook my head. "Time travel is not possible in my time
either, or so I thought. All I know is I travelled through a
portal in Paris and ended up in Ramia eleven years in
the past."

"Are you sure?" she asked, doubtfully.

"I'm struggling to believe it myself, but if that date is
correct," I said, pointing to the calendar on her desk, "It's
eleven years before I entered the portal that brought
me here."

She looked stunned. "I am sorry, but I really don't know
how I can help you."

Dear, wonderful Leylana. I had presented her with the
impossible and yet she was still considering what she could
do to help. I began to realise that even though we were in a
different time, the people were essentially the same. I felt
that same connection with Leylana I had felt when I had
first met her, and it gave me hope to think that, should I be
stuck in this realm for good, the connection between myself
and Ahran might also be the same.

"Perhaps I could speak to the person in charge of portal
travel, maybe they can shed some light on what might have
happened? If there is nothing that can be done, then I will
accept my fate and not trouble you any further." I tried not
to think about what I would do if this was the case and
looked at her pleadingly.

"This is all very irregular and I'm not sure the King
would sanction this."

She was wavering and I could feel my chance slipping through my fingers.

"You are a caring and compassionate Queen, my lady. *Please* find it in your heart to help me just one more time, I have no-one else to turn to."

She thought about it for a moment before letting out a sigh. "Very well. I can't see what harm it would do to ask a few questions."

I released the breath I had been holding. "Thank you!"

LEYLANA GRANTED me a meeting with Stannad Drysda one of Dinara's top engineers and scientists, the following morning, so I didn't complain about being locked in my room again that night. The only problem was that when I was alone it gave me too much time to think about Ahran. It had been an eventful day and I hadn't had time to dwell on how much my heart ached for him. I was struggling with the fact that yesterday he had no idea who I was, nor seemed to care. What if I couldn't return to my rightful time? I recalled the way he had looked at me. Did I have any chance of winning him around *again*? The intensity with which I missed him caused my lungs to feel tight and I struggled to fight the tears. I wiped at my eyes impatiently. I wasn't ready to give up yet.

The following morning a servant escorted me to Leylana's office for my meeting with Mr Drysda. We walked to the other side of the palace, to the royal suite of offices and traversed the palace's entrance hall only to find

Ahran casually pacing and talking on his phone, a flight bag by the door. I stopped abruptly. I had been so focussed on my meeting with the scientist, that seeing Ahran nearly knocked me for six. I stood there for a moment, every cell in my body compelling me towards him. For a split second, it was as if there was a spark of recognition in his eyes, maybe something more. I consoled myself with the idea that perhaps our souls were destined to meet and no constraint of time could prevent it from happening. And then a thought occurred to me; maybe the same souls were attracted to each other, time and time again between now and eternity. But maybe it was just a romantic notion conjured up by the craziness of the last couple of days. I was so love sick for Ahran that I had more than likely misinterpreted his expression as something more than just vague recognition. Even though I smiled and tried to focus on the meeting I was about to have, everything had become blurry and I lost all sense of purpose. Ahran seemed to no longer notice I was there and the servant accompanying me urged me on. All of a sudden, my impending meeting with the scientist had become more important than ever.

Leylana and Stannad Drysda were waiting for me in the Queen's office.

"Good morning and thank you," I said to Leylana, trying to convey my gratitude for what she had done for me. She dipped her head in acknowledgement.

"It's a pleasure to meet you Mr Drysda," I said whilst offering my hand.

He shook it. "The pleasure is all mine."

Stannad Drysda was a tall, slim, grey-haired, intelligent

looking man, whom Leylana had obviously briefed because he eyed me with great interest.

"I have relayed to Stannad what you have told me and he wants to ask you some questions," the Queen said.

I nodded. "Yes of course."

"If you'll excuse me, I have other business to attend to." And with that she left the room, although Yula lurked in the background. I gave him a brief smile and he nodded his head in return.

"Please sit," Stannad said, indicating to the chair next to him.

I sat down and put my hands together as if in prayer, everything was riding on whether this man would be able to answer them.

He placed a small tablet on the table next to me. "I want to record our meeting so that I don't miss anything," he said. Even though he seemed very composed, there was an air of excitement about him.

"No, absolutely," I replied.

"So, talk me through what happened," he said.

"It's a very long story," I said with an apologetic smile.

"I'm listening," he encouraged.

I stuck to the facts and started at the beginning. I told him about the faulty portal in Paris, when Ahran, Toby and I first arrived there, the same one which had prevented us from returning to Ramia straight away. I told him about the Ramian who had been lost whilst travelling through the portal before that and my theory that maybe he had time travelled too. I explained that it had taken Stannad's department a few days to fix it and just when we were about to use it to return to Ramia, discovered that someone had tampered with it. I skipped the bit about Ahran being shot and told him how it felt like I had been sucked into the portal. I described the hurtling, spinning sensation, and finished by saying how I'd ended up on Ramian soil, eleven years in the past.

Stannad nodded, listening intently. "You say you felt like you were sucked in?"

"Yes, just after Ahran had been …" I couldn't bring myself to say it.

"Did you see or hear anything?"

"No, nothing. I can only liken it to being in a washing machine, blind-folded."

"Could you feel anything?"

"No," I replied.

"How long do you think you were in the portal for?"

I shrugged. "I honestly can't tell you, it could have been seconds, it could have been hours, days even. I lost consciousness and with that, all sense of time."

He nodded.

I paused for a moment trying to recall exactly what had happened. "I remember having flashbacks," I said, recalling the jumble of images that had flashed through my mind before I'd passed out.

"Go on," he prompted.

I dredged up the moments following Ahran's death, but the emotions were too private, too painful. "I'm not sure I can remember," I said, having second thoughts about sharing them.

"It's important that you try."

I sat for a moment struggling with the memory and shed tears I couldn't stop. I tried hard to suppress all the hurt and pain I was feeling and managed to recall one of the images, which had been of Katie. "I think I may have thought about my sister."

Stannad leaned closer. "What about your sister?"

I tried to think, but my mind had gone blank. I shook my head and shrugged.

He sat back, looking disappointed. "Thank you, Grace. It has been most interesting."

"Is that it?" I said, feeling terribly dissatisfied.

"For now."

"Do you know how I travelled back in time?" I asked, feeling desperate. I had expected answers and was beginning to worry that he wasn't about to give me any.

"There could be a number of explanations."

"Will I be able to go back to my own time?"

He looked doubtful. "I'm afraid I cannot promise anything at this stage."

I closed my eyes to the black hole of hopelessness that seemed to be swallowing me up.

27

The next few days passed by in a miserable fog. I met with Stannad on numerous occasions for several hours and was never quite sure where he was going with all his questions. There was still no sign of the King and other than being allowed into the palace gardens for some fresh air accompanied by a bodyguard, I was confined to my room. Surely I couldn't stay here indefinitely. What was I to them? Maybe I could persuade Leylana to allow me to go back to Earth. But if I did, then what? Could I exist alongside my eighteen-year-old self? I had no idea of the implications and unable to come up with any answers continued to grieve for Ahran, Toby, my sister and now my present.

On the third morning, I was sat at the window picking at my breakfast, when a knock at the door brought me out of my miserable reverie. It was Deeta, one of Leylana's assistants.

"My Lady would like to see you."

I stood up. "Okay," I said, straightening the hem of my top. Maybe now was my chance to plead my case for her to let me go.

We walked through the corridors of the palace. Stupidly I hoped I might bump into Ahran again, but there had been no sign of him since I had seen him a few days ago. What I would do to feel his arms around me?

Deeta, knocked gently on the door and Leylana called us in.

Stannad was with her and he stood up as we entered the room. My heart lurched hopefully.

"Your Highness," I said. "Mr Drysda, it's good to see you again."

Leylana smiled. "Good morning Grace. Mr Drysda has some good news for you," she said.

My heart leapt into my throat.

"My team and I had always suspected time travel was possible," he began. "It was something we have been working on for years, but it wasn't until I began to talk to you that I was able to discover a large piece of the puzzle that had eluded us." His excitement was almost palpable.

"Do you know how you can send me back?" I asked, not overly bothered by the detail, but desperate to know if it was possible.

"In theory," he said.

"Oh my God!" I clapped my hands over my mouth. I couldn't believe it. I had all but given up hope.

"The Queen has given me permission to go ahead if you are willing, although I must warn you, it may not be safe."

"I'll try anything," I said, enthusiastically, knowing I had nothing to lose. I turned to Leylana. "Thank you! Thank you so much!"

She smiled.

"So how does it work?" I asked, turning back to Stannad and giving myself a stern telling off for having doubted him.

"In simple terms, I believe you entered the portal in Paris as it closed and it is the nature of a closing portal that presents the possibility of time travel. The magnetic field that is created in these circumstances, transcends the laws of time. Do you understand anything about wormholes?"

"I've heard of them."

"Well then, it is enough to say that a closing portal momentarily creates a vortex, its own wormhole in effect. I had always believed this was the case, but had no way of testing it without risking someone's life. Happily, your experience has proven that not only was my theory correct, but that a person can pass through one of these temporary wormholes seemingly unharmed."

"I see," I said, trying to absorb what he was telling me, but too excited by the prospect of being reunited with Ahran.

"We knew we could recreate the conditions for another wormhole, but we had no idea how to pinpoint the time one might want to travel to."

My excitement began to fade.

"But," he said, raising a finger. "After talking to you it occurred to me that perhaps the time could be determined by the frequency of thought."

I shook my head, "I'm sorry, you've lost me."

"Let me explain," he said, enthusiastically.

He touched the desk. "The atoms within this desk are vibrating continuously at a certain frequency. Every cell in our body is vibrating at a certain frequency." He paused for a moment. "And this is the key," he said with excited emphasis. "If the frequency of our physical body affects the geographical plain then perhaps the frequency of our thoughts affect the field of time.

I looked at him in bewilderment.

"The energy of our memories must have some kind of time marker that anchors it to a particular time," he explained further.

Feeling incredibly stupid next to this man who was clearly nothing short of a genius, I had only grasped the basics. "But I was thinking I wanted to go back to Ahran in Paris?" I said.

"Yes, but at the point the wormhole opened you must have thought of your sister which set the time frequency and you were transported back to that specific moment in time. Can you remember what it was, where you were?"

As soon as he said it I knew. "Paris was the first place I visited on my year out," I said, slowly. "I had a random memory, a good memory, of the time I had spent with my sister just before I went travelling."

"That's it!" he said, animatedly.

I stood for a while staring at him blankly, struggling to comprehend, until what he was suggesting began to percolate through. Evo had closed the portal as I entered it which had created the wormhole that sent me back in time. It was all coming back to me now; the frequency of the thought I had about my sister at the moment the wormhole opened sent me back eleven years in the past to the time we were goofing around at Madame Tussaud's.

I felt like the air had been knocked out of my lungs. I began to pace around as a stream of thoughts hit me. "Good Lord! This could change everything," I said. The magnitude of what he was suggesting was only just starting to sink in. "The possibilities are endless." I paused for a moment as one thought careered into another. "Hitler could be stopped, diseases could be prevented, the impact of natural disasters could be dramatically reduced..." It was difficult to contain my excitement.

Stannad held up his hands in an attempt to temper my enthusiasm. "We must not get too excited," he warned. "We are limited to the memories people have, we could not go back further than the memory of the oldest person alive, nor could we travel ahead to the future. What we must also consider is whether it would it be right to interfere with God's work in this way?"

His answer surprised me as much as it worried me. Firstly, Ramians didn't often talk about religion and secondly, in trying to save Katie and Tagan, hadn't I played God? I didn't want to think about what the reverberations might be so I shoved my concerns to the back of my mind for the time being. "But think of the lives that could be saved," I said.

"You are right, but should we change the pattern of history? Things happen for a reason. Light comes from the darkest tragedies; innovation, invention, acts of great courage and kindness. What would our worlds be like if we sanitised everything that had gone before us? In life, there has to be balance, who knows what would happen if we upset that balance?"

"Will I be able to return to the future, I mean my present?" I asked fearful that after all that I wouldn't be able to return to my rightful time.

He smiled. "In your case, yes. You have come from the future, you have a memory of it, therefore you should be able to travel back there, if you are prepared to take the risk."

Suddenly, I felt all the strength drain out of my legs and I sunk to my knees. I sobbed tears of relief. All the anguish and fear and worry of the last few days began to dissipate. I had dared to hope, but there had been a large part of me that hadn't believed it would be possible.

"I'm sorry," I said between hiccups. "I just...just can't believe it!"

"I cannot emphasis enough however, that there is a great risk. Whilst we understand the theory, there is no telling whether it will work in practice, it will be the first time anybody has ever attempted to travel through time in this way and I cannot guarantee your safety."

I nodded through my tears. "I understand." Little did he know that there wasn't anything I wouldn't do to return to the Ahran who knew and loved me, my precious nephew and my life as it was because there was nothing for me here.

"Good, as long as you understand the risks, I am prepared to attempt it."

"That is wonderful. So amazing! I cannot thank you enough!" I said as I sat there on my knees, feeling like I should perhaps pray down to him.

"You have helped us solve a scientific enigma, the least we can do is try to help you get back to your own time," he said with a sympathetic smile. "After that, what we do with this information, is for more important and wiser people to decide."

Stannad Drysda was not only a great scientist, but he was obviously a great thinker and I was humbled by his modesty. In the light of such a big discovery, I was feeling rather guilty that I was selfishly rejoicing the relatively insignificant event, of being reunited with my boyfriend and family.

I wiped my tears and felt wobbly as I got to my feet. "If I am able to go back to the future," I said, "Won't there be two of me?"

He shook his head. "I cannot say for sure, but I think this unlikely." He proceeded to explain the differences between time continuums and priority energies, which quite frankly went right over my head. All I could think about was that not only would I be returning to Ahran and Toby, but I may well be reunited with my sister. There was also the possibility that I would finally get to meet Tagan, properly. I was beside myself with happiness. Who cared if I had played God?

I spent a frustrating few days waiting for a new portal to be opened. I did as Stannad had instructed and tried to train my mind to focus on one particular event. Fortunately, or unfortunately, depending on which way I chose to look at it, watching the man you love gunned down right in front of your eyes wasn't something that was easily forgotten. I hoped beyond all hope that what I had done to save

Katie would mean that the sequence of events that led to Ahran's death would not happen, so I requested to be transported back to Hatherley, walking back into my life at exactly the same time as I had entered the portal in Paris. Stannad explained that there would probably be gaps in my memory, but other than that I should be able to carry on with my life as if I had never been away. I tried not to panic too much about it not working and coming to what could possibly be the stickiest of ends. Stannad had assured me that they were doing everything they could to ensure my safe passage and I comforted myself with the thought that he and his team were brilliant scientists in a technologically advanced world. Stannad's confidence that they could pull this off had caused my pain and sadness to lessen and although I felt somewhat bruised, I looked forward to the moment when I returned to the time where I belonged.

A SMALL FAREWELL party stood on the steps at the front of the palace, consisting of just Leylana and Deeta. Yula was to take me to the headquarters of portal travel where the portal had been opened and where I was to receive further instruction about my journey.

I turned to the Queen. "I cannot thank you enough for what you have done for me your Highness. I will never forget your kindness."

She smiled. "You never know, we may meet again in the future."

"Yes, you never know," I said, returning her smile. I took her proffered hand and gave it a squeeze. "Goodbye."

"Goodbye Grace and good luck."

I climbed into the waiting car and Leylana waved, before turning and making her way back into the palace. I took one last look at my surroundings, hoping that if all went well I would be returning here very shortly about eleven years from now.

On the drive to the high security science park, I struggled with my nerves. As excited as I was, fears about it all going wrong had started to worm through my mind. Best case scenario, I would end up back in my home village in eleven years time. Worst case scenario, I would end up in a million pieces circumnavigating whichever planet's solar system I had been sucked into.

Twenty minutes later, the gates to the science park swept open and we drove down the avenues between the large modern buildings. Stannad was waiting with a colleague at the entrance of one particularly, modern and non-descript glass building and I got out of the car to greet them.

"Mr Drysda, it's good to see you again."

He shook my hand enthusiastically. "Miss Grace, this could be a momentous day."

"Yes, let's hope we can discuss it, eleven years from now," I said, sounding more confident than I felt.

"Indeed," he said, smiling.

"This is my colleague, Hercka Strool, she will accompany you to the portal."

I nodded and shook the hand of the officious looking Ms Strool. "It's good to meet you."

"And you," she replied.

"First, we will take you inside for a short briefing," Stannad said.

"Lead the way." I was eager to get on with it before I completely lost my nerve.

Stannad and Hercka led me to a small conference room where they proceeded to explain everything that was about to happen. They reminded me of the importance of staying focused on the memory that would take me to the time I wanted to return to. That I would be given several injections which they hoped would help me withstand the radiation and forces I would be subjected to and they asked me whether I wanted to be sedated so that I would be unconscious throughout it all. The last thing I wanted was to not wake up, so I declined this. Better to stay conscious at all times, I thought to myself, not that I would be able to do much if anything went wrong.

"Are you ready?" Hercka said finally.

I nodded. "As I'll ever be."

"Goodbye Grace," Stannad said. "It was an honour to meet you."

I gave him a hug. "The honour was really all mine."

"Good luck," he said before returning to the control centre. Hercka administered the injections before taking me outside to where the portal had been created. I had another momentary lapse of faith and for a split second began to question whether I should just stay in Ramia and try to carve out a different future. My hand went to the pebble at my throat and it gave me the strength I needed to listen to Hercka who, after being given the go ahead, began counting down the seconds to the moment when I would have to walk into the portal.

"…three…two…one."

I put my fears to the side and took two steps forward as I had been told to do, my mind totally focussed on Ahran in those last few moments in Paris. Suddenly, I felt a cold blast as I was sucked in by something more powerful than I could ever imagine and lost all sense of reality as I spun and turned until I couldn't tell the difference between my feet or my head. The constant, violent motion caused me to black out.

I CAME TO, lying on the ground, feeling like I'd just been hit by a bus. I didn't throw up thanks to Hercka who had given me something to combat the sickness, but I felt battered and bruised. I drew myself up onto all fours and crawled a safe distance away, just in case I was sucked back in. I sat back on my heels, taking a moment to catch my breath. Thankfully I was still in one piece and silently rejoiced that I hadn't just become a distant star. Was I really sitting in the middle of my wood, in my rightful present, eleven years ahead of where I had been when I woke up this morning? The journey had been just as turbulent as the first time, but I had come round feeling a little less disorientated and felt none of the shock. Maybe it had been to do with the injections, but maybe it was because this time I had everything to look forward to.

I staggered to my feet and looked around. I'm pretty sure

the wood looked the same as I remembered, although it was hard to tell. To the untrained eye, does a wood change that much? I reached out to a nearby tree to steady myself and took a few deep breaths, but driven by my need to see Ahran, my sister and Toby, I began to fight my way through the undergrowth, increasing my pace to a jog once I reached the path leading to my back gate. The key was under the plant pot by the back door where it always was. I opened the door and surveyed the kitchen, other than a picture I'd never seen before and a different dinner service on the dresser, everything was pretty much the same. I ran into the hallway and saw the post on the mat. My pulse raced as I picked it up to look at the date stamps.

"Ho-ly mo-ther of all Gods!" I said out loud. Feeling decidedly wobbly, I made my way into the lounge and sat down heavily on the sofa, still staring at the date. It had worked! It had only bloody worked! I laughed out loud. I had travelled back to where I should be with little more than a hair out of place. It was then that I noticed the unfamiliar photo frame on the mantelpiece; it was a photo of three people. I slowly stood up and walked over to it. I felt like I was in a dream and my hand covered my mouth to stifle a sob. "Oh my God," I said, laughing through my tears. It was a picture of Toby, Katie and Tagan; Toby with his mop of brown curls, Tagan as handsome as he had been when I had seen him only a few days ago and my dear, darling sister looking tanned, relaxed and happy. "You're alive," I whispered as I touched her image, not quite able to believe it was her. I sank to the floor in a crumpled heap, clasping the picture to my chest and crying tears of pure joy.

TAGAN'S CHANCE
Book 4

I had achieved the incomprehensible! I had just travelled through time and back to my rightful place in it. Back to my hopes and dreams for the future, back to Ahran, to Katie and Toby. Now that I had made it, I was able to admit to myself that there had been a big part of me that had struggled to believe it was possible, which is why I could be forgiven for sobbing like a baby in a heap on the floor. It was some time before I eventually gathered myself together and stood up. There was no more time to waste. I put the picture of Toby, Katie and Tagan I'd been clutching back on the mantelpiece and took the stairs two at a time. I needed a shower and a change of clothes in preparation for my reunion with those I loved the most.

I entered the bathroom thinking that the house felt different to when I had been here the morning MI5 had come knocking on my door; less empty, more lived in. I caught my reflection in the bathroom mirror and grimaced. I looked a mess. I combed my fingers through my hair, no more enamoured with the colour now than when Ahran had dyed it for me, what seemed like a lifetime ago. I began to rifle through the bathroom cabinet hunting for the high-lighting kit I sometimes used in the winter to give my hair a lift. I noticed some of Ahran's toiletries in the bathroom cabinet and smiled before locating the hair bleach and ripping the packet open. Dying my hair back to its natural colour seemed the right thing to do. Back to blonde, back to before this terrible nightmare had begun. I rubbed the cream into my hair. I really didn't care what the end result would be because anything that helped me to forget the last few weeks could only be a good thing. I brushed my teeth and paced the bathroom floor, beginning to regret my hasty decision. What was I doing!? I hadn't seen my sister since her fatal accident and I was pretty sure Ahran wouldn't care whether I was blonde or brunette. Why was I wasting time dying my hair?! I reassured myself that a change in image was a sensible move, after all I didn't want Tagan, or Ahran for that matter, recognising me from my sortie into the past and so I shrugged it off feeling justified that it was time well spent. If I was honest, it gave me the time to pull myself together, it wasn't every day you were faced with the prospect of seeing your sister who had died three years ago and the love of your life who, after being gunned down in cold blood, nearly destroyed you by not having a clue as to who you were. It was a lot to take in and there was a certain amount of re-adjustment to be done. There had been so many times over the last few days that I'd doubted Stannad, but he had come up trumps and I owed him *everything*.

Once I'd showered and rinsed my hair, I wrapped myself

in a towel and went into the bedroom. I chose a sleeveless wraparound dress that I couldn't remember buying. Stannad had warned me that there would probably be some inconsistencies in my memory, but nothing I wouldn't be able to handle. I dried my hair which turned out more of a muddy yellow than blonde and I quickly applied some make up. My final assessment in the mirror returned a verdict of *'Not bad given the time and effort spent.'*

Feverish with anticipation, I made my way downstairs before locking the back door and heading to the portal. I approached the trunk of the big oak apprehensively, however the desire to see Ahran and my precious family overrode any loss of confidence I now felt in portal travel. I reached out my hand and met no resistance as I hurriedly entered the gateway.

I WELCOMED the usual rollercoaster sensation before stepping out into the warm Ramian sunshine only to discover that there were two guns pointing at my head. I squinted in the light.

"Nadara!" One of the gunmen shouted.

I instinctively raised my hands. "It's…it's me Sophie McAllister," I said to the two guards who were dressed in dark, combat gear.

One signalled to the other to lower his gun. "Forgive us Miss McAllister, your hair is different."

I was relieved they now recognised me and dropped my hands. I gave a nervous chuckle. "Oh yes, a last minute

D.I.Y. job," I said, without further explanation. "May I pass?"

"Of course," one of them replied. They both stepped aside.

"Thank you." Never had I been met by an armed guard before. I wondered if extra security measures had been put in place as a consequence of me unexpectedly appearing in Ramia, more than a decade ago. It was probably no bad thing I thought to myself, and continued with my journey feeling as nervous as a kitten.

The distant echo of music drifted on the air. It sounded like there was an event taking place at the palace and I could only hope that Ahran, Katie, Tagan and Toby would all be there. I hadn't a clue what it might be in aid of. I looked down and brushed a leaf from my dress, I was at least glad I had spent some time on my appearance. I took a deep breath and made my way across the palace grounds to one of the side entrances. In reality, it was less than a day since I had been here last, but it felt like a hundred years had passed. I paused for a moment in the courtyard and closed my eyes letting the sun's rays wash over me as if it was performing some kind of celestial baptism, anointing me back into the world where I belonged. With renewed excitement, I entered the palace and began to make my way through the corridors, passing several of the palace staff who nodded respectfully. With every step, my heart beat harder and harder. It was a beautiful day and it seemed the guests were being entertained in Leylana's favourite part of the gardens, the same place where Ahran had carved his name on a tree as a boy and the spot where Elaya and Tigor had been married. I headed towards the music and the murmur of the guests. I recognised one of the servants coming out of the marquee carrying a tray of empty glasses.

"Fala, have you seen Katie or Ahran?" I said a little breathlessly.

She didn't speak English, but she understood a bit and nodded her head towards the marquee and smiled. My pulse raced as I passed through the vine covered walkway to the bottom end of the marquee. *This was it!*

Standing in the doorway, I scanned the guests for the faces I'd thought I would never see again. A flood of emotion swept over me and I took a deep breath, if I didn't keep myself in check, there would be tears even before I saw them and I didn't want them to suspect a thing. I had to try and act normal; this may be a momentous occasion for me, but for them, nothing had changed.

There were little more than a dozen people in the marquee, clearly most of the guests had chosen to sit at the tables out on the terrace to take in the view of the mountains and the town below. As hard as I searched for Ahran, it wasn't long before I realised he wasn't there. He was always so easy to spot, so tall and striking even among his fellow countrymen. I was about to make my way outside to see if he too was out on the terrace, when my gaze settled on an achingly familiar face. I stopped in my tracks. She looked like a little ray of sunshine in a pretty lemon-yellow dress, her blonde hair piled up on her head with tendrils bobbing happily as she chatted to the lady in front of her. I couldn't move and dared to breathe. She turned to put her empty glass on a passing tray and I exhaled a long breath as if I had been holding it for the last three years. There was my sister, whose life hadn't been tragically snuffed out one winter's night on a dark country lane, but my beautiful sister who was very much alive *and* very pregnant! For a moment, I stood feeling a little confused as my brain tried to process this new piece of information. My first thought was that I hadn't come as far back into the future as I had hoped and that perhaps it was Toby she was carrying, but I quickly dismissed this idea, I'd had confirmation of my place in time from the date stamp on the letter and the photograph on my mantelpiece. No, this pregnancy was a different one and I was overjoyed at the thought of becoming an auntie again.

I walked over to her, my heart slamming in my chest.

"Katie," I said, my voice catching in my throat.

She turned towards me. "There you are!" She paused. "What on Earth have you done to your hair?!"

I was speechless. There were no words to describe how good it was to see her, standing there in the flesh and looking so radiant. I could no longer hold back the tears that began to roll down my cheeks.

"Sophie, are you alright?"

"Yes, yes, I'm absolutely, perfectly alright," I said, throwing my arms around her half crying and half laughing. All the times I had wished she had been here and cursed God for taking her away from me, and now as I clung to her, all those dark, horrible, hopeless times just melted away.

"Hey, you're squashing the baby!" she said, pulling away and looking more than a little puzzled.

"Oh my goodness the baby! When's it due?" I asked, enthusiastically wiping away my tears.

She took hold of my elbow. "Excuse us for a moment," she said to the lady next to her and steered me away to a quiet corner.

"Sophie, what is *wrong* with you?" she said, sounding concerned and more than a little bit cross.

"I'm sorry," I said, chuckling. I'd fully intended to act normal, but how could I when I was so happy to see her alive and *pregnant*? I had tried to prepare myself for the holes in my memory, but I could see now that nothing could have prepared me for this. Katie was not only alive, but doing a very good job of growing another life inside her; it was beyond anything I could have wished for. I stared at her, my mouth opening and closing like a goldfish as the reality of what had happened began to sink in.

She looked at me with a confused expression. "Are you okay?"

I knew I was going to have to come up with something to explain my strange behaviour and *fast*.

"I'm sorry," I said. "I…I hit my head this morning and now I don't feel so good."

Her expression changed to one of concern. "Here," she said, pulling out a chair for me. "It must have been a hefty knock."

I sat down and gazed up at her. "It's just *so* good to see you."

"Sweetheart, we only saw each other yesterday." She placed the back of her hand against my forehead like one's mother does when trying to assess the extent of illness. "How did it happen?"

"Oh, it was stupid," I said, stalling whilst trying to

353

concoct a half reasonable explanation. "I…I was carrying some washing down the stairs and fell, the next thing I know, I'm lying at the bottom of the stairs." I shook my head as if my carelessness was just as much a disappointment to me as it would be to her.

"Jesus Sophie! You could have seriously hurt yourself. I'll call a doctor."

"No! No, I'll be fine," I said, grabbing her hand.

"Hey Sophe. Is everything okay?" said a voice from behind me and it immediately stirred up a mixture of emotions. I turned in my seat excited to see him, but a little worried he might recognise me from our brief meeting in the past.

Tagan looked happy and relaxed, dressed in a lightweight suit and casual shirt. He slid his arm around Katie's swollen waist and kissed her hair. It was a subtle, intimate gesture. Suddenly, I had a flashback of Tagan's diary and the entries he had made about Katie those first few times he had met her. I smiled up at them both enjoying their display of togetherness, somehow it made the ordeal I had just been through that much easier to bear.

I stood up and kissed him on both cheeks. "Everything's fine," I said, grinning like a Cheshire cat.

"Everything is not fine," Katie said disapprovingly. "Sophie has fallen down the stairs and hit her head and she seems confused, I'm worried about her."

"I'll call the doctor," Tagan said, taking matters into his own hands.

"Please, I'm fine, I'm sure it's only temporary." I

couldn't have felt better, but my attempted reassurances obviously weren't having the desired effect.

"You look different," Tagan said, eyeing me whilst attempting to work out why.

Did he recognise me?

I touched my hair nervously. "I thought I'd try something a bit different."

"It er...suits you," he said, clearly bemused by the vagaries of female vanity, but trying to be polite, even though he wasn't convincing any of us of his sincerity. I breathed a sigh of relief, there didn't seem to be any sign of recognition in his eyes.

"No, it doesn't, it's too short. But, it'll grow," I said. Suddenly the state of my hair was of little importance. I took a moment to examine my handsome brother-in-law. He looked just as I remembered; strong, athletic, and gorgeous, although not quite a match for his cousin.

"Where's Ahran?" I said, unable to contain my excitement.

"He'll be here shortly," Tagan replied.

I felt a crushing wave of disappointment. "Oh." I guess I'd waited what seemed like an eternity, a few more minutes wouldn't kill me.

"And Toby?" I was anxious to see my nephew again, it had been hard being separated from him, like a part of me had been missing.

Katie looked around. "He was here a minute ago, I think he and Salom might have found a quiet corner with their computer gadgets."

I nodded and surveyed the guests to see if I could see

him. As wonderful as it was to be here, it felt odd, like I had been spun around a few times and was struggling to orientate myself. I leaned closer to Tagan. "And why are we here exactly?" I whispered.

"It's Ley-lana's birth-day," Katie said, speaking slowly and a little loudly, as if I was the deaf, slightly batty, old Aunt.

"I think she might have amnesia," she said, turning to Tagan.

"Yes, that's it!" I said fervently. "I hit my head and I have amnesia!"

Toby came to join us, interrupting our awkward conversation. His hair was longer and he looked in exceedingly good health. Was he even taller than I remembered?

"Ah, there you are! Auntie Sophie was wondering where you were?"

He was a sight for sore eyes and I pulled him towards me in a bear hug. "I can't tell you how good it is to see you sweetheart." I planted a big kiss on his cheek.

"What's up with Auntie Sophie?" he said to his mum when I finally released him.

"She's had an accident and we think she's lost some of her memory," Katie explained.

"Oh," he said, not appearing overly perturbed.

"Grams wants you," he said to Katie.

"Tell her I'll be there in a minute."

"Where is the Queen?" I said, surveying the people in the marquee. She was the only person who would understand what was going on and I was desperate to see her.

"I think you need to see a doctor first," Katie insisted.

If I was to be at all convincing, I had little choice, and so gave in. Fortunately, I was seen by the palace doctor almost immediately, who after a brief examination returned an inconclusive verdict. I was released on the proviso that I would have further tests in the coming days. I suppose amnesia was the obvious ruse, it helped explain my blind spots nicely, although the doctor was puzzled by no obvious signs of head trauma.

I linked arms with Katie as we walked back outside to where the festivities were in full swing. I wanted to pinch myself; I had my dear sister back, she had Tagan and when Ahran arrived my world would be complete. I squeezed her arm. There was a big part of me that felt relieved that I would no longer have to make difficult decisions about Toby because he had his mother back too. I felt completely vindicated for doing what I had done.

"I'm just going to sit down for a bit, I feel a little light-headed," Katie said, heading for a vacant seat.

"Are you okay?" I asked.

"I'm fine," she replied. "It's a tight squeeze in there now," she said, running her hands over her swollen belly. "And it's making me breathless."

I took the seat next to her. "When is the baby due?" I now had a good excuse for the gaps in my knowledge.

"In a couple of weeks' time," she said. "Although if he or she decides to put in an early appearance, I wouldn't mind that much."

I had been so pleased to see her earlier that I hadn't noticed the tension around her eyes. "You must take it easy," I warned.

"I know, it's just all this house business, it should have been finished by now."

I looked at her blankly.

"Tagan and I are having a house built," she explained patiently. "I just hope it's finished when the baby arrives. Halsan and Leylana have been wonderful, but I'm looking forward to having our own space again, away from the palace."

I nodded. "So, you are living here at the palace?" I was doing my best to piece it all together.

"Yes," she replied.

Our conversation was interrupted when Leylana and the King entered the marquee. Halsan called for hush. It was the first time I had seen the Queen and she waited whilst the King introduced her. She stood in front of her guests, waiting for her husband to finish and looking stunning in a pale green fitted dress. She began to speak and as I listened in ignorance, I noticed how much younger she looked, happier, as if a great weight had been lifted off her shoulders.

I was so overwhelmed to be here, that much of what she said went over my head, but I did join in with the toast. "Hatcheena!" I cheered along with everyone else.

It was then that I spotted him.

Tagan's Chance is available on Amazon now

BOOKS BY AMELIA FORD AND THEIR ORDER:

Coming Soon

Damned and Damaged

For more information about Amelia and her books visit

www.amelia-ford.com

www.facebook.com/AmeliaFordAuthor

Note to Reader

Hopefully you've enjoyed reading Tagan's Chase. Please would you take a few moments to review it on Amazon? Many thanks.

FREE BONUS MATERIAL

Get exclusive, FREE bonus material about the characters and their lives, PLUS giveaways and book news when you sign up to the author's mailing list.
To get started:
www.amelia-ford.com

56112629R00220

Made in the USA
Middletown, DE
19 July 2019